REDEMPTION DAY

by

STEVE O'BRIEN

REDEMPTION DAY

First Printing 2012

Author services by Pedernales Publishing, LLC.
www.pedernalespublishing.com

Distributed by:
New Shelves Distribution
103 Remsen Street #202
Cohoes, NY 12047
(518) 391-2300
www.newshelvesdistribution.com

ISBN 13: 978-0-9820735-2-0
ISBN 10: 0-9820735-2-6

Library of Congress Control Number: 2011917728

Printed in the United States of America

10 9 8 7 6 5 4 3 2 1

www.AandNPublishing.com

Also by Steve O'Brien

Elijah's Coin

Bullet Work

Critical Acclaim for *Bullet Work*

O'Brien weaves this tale of exciting characters, breathtaking horse racing action; right into our lives...He opens up the equine world to readers, with the grace of an artist sweeping his brush across a canvas.

—US Review of Books

Poetic ruminations about randomness punctuate the action in this mystery...These philosophical, foreboding passages transcend the novel's specificity—its insular, transient community of racetrack devotees who endure long hours and low pay to be near the creatures they adore—to become insightful analysis of character and motivation. O'Brien refuses the pat, satisfying wrap-up mystery readers may anticipate.

—Foreword Magazine

This is a wonderful tale, full of stories of the people behind the scenes. People are often interested in the "horse whispering" phenomena and O'Brien brings it to another level...[A] must read for the Dick Francis fans, another direction for the aficionados of the horse racing field.

—Seattle Post-Intelligencer

The manner in which O'Brien introduces each of these characters in brief focused chapters is a stroke of writing genius, a polished version of the manner in which some other novelists such as Cormac McCarthy have always used. O'Brien continues to impress with his skills as a writer and his underlying concern for humanity that is so lacking in the work of other writers of this genre.

—Grady Harp, Amazon Top Ten Reviewer

Critical Acclaim for *Elijah's Coin*

Elijah's Coin by Steve O'Brien is a very thought-provoking book of change. It will make you look at who you are, what you want and where you are going.

—Chicago Sun-Times

This story is spiritual, moving and incredibly hopeful. It is about finding your way in your life, even if you don't want to anymore. It's about finding the good in people, but more especially, it's about finding the good in you. The author has written a wonderful, wonderful story of possibilities and love and I absolutely devoured it.

—Front Street Reviews

This is a deceptively simple, feel good story that is a sheer delight to read...The quality of Steve O'Brien's writing cannot be bettered. . .[A]lthough written as a novel it could easily share space in the psychology or self help sections of the book store.

—Blogger News Network

Nick, this one is for you; my real life Nick James.

They shall be for you a refuge from the avenger of blood. He shall flee to one of these cities and shall stand at the entrance of the gate of the city and explain his case to the elders of that city. Then they shall take him into the city and give him a place, and he shall remain with them.

Joshua 20:3-4

REDEMPTION DAY

Prologue

Killing by an empowered government was deemed justice. Be it a convicted death row inmate or an unfortunate battlefield enemy, death was righteous. David Allen Wolfe agreed with the premise. Where he disagreed was with which government was authorized.

That made all the difference.

Wolfe grabbed the long neck and killed the remainder of his beer. A loud burp erupted, and he signaled the waitress for another round. He leaned forward on his elbows and scratched his three-day-old stubble. Two men sat across from him. At six foot four and two hundred forty pounds of twitching muscle, Wolfe towered over them even while seated.

"You got wheels, Brother Kevin?" Wolfe asked.

Kevin Landers nodded. "I got a guy."

"I don't give a shit if you got a guy. Do you have the vehicles?"

"Yeah, Jesus, yeah, I got the vehicles," Landers said at first looking at Wolfe, then staring down at his beer bottle.

"This is getting serious. We gotta have clean communications. I don't need no bullshit. I ask you something, you tell me. Got it?"

"Yes, sir," Landers said sheepishly.

The waitress, a chunky blonde trying desperately to look like she was still in her twenties, placed three more beers on the table. As she reached forward to gather the empties, Wolfe slipped his hand up her backside. She jumped forward and jerked away, giving him a stern look. Wolfe laughed heartily and blew her a kiss.

"The fuck you laughing at?" Wolfe said to Gibson, the smallest of the three with round wire rim glasses framing his eyes like fishbowls. Gibson stuck the beer bottle into his mouth to wipe the grin.

Though early afternoon, the tavern was dank and shadowed, a hole with a small bar, where two geezers occupied all but one seat. One vacant booth separated the trio from the front door that hung precariously on worn hinges. Chicken wire covered the sparse windows, and mildew was the fragrance of the day.

The waitress was the only thing about the place that drew any interest from Wolfe. She was his type. Female.

"Talk to Merton?" Wolfe said to Gibson.

He swallowed hard, "Yes, sir, spoke to him this morning. We've got a secure line set up—"

"Secure line, my ass," Wolfe said leaning against the table with a menacing stare.

"We're set," Gibson said, avoiding eye contact. "We can upload from the compound, and it's designed to route through several sites. Not traceable."

"Everything's traceable."

"Well—it would take a hell of a long time to figure it out. By the time anyone does, we're gone."

These guys were good, Wolfe knew, but leaders imposed their will at all times. He knew that was what kept leaders in charge, but in his field what kept them alive.

"Mert okay with it?"

"Mert's good. He's the last man in the chain, so they'd have to walk it back from him."

"He won't give them shit. Mert won't talk. He's solid."

Gibson nodded.

Now back to Landers. "We're gonna have a run-through tonight. Get the vehicles there. We're gonna practice til it's perfect. I got Jackson's boys meeting up later tonight. Those guys seen time in Baghdad and Irbil. They got skills. They won't be at the compound. But even if they come around, nobody goes to the shack, 'cept us. Got that? Nobody."

Wolfe took a long pull on his beer. He let out a sharp whistle and motioned to the waitress for the check. "When this goes down, we'll have those lawless bastards, FBI, justice, sheriffs crawling up our asses. Nobody goes to the shack without my okay and nobody talks about the shack."

"What shack?" Landers chuckled.

"Damn straight."

~

Sarah rang the register, waited, and ripped the receipt from the machine. After slapping it into the plastic check holder, she walked it over to the table where the men sat. She made sure to keep her distance from Mr. Grabass. Without so much as a thank you, she moved across the room back toward the bar.

She had to put up with idiots like this. Over time Sarah had learned how to diffuse a bad situation. That meant dealing with morons like this guy for minimum wage plus tips.

Tips, yeah, that was a joke.

I don't need this to escalate, she thought, particularly since it's just me and Zeke running the place today.

Zeke was a good friend, but hadn't been in a fight since the early days of Vietnam. No, if things went south, Sarah was going to be on her own. The only other inhabitant of the bar was old Luke Skinner. At somewhere north of eighty years old, the best he could do was fall off the bar stool and cause someone to stumble over him.

She'd thought about moving out of the county, up to Winchester, get her a real paying job. But the rents they charged up in Winchester always backed her off. At least here in podunk, Yellow Spring, her mobile home was paid for, and all she had were community fees for a place to live. The one thing she got in the divorce that was worth a damn. Well, other than her daughter.

Heck, what was she thinking? Kelly was still in school, would be for a bunch of years. No moving to Winchester. It wasn't going to happen anytime soon. Jobs were hard to come by in Yellow Spring, so it was in her best interest to just keep this job until something else came along.

The men sauntered past her toward the front door. She ignored them, though making sure to keep them in her peripheral vision. From the corner of her eye, she saw Grabass staring at her. Then he stopped, about four feet away. She froze.

"See ya, sweet cheeks," he said.

She looked down, wiping imaginary water droplets off the bar.

"I said see ya, sweet cheeks," Grabass said, this time in a booming voice.

She looked over and stared directly into his eyes, mustering all her courage. For a second, they were locked. Though attractive enough and unlike the losers she had to date in this area, his eyes were grey and electric. It was like the eyes didn't connect with the rest of the body, like they were controlled by some other being.

After three seconds that seemed like three years, he started moving again. Eyes were still on her, but at least he was moving toward the exit. When he finally turned his head to leave the building, she exhaled fully.

The men piled into a rust-colored GMC pickup, Grabass, of course, driving. What a creep. He was still staring toward her from behind the steering wheel. He put the truck in reverse and backed away in a wide arc. The truck was shifted and burned rubber, spitting gravel as it careened onto the highway and out of sight.

Never seen them before; hope they never come back. Sarah ambled to the booth the men had occupied, slipped the check wallet into the front of her jeans, and plucked up the bottles. She wiped the table down holding the three empties aloft.

Zeke and Luke were engaged in a deep conversation about when old man Tucker closed up the hardware store, before or after the drive-in shut down. They always rambled on about some nonsense. The bottles chinged and thudded as they went into the oversized plastic rubbermaid.

No tip, she was convinced. She slipped out the wallet, opened it, and stared. Then she turned it slightly sideways and stared more. Zeke and Luke turned their attention toward her. She lifted the multi-colored document out of the wallet and examined both sides of it, holding it in the air like a flattened earthworm.

"What in hell's name is this?"

Chapter 1

April 15

A white-haired man in red striped suspenders appeared in the doorway. With hands on the door frame, he leaned in. The message was simple. "You're fired." Then he was gone.

Nick looked up from his desk at the empty doorway and exhaled loudly. The footsteps clicked two doors down the hallway. "You're fired." The clicking of heels became more distant and a final, "You're fired" was delivered. All became silence.

A bespectacled imp of a man walked through Nick's doorway with a clipboard and tossed a document on his desk. "This is your severance agreement, Mr. James. You have 21 days to sign and, if you agree, your severance will be paid on the eighth day following receipt."

"Get out, Briney, you blood sucking ferret."

Briney continued undeterred. "I must remind you of the obligations of the covenant not to compete which you signed with the company. Your network account is being—"

"I know the drill."

"Terminated. Please leave all papers and materials with your desk. We will review everything and mail your personal belongings—"

"Okay, okay, enough with the good Nazi routine."

"To your residential address on file. Your security badge

for the building has been deactivated, so once you leave, you won't be permitted access."

"Get out of here."

"It's been a pleasure having you work with us at Center Tech and I wish you the best of luck in the future."

Having read Nick his rights, the man spun around and scurried two doors down the hall. "This is your severance agreement—"

Nick leaned back in his chair and surveyed the paperwork on his desk.

Should I call someone? Who would I call? Kate? No, can't call her.

He picked up the document the ferret had left behind and scanned it. Twenty-two thousand five hundred dollars—three years of work and this was the final insult.

His report on domestic terrorist groups lay unfinished on his desk. He stared at it briefly, then disengaged. He tapped his computer, and his email had been erased, his network connection had been shut off. Damn efficient. They've had a lot of practice.

A head appeared around the corner of his door frame. "You okay?"

"Yeah. I guess."

Dave Winters walked in and plopped down in the client chair next to the desk. He was twenty pounds overweight with a receding hairline accentuated by no evidence of a comb or brush having passed by recently. His black pants and white shirt looked like he'd slept in them, and the knot of his tie never quite made it to the top of the collar, which was okay since the top button was missing anyway. "Sorry, man. I didn't know."

Nick nodded. Dave was from the adjoining office. The one who had been skipped over in the massacre. "Pays to be on the fed payroll."

Dave nodded this time.

Winters was actually employed by the Department of Homeland Security, a lifer. Nick was a contractor or had been until three minutes ago. The agency had "feathered" contractors from Center Tech and lifers in adjoining offices down this corridor of the massive limestone building on Pennsylvania Avenue.

Feathering, Nick thought. Nice expression. What it meant was the lifers were surrounded by people who actually did the work and had performance expectations. Lifers were the ornaments on the Christmas tree. Contractors were the tree that held up the ornaments. The tree always died and a new tree would be brought in to hold up the shiny, glittery baubles.

Firing a lifer was next to impossible, Nick knew. Unless they bludgeoned their supervisor with an axe and the full College of Cardinals happened to be eyewitnesses, they were invincible.

Even if they force fed the boss into a wood chipper, the union challenges and Byzantine process to terminate them would run through the offender's expected retirement date, which was damn early anyway and loaded with lifetime benefits.

Productivity didn't matter, he thought; intelligence didn't matter, competence didn't matter. They were cloaked with the impenetrable shield of "the civil servant." Lifer's could play Texas Hold 'em all day on their computers or run pornographic websites from their taxpayer financed server. The worst that could happen was "reassignment."

Winters had been Dave's advocate and friend. He was more of a mentor than a co-worker. He knew the politics and where the battle lines had been drawn on each of Homeland's initiatives. Winter's sage and candid advice had kept Nick out of more than a few scraps over the years.

Winters had taken Nick under his wing. He became the sounding board for Nick's research. The subtle shake of his head could alter Nick's strategy and a favorable word could elevate an otherwise ignored research report. Winters knew the game. He'd played it more than two decades, first at State, now at Homeland.

He was the only person Nick could truly confide in, the only person Nick had ever told the true story about his father. Of all his co-workers, Winters was the one Nick would miss most as he emotionally packed his belongings.

"Briney's a piece of work, isn't he?" Winters coughed at him as Nick shook his head.

Another head appeared in the door frame. This one with long brunette hair and tears. Nick waved her in.

"It's not right," she said, snuffling.

"Doesn't matter what's right. It is what it is," Nick said. "It was the DOMTER contract. When that got defunded, it was just a matter of time before Center Tech reacted. Kind of surprised it took this long. Hey, at least we got fired by Galbert himself. He didn't send some pin striped, Ivy League lieutenant to do it."

She slid along the door jamb and entered the office leaning against the wall with her arms folded. She was five feet tall, if she stood on tiptoes, with a white blouse and blue knee length skirt. A jangle of bracelets adorned one arm that rattled and clinked as gravity dictated.

"What am I going to tell Rick? He's going to be so pissed off. He just bought that damn boat last week." She tried to laugh, but couldn't quite make it and covered her mouth.

"You'll be okay, Kathy," Winters said. "You've got SCI with a bunch of tags. That kind of security clearance is worth plenty, at least in this town. Somebody will pick you up. You, too, Nick."

Nick laughed and shook his head. "Did my full lifestyle poly two months ago. Bastards. Not sure it was worth going through all that crap if I was going to be laid off. Good planning on their part."

"What about the non-compete?" Kathy said.

Winters turned toward her. "Those things aren't worth shit in this industry. Just sound nice to shareholders and investors. They aren't going to enforce it; you watch."

"Easy for you to say," she said.

Winters tossed his hands in the air and turned back to Nick for validation.

"Probably right."

The sound of heels clicking on the granite came echoing down the hallway. Kathy snuffled again and rubbed her eyes. They waited.

Peter Logan stepped into the doorway. Based upon the prior footsteps and location of his office, he was the third of the Center Tech terminations in their wing. He was tall and lean with his blond hair brushed back perfectly. Peter stood there wearing his pink dress shirt and navy sport coat with hands on his hips. No trace of anger or disappointment framed his face. He quickly scanned the people in the office. "Anybody want to get a drink? I would have sent an email, but—." He shrugged.

Nick looked at his watch. "One-thirty? What the hell. We'll beat the happy hour crowd."

Chapter 2

Two rounds of drinks and a chorus of gallows humor later, Nick picked up the tab. It was only fair. Everyone else had family and spouses that they had to break the news to. Nick didn't. He rode the pre-rush hour Metro to DuPont Circle. His mind was muddled.

Thoughts about polishing his resume; would he tell Kate? What about his mom? He kept his emotions toward Center Tech on an even keel. It did no good to be angry. The deal was done. Now he had to move forward.

An adapted Groucho Marx line coursed through his memory. *I wouldn't want to belong to a club that would have me as a member.* Nick's version was he didn't want to work for a company that would fire an employee like him.

The cancellation of the DOMTER contract was all this was about. Some senior official in some administrative office decided to move some numbers on a spreadsheet. The cascading effect of that change resulted in Nick and a half dozen other folks walking home with a pink slip. He was merely collateral damage in a battle waged on a different plane.

The streets of Georgetown were quiet as he walked across the Q Street Bridge toward home. *What you see will always be.* That was the mantra of Georgetown and the resident association did everything in its power to ensure that was followed—from deciding what color a front door could be painted, to what trees could be planted, to what kind of paver bricks were in the driveway.

Stately federal townhomes were the custom of Georgetown, some small, some massive, but all considered exclusive. Jammed next to one another and polished like a news anchorman's teeth, the village thumbed its collective nose at the rest of DC.

Orange dust from tree pollen covered the windshields and trunks of the cars that hadn't moved for a few days. On high pollen count days, nature could clog up the healthiest of sinus cavities. It could bring a charging bull moose to its knees.

A panhandler shook the loose change in a grimy Starbucks cup from his perch on a produce crate. Nick handed him a dollar bill. The contribution earned him a "God bless you, young man."

Nick was familiar with many of the homeless who worked the Georgetown streets. This gentleman was new to Nick. As he continued down the sidewalk, Nick smiled and pondered that he and the panhandler were now in the same boat employment-wise, just that the panhandler's job paid more at the moment.

Nick walked past the stairwell that led down to the entrance to his English apartment and continued up the street, past two more homes. He climbed the front stairs onto the intricately carved wooden porch and pulled open the door.

"Mrs. Mackenzie, it's me."

"Oh, Nicholas, I'm back here in the library."

Genevieve MacKenzie, one of the grand dames of Georgetown, was one of two people who referred to him as Nicholas. The other was his mother.

The Victorian style home was impeccably designed, if 1950 Americana was the definition of perfection. Dark wood wainscoting covered the main floor with red and white designed wall paper in the entry way.

Each room started with the wood base, but another primary color adorned the walls. Photos of DC dignitaries littered the walls, climbing up the stairway. Presidents, Secretaries of State, Vice Presidents, and political figures too many to count pasted the walls. Many of the photographs had been snapped in this very home by Cecil, her husband of fifty years. Prostate cancer had taken Cecil the year before Nick moved to the neighborhood.

Nick walked through the living room and entered the library. Mrs. MacKenzie sat holding a book in her lap and pinched a cigarette holder in her fingers.

She was petite, white haired and on first glance looked every bit her eighty years. But there was electricity in the old gal. What some might describe as frail, Nick saw as wiry. The heart of a grandmother, he knew, with the spirit of a rodeo clown.

"Your one indulgence for the day?" Nick joked. Her one indiscretion was smoking. She claimed one per day. Nick knew better.

"Yes, child, you happen to come by just as I'm having my daily constitution. But you're home from work early; something you need to tell me?"

"Nah," he said, giving her a wave. "Guys like me, we come and go as we please. Gives other folks a chance to catch up to us gunners."

She coughed a laugh, covered her mouth with a fist momentarily, then replaced it with the other hand and took a deep drag.

"I thought since I have some time, I'd take Kiki for a walk and clear the outdoor fireplace. With Spring coming you'll want to sit outside in the evenings and the fire can keep you warm while you—what is it? Have your daily constitution?"

A blushing smile crossed her face and she waved him away.

Kiki was a mutt terrier that made rattlesnakes seem charming. No bigger than a muskmelon on legs, she would take a bite out of anyone just to see how they'd react. Kiki growled at Nick like he'd invaded the home. Fact was, Nick walked Kiki three or four times a week. There was apparently a long warming up period from her perspective.

Nick had learned how to deal with her. He said, "Oh, Kiki girl, how are you?" as sweetly as he could, while slipping closer and snatching her from behind, holding her by the knap as she snarled and tried to bite his arm. He clipped the leash to her and dropped her on the ground. She quickly headed the door as if nothing happened between them. Devil dog, Nick thought. Kiki scampered down the steps onto the pavers of Volta Street, ready to attack whatever came in sight.

Mrs. MacKenzie and Nick had become friends shortly after Nick moved to Georgetown. Kiki took a chunk out of his chinos the first time he'd walked by.

Mrs. Mac had more money than the rest of the neighborhood combined, but she wouldn't spend a nickel frivolously. She had apologized to Nick for the assault by her dog, and the two had become odd couple friends.

For Mrs. Mac, she had a neighbor who didn't fear her dog and would help walk the beast, which was becoming more difficult for her with each advancing year. For Nick, he wasn't sure. Mrs. Mac just felt like family; something he longed for.

In a town like DC, having someone with hard worn values, a stern sense of right and wrong and the occasional meal, helped keep him balanced. In a strange way, they needed each other.

Nick decided to change clothes, so they ducked down the stairwell to his door. He stopped suddenly. The front door was ajar. Nick pushed it open with his fingers. Now was the time that Kiki could turn into a yapping monster, but she was infatuated with a tattered piece of newspaper that had blown down into Nick's entrance.

He yanked on the leash, and the two entered the apartment. There were only three rooms—a main room, where his hide-a-bed was located, a kitchen, and a closet of a bathroom. Nothing appeared to be moved. The TV was still there, stereo where it belonged. Nick edged toward the bathroom and in one move flung the door open, preparing to battle whoever was in there.

It was empty. He turned and looked around the apartment. Everything looked as he'd left it. After his breathing returned to normal, Nick walked back and pushed the door closed. He quickly changed into jeans and a T shirt.

One thought went through his mind. He got down on his hands and knees and peered under the hide-a-bed. The wooden cigar box was where he'd left it. He peeked inside just to be sure. Of course, it no longer housed cigars, but something more valuable, something recently legalized in the city.

Convinced that he'd just forgotten to pull the door shut when he'd left that morning, Nick took Kiki on that walk he'd promised.

Chapter 3

The sun dipped its head below the tree line along George Washington Parkway as the black GMC SUV powered in the left lane. The two sun-glassed suits with earpieces didn't speak, as was their routine.

Agent Gray, the navigator, gazed out the right window at the sleek, white boats congregating near the three sisters, an outcropping of rock that poked out of the Potomac. Across the river, the towering spires of Healy Hall at Georgetown University stood radiantly.

The sole passenger in the back, though looking in the same direction, didn't share the concern for the scenery. He pondered the Sixth Amendment argument presented by the brief he held in his left hand while chewing on the ear piece of his glasses held in the right.

The Bryant exception was flat wrong; he'd been in the minority on that opinion three years before. It was the law of the land, however. He'd sworn to uphold it, but an extension to include excited utterances in routine investigations was too much. It swallowed the whole amendment. Bryant made a mockery of the Confrontation Clause.

Where had the Court gone? Where was it headed?

So much had changed since Silvio Caprelli had taken his seat on the highest court in the land. Strict constructionists like him had ruled the day. Over the years progressives, or those known for "evolving" Constitutional rights had become the majority. Splits among the justices had become common and were eerily predictable.

Evolving Constitutional rights? Caprelli shuttered at the thought. Constitutional rights were what the framers set them out to be; no more, no less. If folks didn't like them, the framers set out a procedure for changing them—amend the Constitution. Such efforts were far too difficult. How could any progressive expect the square states to approve changes to the Constitution? No, the easier way was to get judges on the bench who would bend the Constitution to meet the objective. For Caprelli, any attempt to "read" things into the Constitution was legislating at best and legal heresy at worst.

Twelve years had flown by since that sun-drenched September morning when he was sworn in on the steps of the Supreme Court Building—twelve Red Sundays, twelve State of the Union speeches, and oddly enough, twelve Supreme Court justices with whom he'd served over the years. In this job for life, he'd witnessed three presidencies and had sworn in the current inhabitant of the White House, though he couldn't think of many topics on which they would agree.

The SUV shifted into the right lane, Agent Jaspers noticed a white cargo van coming up quickly from behind. The van shot past and moved into the right lane as well.

"What the hell?" Jaspers said, glancing to his left as a similar van, this one red, pulled long side. He hit the brakes as the van in front slowed. "Guy goes past me like a bat out of hell, then slows down. Then I've got this idiot," thumbing to his left, "on the—Jesus."

The red van in the left lane slammed into the SUV, knocking it askew. The brief was knocked from Caprelli's hands, scattering pages across the backseat and into the foot wells.

Agent Gray reached for the weapon on this belt as the escalade was hit again. "Shit." He knew what was coming down. Jaspers tried to slow down and get out of the box between the two vans. His eyes locked with Gray's momentarily. Gray reached forward and hit the button low on the console.

The red van slammed into the SUV again, this time keeping contact and pushing to the right. Jaspers saw the exit to the Glebe Road overlook ahead. They were pushing him off the parkway and onto the entrance to the overlook.

Glebe Overlook was a short span of roadway, about three hundred yards long with parking slots painted on the asphalt. It served no purpose other than to allow bored travelers to look a hundred feet down onto the Potomac River. No vehicles were parked in the overlook.

The white van slowed and gave Jasper no choice but to follow. They had to hold out for three minutes. The signal had been sent, and cruisers would be coming at high speed. Three minutes.

"Get on the floor," Gray yelled over his shoulder. The justice complied.

The lead van stopped, completely blocking the path of the SUV. Jaspers hit the gas and rammed the van from behind. The cargo van crumpled, but with brakes locked, the SUV couldn't escape. The red van angled to the left and behind the escalade; no escape.

Jaspers and Gray had handguns drawn. Their task was to delay. Help was coming. They had to hold out.

Two men in knitted black ski masks jumped from the side of the white van and spread apart. One in a green western shirt had an automatic weapon. The other in a blue T-shirt was carrying a bucket. A third man bailed out of the red van carrying an assault weapon and circled to the right.

Grabbing the pail with both hands, the man in the blue

T-shirt flung its contents onto the windshield. Black paint darkened the vehicle followed by the repeating discharge of an assault weapon—several assault weapons.

The reinforced glass popped and cracked. Blinded and unable to return fire, the agents ducked down. Though not bullet-proof like the President's limo, the windshields in standard service vehicles were built to withstand significant impact, but it wouldn't hold out for long.

Where the hell is back up?

~

The two men scrambled to either side of the vehicle and continued firing. The side windows blew out quickly. Agent Gray fired his weapon once, Jaspers not at all. In a matter of seconds, their bodies were bloodied and riddled with bullets. The men ran to the back door of the escalade. It was locked.

One of the men reached through the space that used to be the driver's side window and popped the lock. The back doors were thrown open. Justice Caprelli, stretched on the floor of the SUV, held his hands forward.

"Get out."

Caprelli started to get up off the floor when a hand gripped the back of his shirt and yanked him out of the vehicle. The man was a gorilla holding the Supreme Court Justice like a puppet. Caprelli's hands were out to the side, his airway constricted by the man with the death grip on the collar of his pressed white dress shirt. He was being dragged to the lead van.

"Wha—what do you—" Caprelli garbled, but couldn't finish.

The man threw him into the side of the van. Caprelli fell to the ground, blood oozing from a cut over his eye from being slammed into the van. A man in a blue T-shirt grabbed the justice's tie and lifted him to his feet.

"Get your clothes off." This came from the tallest of the three in the green shirt and jeans, the one who had ripped him like a rag doll from the SUV.

"What? What are you—?" The assault weapon's butt hit him square in the face, knocking him back into the van. Pain seared through his face, between his eyes. He slid down the side of the vehicle into a seated position. The tie grabber picked him up again.

"No questions. Get your clothes off. *Now!*"

Caprelli was dazed and disoriented by the blow, but fumbled with his fingers to get his shirt and pants off. He trembled, not from the cool air, but from sheer terror.

One man ran back to the red van and pulled out a whiskey bottle. He reached inside the SUV's broken window and shattered it against steering wheel.

"Everything," green shirt yelled at him.

The justice slid his boxer shorts onto the ground and tugged off his socks. Completely naked, he covered himself with his hands.

"Get in," he said, motioning to the open side compartment.

The man in the blue T-shirt reached down and pulled the wallet from the pants. He started to examine the contents as the man in the green shirt slapped it from his hands.

"Hey, the cash," blue T-shirt pleaded.

"Ya dumbshit." Green shirt threw the wallet into the van and pushed the justice in behind. "Let's go." He nodded to the man standing by the bullet-riddled SUV. That one fired up a Zippo and tossed it into the front seat. Flames erupted, dancing inside the front seat of the disabled carcass.

The vans burned rubber accelerating through the overlook, shooting back onto GW Parkway. Moving at high speed, dodging back and forth in the lanes, they shot past other vehicles.

At the McLean exit, one van got off the parkway, the other kept speeding westward.

~

Caprelli had fallen face forward and was kicked and bounced as the van rocketed up to speed. His upper body was pinned between the back of the driver seat and a smooth flat, object to his left side. His heart pounded; he was breathless and certain that his nose was broken. He pressed it between his fingers to staunch the bleeding.

Who were these guys? Where were they taking me? What did they want?

Questions swirled. He knew all of the answers were bad.

Terror surged through him like an electrical current. *How long before anyone will know I'm gone? How much money do they want? Will Stella be able to get the money together? Stella. Oh God. What's going on?* Blood rolled down his cheek and into his mouth.

Be calm, he thought. He took two deep breaths. Be smart. You'll get through this, whatever it is. Be calm.

He rolled onto his shoulder and pushed himself into a seated position. He was going to confront his captors. He opened his lips, but before sounds could come out, he froze. The sheer terror of the attack was nothing compared to what he saw now.

He stared at the smooth flat object next to which he had lain seconds before. Caprelli's breath was trapped in his throat as he stared, unable to remove his eyes.

It was a wooden casket.

Chapter 4

Javier Lozano was an American.

Though the oldest child of Spanish surnamed parents, he wasn't Latin American.

Though his birth certificate identified him as Javier Lozano Castaneda, he wasn't Hispanic American.

Though born in the Montaverde mountains of Mexico, he wasn't Mexican American.

Javier Lozano was an American.

Despite a distinctively ethnic name, he didn't engage in ethnic culture. Despite his love and loyalty to family, he was committed to them as individuals, not their race.

The coyotes had brought Javier and his family across the Rio Grande. Javier was two years old. Jorge, his father, wouldn't discuss their journey, but Juanita, his mother did.

Coyotes were a necessary evil. If they wanted into the US, they needed a tour guide. Coyotes could never be trusted. To make it safely, they slept with their eyes open.

Jorge and Juanita spent all of their savings and all the money they could scrape together to get into the caravan. At least that's what they'd told the coyotes.

Coyotes knew better. Nobody went penniless into the US. Everyone in the caravan said they'd given up all their money. They'd all lied.

The Lozano family headed out from the hills outside

Algodones for the three day journey to America. Six others paid their life savings to travel with the three coyotes.

The second night, the couples were separated and the shake down ensued. Jorge had prepared Juanita for the trap. Just play the part; all will be fine.

The coyotes had pulled money out of two of their traveling companions. One man was brutally beaten. Jorge had sewn ten US twenty dollar bills into the sole of his boot. He didn't tell Juanita. It would be better if she didn't know. She just knew he had money. She didn't know how much or where.

The last night the coyotes met up with the border compadres. These were the guys who could get them across the river. Of course, no one bothered to tell the clients that there was another toll to pay. The amount they paid the coyotes was to be all-inclusive, but with mock shrugs they were told that "things change."

The smelly and tattooed man wrestled Javier away from Juanita and held a knife to the boy's throat. He didn't give a damn whether they made it to America. If they wanted to save their son's life, they would come up with $100, pronto.

Jorge knew if he pulled out any money, they would just kill them all. Better to show resolve than die displaying weakness. Juanita and Jorge were separated, Jorge restrained by two of the coyotes, while tattoo man and Juanita had a private discussion.

Sweat oozed down Jorge's face as the men laughed at him. They never discussed what happened. They didn't have to. The next day they were driven to the edge of the river and, on the signal from the coyote with the binoculars, they crossed onto American soil.

They spent two nights in Brownsville and then were off to Virginia by bus. Jorge found work, and their American dream had taken root. When Javier entered public school, his teacher suspected that he was mentally challenged because he didn't speak a word of English. When the counselor translated the problem for the parents, they were shocked and embarrassed.

From that day forward, his parents never spoke Spanish again in the home, only English. Many of their early conversations were primitive and mono-syllabic, but it was all in English.

Javier enlisted in the Army right out of college. September 11 changed his life, but not in a predictable way. Being in the service meant he would complete a tour in Iraq, that was a given. But in the wake of the 9-11 attacks, the President had, with little fanfare, signed an executive order announcing that the military was engaged in a "time of conflict."

For the masses, the phrase didn't mean much. For Javier, it meant he could become a US citizen under Section 329. It was a little known provision that permitted naturalization for service members regardless of whether they entered the country legally. Becoming a naturalized citizen gave Javier opportunities that never would have been available otherwise.

Law enforcement was his interest, and he knew that red-blooded Americans worked for the FBI. With his language fluency and top scores at Quantico, he was recruited into the Counterterrorism Division.

Step and grade promotions came quickly and easily as he outworked and outperformed his fellow Special Agents. He'd been fast tracked for advancement, and his ethnic background was a bonus, though Javier refused to acknowledge it.

No one ground their casework harder than Javier. Intra agency assignments with CounterIntel, Cyber and Hostage Rescue gave him the perfect credentials for the Caprelli kidnapping.

The siren wailed as two black sedans thumped forward, left wheels in the median, right wheels on asphalt. George Washington Parkway had been closed in the northbound direction soon after the kidnapping had been reported. Two lanes of traffic sat and moved forward in intermittent increments. The backup stopped traffic all the way onto the Roosevelt Bridge.

Fifteen minutes after the kidnapping, Javier got the call from William Ford Jannsen, Director of the FBI. This was big. All eyes would be on him, and getting the Justice back safely was the highest priority. It wasn't just about one man's security; it was about the mental well being of a nation. Terrorists can't kidnap government officials and get away with it. The answer was just that simple.

Javier had said thank you to Jannsen. It stunned the FBI Director. "Don't thank me," Jannsen said flatly. "Just get that guy back. And in one piece."

The fire engine came into view first. Javier knew it was there, but he shook his head anyway. All that water will damage the crime scene. Any trace evidence would be gone, and simple evidence like shell casings would all be washed from their original location.

Guys were pros.

It made no difference whether the dead Secret Service officers were burned or not. The only reason for the fire was to get us to cover their tracks. That's one for the bad guys, Javier thought.

The sedans stopped just short of the entrance to the overlook. Javier was followed through the standing traffic by four other FBI agents. His jet black hair was trimmed and swept back, signaling a man on the move. His inherited Hispanic features were accentuated in a starched white dress shirt and dark grey suit. Like a jackal on the prowl, he led the pack of agents toward the scene.

The fire truck blocked the entrance, three Arlington Police cars and one US Park Police vehicle sat on the grassy area dividing the overlook from GW Parkway. Several officers milled about in various stages of investigation.

"Who's the OIC?" Javier shouted.

An athletic police officer with dark hair and matching mustache stepped forward. "Detective Sergeant Milbank," he said, approaching the FBI agents.

Javier flashed his creds. "Special Agent Lozano. This is my crime scene now."

Milbank nodded. Normally the locals wanted to argue over jurisdiction. This guy didn't. Javier knew Milbank didn't want any part of the kidnapping of a Supreme Court Justice. He could handle the occasional drunk driving Senator or car crashes involving diplomat kids, but he didn't want this case and appeared more than happy to pass leadership on to the feds.

Steam and whiffs of smoke drifted from the incapacitated SUV. The air hung heavy without a breath of wind. The unmistakable stench of burned flesh wafted from the vehicle. Water dripped of the vehicle as though it had just run through a manual car wash.

Javier shook his head and scanned the area. He quickly pointed right. "Hey, what's that guy doing?"

A uniformed officer was circling the front bumper of the burned out SUV, peering at the ground.

"That's my guy," Milbank said. "I asked him to do a spiral search of the—"

"You," Javier shouted toward the man. "Yeah, you! Get off my crime scene."

Javier turned toward Milbank. "Any wits?"

"Yeah, got three witnesses who were driving by. Being questioned over there." Milbank motioned to the far end of the overlook.

"Thank you, Detective. We've got it from here." He turned and faced the officers behind him. "I want a two by two grid search starting over there and extending six feet beyond the overlook."

He turned back to the scene and motioned. "I want photos from here and there, panoramic shots. I want three foot grid photos of the entire overlook, one foot grid shots of the interior of the vehicle. I want perspective shots—all directions from the vehicle. We got three wits over there; get a complete run-down." He stepped forward, motioning to his left. "And get that damn fire engine out of here. I want every shell casing, cigarette butt, sunflower seed, everything bagged and tagged."

"Yes sir," they said nearly in unison.

"Find out where the water runs and pull the drains and see what can be salvaged. And get the M.E. on the phone. No reason to keep the bodies here. That's not going to tell us anything. See if we can lift any prints from the exterior of the car." Between the baptism of fire and water that the SUV endured, the likelihood of usable prints was distinctly remote.

With this assignment Javier had unlimited resources and a nation watching. Remote or not, he wasn't going to miss a trick.

He looked to his right down the parkway where stationary cars stood end to end as far as the eye could see. "We're gonna be here awhile."

Chapter 5

Elliott Galbert wheeled his white Escalade out of his four stall garage and backed into the cul de sac. The rims glistened in the sunlight. Everything Galbert owned glistened and gave the appearance of perfection. People judged others based on appearances. Galbert's mannerisms screamed success and power.

He gunned the engine and wove through the curvy pre-planned neighborhood toward the guard house. McMansions lined the streets, set back a suitable distance from the road to create maximum impression.

The Reserve in McLean existed for the new rich. A smattering of hi-tech executives from the Dulles corridor were in residence in The Reserve. A few double dipping government retirees lived there. Rich with a government pension and lifetime benefits, these folks started second careers, some in the private sector and many in the intelligence field. A married couple both double dipping equated to nearly four incomes to support their enclave in the suburbs.

Galbert and other residents were business folk. In this neighborhood, government contractors, like Galbert, had the resources to occupy these houses of distinction.

Galbert slowed ever so slightly as he shot through the gatehouse. The man in the grey uniform waved. Galbert ignored him. He approached Georgetown Pike, slowed, tapped his brakes, then turned left toward Great Falls.

Galbert sped west along the winding wet asphalt of the
Pike. He made a mental note to have his car washed. The
damn road would leave water spots on the lower half of his
vehicle.

Galbert was a creation of the federal government. Like
many contemporaries, he started a government contracting
business. Small business set asides allowed him to get his
first contracts. SBA loans flowed easily, and his business
flourished. In a matter of seven years he held contracts
totaling nearly ninety million dollars, with unexercised
option years. He worked for DOE, GSA, CMS, DoD, and
several intel shops.

He started with IT services, rode the wave of wiring the
US government for personal computers. Along the way he'd
acquired a few other contractors who had expertise valuable
to the world's largest client, but who couldn't operate a
business with a Sherpa and a flashlight. He picked them up
on the cheap and added to his collection of contracts like a
stack of poker chips.

Then, as many successful contractors learned, Galbert
hit the wall. It wasn't a wall he could overcome with business
savvy; it was a wall created by FAR, the Federal Acquisition
Regulations.

Galbert's business had just flat become too successful.
So successful, in fact, that he would no longer qualify for
small business set asides. He was too small to be big and
too big to be small. He would have to compete on the same
field with the multibillion dollar boys, no advantage going
forward.

So like others before him, he picked up his poker chips
and sold them to the highest bidder. Lockheed Martin paid
him just a shade under two hundred million dollars for the
business, gave him a board seat on a corporate division that
never met, and bought a three year non-compete.

Galbert, being young and naïve, shared the largesse with his most trusted employees and still pocketed a shade over one hundred thirty large.

He took his trophy wife, his second, on lavish vacations to exotic resorts and locations, but hated every minute of it. Like a clock ticking in his head, Galbert was waiting for one thing, for that moment when his non-compete expired. Then, like all successful government contractors, he started over.

He was once again a qualified small business with the ability to pickup set aside contracts like poker chips. It was known as the McLean shuffle. Form small business, acquire federal contracts, acquire smaller businesses, cash out, repeat as necessary.

This was the only line of business where one acquired promises from the government, then bundled them up as assets and sold those promises to the highest bidder. It was a beautiful business model and one that made Galbert a wealthy and powerful man.

This incarnation of the McLean shuffle was called Center Tech, Inc. or CTI in the world's capital of abbreviated names. Rather than naming the business after himself as some losers did, Galbert wanted a name that sounded stable and hi-tech, not some goofy mission oriented description of a name; just one that worked in this town.

Many of his minions from his former business were ready to get back to work. They had blown much of the money Galbert had given them. They had ridden Harleys through Colorado, sky dived in the desert, and blown cash on the latest Dulles corridor hi-tech software company pretending to be venture capitalists. They were ready to get back into business. This time they wanted a piece of the action.

How bold of them, Galbert thought.

So he made them put their own money up for ownership in Center Tech. That caused about half of them to give up the ownership idea and just hire on as employees. The few who ponied up cash had acquired less than fifteen percent of the company.

It was still Galbert's game to run, and he was a master of it.

He drove until Georgetown Pike hit a dead end at Route Seven. The Escalade merged smoothly onto the highway, made an illegal U-turn and dove onto a gravel road leading to Paddy O'Shea's Driving Range.

Great, he thought. Now he'd have a little mud to go along with the water marks.

Galbert had a problem. He hated problems. A man of his importance didn't have time for problems. They interfered with his sole motivation, making money.

At the end of the parking lot he swung into a space. One man stood at the end of the range dribbling shots off the driving mat. Galbert pulled a set of clubs from the back of his vehicle and marched toward the man. The tassels from his Italian loafers slapped as he walked.

"You suck at this," Galbert said to the man, who topped a ball about thirty yards off the rubber tee. The man turned and smiled. He wore a loose-fitting blue windbreaker over jeans and running shoes, no socks. Galbert set the clubs on the wooden frame next to the man's set.

"You're late," the man said.

"I'm on time wherever I am. You weren't going anywhere, Weasel," said Galbert.

He paused before his next swing and turned to look at Galbert. "My friends call me Haden. But you can call me Mr. Maxwell."

"I'll call you whatever I want. Weasel fits nicely."

Haden smiled and turned back to the ball. "Look at

us," Haden said. "Just a couple of pals out hitting range balls." He skittered a ball along the ground.

"Hardly," Galbert said. He looked down the range. One other golfer stood ten mats over. He powered balls into the distance one after another. "I don't like all this international bullshit I'm hearing."

"Relax, I've got it all covered, my friend."

"Costing me a fortune and you say relax. That's choice," Galbert said.

"We need the media exposure. The international terrorist talk is red meat for the media. The specter of foreign agents will rile up the natives. Get them in a fever pitch. Trust me," Haden said as he finally connected on a shot. He looked back over his shoulder. "Gotta play these guys. When the time is right, the truth will come out," he said with a laugh. "Our truth, that is."

"I want to know who's in on this," Galbert said. He leaned down and flicked a speck of mud of his tasseled loafers.

"You don't need to know. You hired me for a result. You'll get the result. You don't need to know how or why. Believe me."

"I checked you out," Galbert said. "You're just a damn GS11. You don't have any swag."

Haden smiled. "I've got more swag than you'll ever know. Your deal with General Dynamics got iced because of DOMTER. I'm getting that back on track for you. That contract alone will be worth triple the face value when you sell. I'm going to make you a wealthy man, my friend. Very wealthy indeed."

"Make it fast," Galbert said. "I'm losing my patience, and when I lose my patience, I stop spending money, Haden. Got it?"

"Chill. I've got everything under control," Haden said.

Galbert spun on his heels and stomped off toward his rig. He fired it up and scattered gravel as he left the lot.

~

Haden sneered as he glanced at the bag of clubs that Galbert left behind. Once back at his apartment, he'd go through the bag. There would be seventy-five thousand in cash tucked in there somewhere.

Damn well better be.

Chapter 6

The FBI's Hoover Building occupied an entire city block in downtown DC. It was constructed with the architectural grace and elegance of an above ground bomb shelter. Underground parking was controlled by reverse ramps that had to be lowered by hydraulic power. Nobody got into that building by mistake.

On the fourth floor of the east wing a dozen federal agents were jammed around a small conference table. Javier was conducting a role call for the interagency task force on the Caprelli kidnapping. Although it was nearly midnight and the calls hadn't gone out until after seven pm, perfect attendance had been achieved. The kidnapping of Justice Caprelli was the only story circulating in the media spin cycle. The heat was building.

Kate Buchanan from Justice was one of three women present. Her brunette hair was pinned back in a sensible fashion, and she wore a navy suit with a white blouse. Corporate looking, Javier thought. Piercing blue eyes, high cheek bones, and a megawatt smile, she could easily pass herself off as a former Miss America. At twenty-eight, she was eye candy for the force. She would be eye candy in any crowd.

"Agent Buchanan." Javier nodded toward her. "She has lead from Justice. We'll work everything through her and her team search warrants, subpoenas, questions on protocol, everything."

He turned directly toward her. "Kate, we'll need a review and detail on every case Caprelli was working on. All his opinions in the past five years. Everything he authored, speeches, presentations. Everything."

"Already on it," she snapped back.

"Officer Jonah." Javier pointed to the large black man across the table from Kate. "He's the liaison with DC Police. Kathy Hernandez is from the Virginia State Patrol. Next to her is Pete McGarrity." A balding head was perched on the bulging layer of fat in a rumpled white dress shirt. He nodded to the group.

Javier continued, "Pete is from the agency. He'll bring us intel on international groups that may be of interest. Next is Wesley Kipling. He's my second in command. Despite his youthful appearance, he served in the military, had a stint at the agency, private contracting and four years here." Wesley smiled and nodded.

Pointing at a long-haired pimply faced kid, Javier continued. "Scottie Palmer is our IT lead." Palmer gave a bored wave to the group. Kid had the social skills of a walnut, Javier knew, but as an IT expert, he was the Bureau's shining beacon. That's why Javier chose him. He could deal with quirky personalities, but he couldn't deal with failure.

Javier continued, "Keep him copied on all reports and intel. Ken Shuller will also work on communications. Dave Winters is liaison from Homeland." He ticked off the last three people, "Kevin Jacobs, Sean Renter, and Maggie Dillman are junior agents. They will provide support, research, anything you need to move forward."

Javier commanded the group standing at one end of the table. Once introductions were done, he lifted a folder. "In the binder in front of you is the write-up on the scene investigation, photos, background on Caprelli and the two officers killed. Memorize it, then let's build a game plan.

One other word. This is highest priority. I know I don't need to say this, but I will. Nothing leaves this group. Nobody talks to media, wives, girlfriends," then glancing at Kate. "Anyone. No interviews. Nothing. Anything released comes through me and only me." Javier paused, making eye contact with each person present.

"Pete, we're going to need background on cell activity in the region," Javier said. "And a primer on suspected international terror groups operating in the country."

Pete leaned back and remained silent. After a few seconds he started gesturing with his hands. "Well, you know it takes some time to get information cleared and de-classed—"

"I don't want to hear it. Just get it for us, and get it now."

"There's only so much I can do quickly."

Javier slammed his hand on the table. "Don't give me that. We need that info, and we need it right now. We've got a Supreme Court Justice who's been nabbed, we've got two dead agents. I don't want excuses, and I sure as hell don't want you playing hide the weenie with us. Get it and get it right fucking now."

Pete nodded, but displayed little enthusiasm.

Wesley looked down at the table, smiling.

"We've got to work together. No barriers, no agency interference. You're on this team and, if you aren't totally committed to it, leave now." He pointed toward the door and glared at McGarrity. "Are we clear?"

They shifted around nervously. Javier let his remarks hang in the air.

"Now," he continued. "We've got four rooms on this wing. Media/tech is on the far end, the next room will serve as a library, this conference room and the room on the other side for operations. Get used to it. Let's get to work."

~

Thirty minutes later they took a break. A solitary task force member left the room and took the elevator to the ground floor. He removed his personal cell from his back pocket.

He had an important call to make.

Chapter 7

The silence was insufferable.

He'd tried screaming. He'd tried kicking. He'd tried pushing. Nothing worked. Caprelli remembered driving for several hours, then the sound of a motorcycle or some kind of small vehicle.

A rag doused with chloroform was the last he recalled. His hands were bound, his legs not. The space into which he was confined had to be the coffin he'd seen in the van.

The initial shock and fear brought out emotional responses from the jurist. Time and silence allowed him to return to his analytical frame of mind. It was his primary strength. If he was going to get through this, he knew it would be with his mind, not physical strength.

He had a water bottle that he was able to pull open with his teeth. A small plastic bowl with a form-fitting lid held some kind of mixture of rice and crisp green beans. The smell of his own urine burned his nostrils and eliminated any appetite.

If they meant to kill me, he thought, I'd be dead already. They wouldn't poison him with the water or food. It made no sense.

None of this made sense.

His wandering thoughts were of Stella and what she must be going through. She would have had a fabulous dinner on the table, as today was their home date night. It was a tradition of twenty-five years.

Redemption Day

She had completed classes in French cuisine, one with Michel Richard, the world famous chef of Citronelle in Georgetown and the other at the L'Atelier de Cuisine in Montepellier, France. It was always a surprise and always delicious. She must be devastated. He was sure the police were with her, and hopefully neighbors were there to console her. His heart ached.

Caprelli had no experiences to help him adapt to his confinement. He'd read somewhere that to keep his senses about him, he had to focus on something. Captives who survived prison camps were able to maintain equilibrium by visualizing tasks, building a wall brick by brick, or remembering small details from their past.

His advantage at this point was his mind, and he had to keep it sharp. He was unable to relax, so he used his mind.

He thought back to his law school days and the techniques he'd incorporated to learn the law. Within his mind he rattled off the exceptions to hearsay evidence. He recited the rule against perpetuities. He counted off the exceptions to the Statute of Frauds. He was able to visualize his outlines for constitutional law, contract law and Federal Rules of Evidence. His mind hummed, and through the mental distraction, he was comforted.

Caprelli knew he needed to sleep, preserve his strength, but he couldn't. He thought back to his days in his law firm in Chicago. There were over 100 attorneys, which at the time was a large firm, not like the thousand plus mega firms that existed today. He started with his corner office and recited the names of the attorneys, paralegals, and secretaries as he moved from one end of the office to the other, then the floor below.

David Jacobson, Northwestern grad. Tax lawyer. Cindy Baker, paralegal for corporate commercial group.

He'd been on the bench for 22 years, twelve on the Supreme Court, five with the US Court of Appeals for the

Seventh Circuit, and five years as a district court judge in Chicago. Caprelli was proud that he could remember the members of his former firm. It had been a long time, but he wouldn't allow himself to forget.

Martha Grimble, secretary to Jacobson and Gary Littman. Littman, Colombia law, securities specialist. Debbie. Something. He concentrated. Debbie Preston; no Debbie Prescott. Yale. Clerked for...somebody. Seventh Circuit. Judge Rueben Grainger. Next was a tall guy... Northwestern law school. Blond hair. Big Chicago Bears fan. Spencer Daly.

In the darkness and silence, he mentally walked the halls of his former office. When he made it all the way around, he started again.

Chapter 8

Nick ambled down 33rd Street toward Megan's on M Street. He dodged in and out of the garbage cans that lined the street. The imposing federal-style townhouses had no back yard access or side access, so despite the pretentious locations, garbage was hauled to the street through the front door.

The red brick sidewalks required some level of focus to avoid tripping over uneven bricks and holes previously occupied by missing bricks. Steps down into English apartments narrowed the path further.

Nick knew the streets of Georgetown. He'd walked them all hours of the day and night. He'd jogged every sidewalk from Foggy Bottom to Georgetown University, from the Potomac River to the Dumbarton Gardens above S Street.

After a left turn on M Street, he walked past two storefronts and into Megan's coffee shop. In a world of globally branded coffee houses with their pre-programmed coolness, Megan's was an oasis. The owner, Megan in fact, was on site nearly every day and served as chief barista at most times.

Megan looked behind her toward the door as Nick entered. Steam from the espresso machine hissed and fogged the air around her. Half a dozen patrons were spread out among the tables in the narrow refurbished townhouse. The smell of roasted coffee filled Nick's senses as the door closed behind him.

"Skinny vanilla latte with a shot, coming up, Nick."

"Thanks, Megan." Nick handed a bill to the girl running the register and placed a copy of the *Washington Post* on the counter as well. Megan's always had free papers lying on tables and chairs, but Nick preferred to buy one. There was something wrong about reading a second hand paper. The news seemed tired and worn as the wrinkled pages. Even though he didn't need to buy a paper, he always did. It was part of being a good customer.

"You playing hooky today?" Megan asked. Her red hair was pulled back into a tight bun. She was what they euphemistically called big-boned. She had striking features, large pronounced cheekbones with lips so full, Hollywood starlets would swoon. She was nearly as wide as she was tall and easily capable of breaking open crates of coffee beans with her bare hands.

It was a Tuesday, after all. Nick was a regular Saturday and Sunday morning guy, but not so much on weekdays. Not wanting to fess up to being unemployed, Nick looked down at his tennis shoes, jeans, and corduroy shirt and said, "Yep. Gotta take those leave days or lose them. Need a day to recharge the batteries."

"I hear you," she said as she turned and slid a mug across the counter.

Nick blew the foam back from the edge and took a tentative sip. "The best, Megan. You're the best." He gave her a little salute with the mug and took a seat at an open table.

The front page of the post was slathered with stores on the kidnapped justice. Photos of the scene, diagrams

42

of the kidnapping, timelines of the events, articles, and commentaries filled the first section of the paper. Who would kidnap a Supreme Court Justice, much less the most conservative member of the bench? It just didn't make sense. No one had claimed responsibility, at least as of the printing of the *Post*. Articles chronicled the careers of the Secret Service officers. One fiancée would live the rest of her life without the man she loved. The other officer left a wife and two small children behind.

These guys just don't get taken out like this, Nick thought. Something's not right.

Nick glanced at the television monitor high above the counter. Breaking news flashed across the screen. The concept of breaking news had fallen so far in a twenty-four/seven news cycle. It could be a car crashing into a McDonald's in backwater Tennessee, or maybe it was a warehouse fire somewhere in Kansas. The Caprelli kidnapping sprung onto the screen and Nick yelled for Megan to turn up the volume.

The perky blonde news reader blathered forward. "The Associated Press is reporting that terrorist group, Sahhallam Brotherhood is claiming responsibility for the kidnapping of Justice Silvio Caprelli. FBI and Justice Officials have yet to confirm the connection. The Sahhallam Brotherhood was originally founded in Yemen and was responsible for the Paris train bombing last year and the triple bombing in Amsterdam six months ago.

"This is the first time the group has struck on US soil," she continued. "Mastermind of the Sahhallam Brotherhood is believed to be Ahmed Ali Akbar, better known as the Sultan of Sand. Akbar was educated in the United States and is believed to have a large number of sleeper cells at his disposal. We continue to follow this story and will interrupt our regular programming as more information becomes available."

"This just makes me angry," Megan said. "Man's got a family. This is just getting so crazy. If they can nab a man under Secret Service protection, we're not safe anywhere anymore."

Nick was shaking his head. "Doesn't make sense."

"What do you mean?" Megan said.

"Guys like this, the Brotherhood and al-Qaida; kidnappings aren't their MO. Suicide bombings and targeted bombings, yes, but not a kidnapping. Certainly not on US soil."

"Yes they do," a woman piped up from the adjoining table. "They kidnapped plenty of our boys. Tortured them, cut their heads off, and videotaped it."

The proverbial "they," Nick thought. Wrap them up in one big stereotype. All Muslims are terrorists, all killers.

He looked at the woman. "What happened in the Iraq or Afghanistan war isn't what I'm talking about. These are terrorist cells."

"Bunch of godless animals is what they are," the woman continued. "We need to drop the big one on the whole place. Bomb them back to the Stone Age."

"Good way to kill a bunch of innocent people," Nick said.

"They harbor these killers. They don't prosecute them or even try and stop them in their home country. They're as bad as anyone. Ain't nobody innocent over there. Now they're sending guys over here, kidnapping folks. Walk right over our borders, 'cause our government don't give a damn about keeping them out. We should have cleaned them out when we had the chance."

No reason to debate with her. She had swallowed the blunt message of media fear mongers, hook, line, and sinker.

This kidnapping was surgical. It was precise. No homemade incendiary device was employed. No sloppy work to kill innocent people. There was no suicide attacker. No, this was different. This didn't have the marker of international terrorism. This was intentional. This had a plan behind it, but what was the motive?

Nick grabbed his phone and turned away from the television, poking the speed dial for a familiar number.

"Nick, how you doing?"

"I'm fine, Dave. Just fine," Nick said.

"Can't believe you called. Was just talking about you," said Winters.

"Me? What are you doing, an autopsy on my career?"

"Nope, got a call for you. Sheriff from Hampshire County, over in West Virginia. Name's Brager. Know him?"

"Brager?" Nick searched his memory. "No, coming up blank."

"Said he met you at a Homeland conference in Richmond last year," Winters said.

"I remember the conference; was on identity scams and the blood suckers who sell them," he said. "There was a pretty good crowd there. Can't say I can place the guy."

"Anyway. I told him you weren't here anymore. Didn't tell him anything else."

"Thanks, man."

"Just want you to know. I gave him your cell number. Still can't believe yesterday. Just plain wrong, Nick. Just wrong."

"Hey, you didn't do anything. When I calmed down, I realized it's just business. It'll all work out."

"You call your mother?" Winters asked.

"What are you, my nanny?"

"Just saying, you're all she's got. You need to reach out. I've got no family left. You do. And with what she's been through, ya know, with your dad and everything. She'll want to know."

Despite the ribbing from Winters, Nick knew he was right. Like the advice from the middle aged uncle to a teenager, the uncle was correct, but the teenager was too irresponsible to follow it.

"I know," said Nick. "Still a little early to be calling Nebraska right now."

"Family's not around forever, Nick. All I'm saying. Just don't miss an opportunity. They don't come back."

"I know. Thanks. But the reason I called; any chance you can shoot me the DOMTER file I was working on before I left? I need some of the research. Might have something to do with this Caprelli kidnapping.

There was only silence on the line.

"Dave?"

"Yeah, I'm here. Nick, you know I'd help if I could."

"You can redact anything classified. Heck, there's nothing in there that would be sensitive."

More silence.

"Nick, I just can't. If you take it up with Galbert or go through channels at Homeland..." He paused. "I'll front run it for you, but if I send anything out of here..." Winters stopped and a sigh escaped. "You know I've only got a little over a year to go for my pension, but edgy as things are here right now, I just can't risk it. I'm sorry, buddy."

"No problem. I understand. I'll take it through channels." Nick knew he wouldn't, but wanted to let Winters off the hook. "Here's something you can do, though. Do you know who's running the investigation on Caprelli?"

"That I can find out. I'll shoot you an email. It's probably going to be one of those inter-agency cluster jobs, I'm sure. You know, spread the blame around."

"Probably right. Appreciate it, Dave. Hey, let's grab lunch one of these days."

"You got it. Let me know."

Nick snapped the call off. That was stupid. He knew Winters wouldn't release anything. It was wrong to even ask.

The talking head on the TV was interviewing a terrorist expert describing how cells have evolved their tactics to include kidnappings and related activities, that we shouldn't be surprised.

"See? I told you," the woman said, pointing to the set.

Nick shook his head, folded the paper under his arm, and moved toward the exit. "Thanks, Megan. Have a good day."

Chapter 9

Wolfe leaned and spat over the cracked and splintered wooden railing. The sun was just beginning to peek through the budding trees that surrounded the cabin. There was no sound save for a few birds flitting among the trees. The cabin was set back a half mile from Miller's Road. The seclusion was the primary attraction of the place. Another quarter mile up the mountain was the shed. The prize was conveniently secured there.

The recession hadn't broken in West Virginia, and that allowed him to rent the place for a song. A fraction of his "off the books" earnings from his stint in Afghanistan had secured a paid up one year lease.

He'd been up before dawn. He always was. The hanging pollen burned his eyes, but didn't prevent him from his daily regimen of two hundred sit ups and push ups. Something he'd done every morning since the eighth grade.

Although he carried a pistol now, he missed the M16 and other weaponry he had access to in what they euphemistically called hell. Wolfe wouldn't serve in the military. That would be treasonous, but his cousin had set him up with an overseas gig with Power Security.

Jim Power understood the struggle, and he didn't care about one's political views. He only cared about courage and making money. Wolfe fit in perfectly. As one of the contract security forces for the US government's effort in the Afghan hills, laying down the law was all that mattered.

Two years had aged him ten, but Wolfe loved it. He didn't give a shit about the soldiers and officers he protected. It was just a job and, if the job required him to kill those godless freaks, that was fine with him. The firefights and ambushes had sharpened his senses. He could smell a set up as ably as anyone on the front, but mostly he could smell fear.

That fear came primarily from the men he protected. They just wanted to survive and make it home in one piece. They feared engagement with the enemy. Wolfe relished it. The rulebook would call him a mercenary. Power dubbed his group PFH-Patriots For Hire. The "for hire" was the only part Wolfe ascribed to.

He lifted the stained mug off the railing and took a slug of coffee. Kidnapping was a trade he learned well in the mountains outside Kabul. Know your enemy, know their pattern, study the intel, and execute the mission.

His former captives had been tribal leaders and their henchmen. Getting information from them was a different matter. Three of his captives had died under his band of thugs, without providing anything of value. He'd learned to back off, increase the fear, amplify the uncertainty. He eventually could get them to sing.

When they sang, more bad guys died. That was Wolfe's job.

Moving cargo from Kabul to Enterprise base was his milk run. Knowing where the insurgents hid and the tricks of their trade became his expertise. He laughed as he thought back. His squad had named the route Wolfe's Highway. Anything that interfered with the route had to be eliminated. At times that involved women and kids, but the job had to be done.

Wolfe had to be spirited away from the front after destroying a school that might have hidden some local misfits. Power Security valued the effort, but the pressure from the media and those losers in Congress had turned the pot to boil. An international storm erupted.

Power apologized to the world community. Wolfe didn't. His base pay had been frozen by the cretins who managed the international banking community. Wolfe was able to carry a backpack of cash through Toronto and into the wilds of Canada before crossing the border into the welcoming arm of the Montana Brotherhood.

Congressional committees and other do-good interest groups shouted for his head, but Power had given him a head start. And that was all Wolfe needed to disappear.

With his store of cash and his new-found connection in Washington, he was able to plan the mission that mattered most.

The mission started with the prize in the shed.

Chapter 10

Nick checked his Blackberry as he turned on 33rd Street and climbed back into the Georgetown neighborhood. A note from Winters awaited him. Guy named Javier Lozano was the OIC on the Caprelli task force. FBI was leading the investigation. That made sense, Nick thought. A phone number was also included.

Nick wouldn't call just yet. First, he had to have something. Right now he only had a hunch, but he knew he was much closer to the truth than what the media reported. He continued uphill into the quiet residential area.

A note from Winters popped up. This one had the phone number for Sheriff Brager. He dialed. Brager answered on the second ring.

"Sheriff, this is Nick James, from Homeland." Could he still say that? Well, it was a small lie and would avoid going into a long explanation. "Dave Winters said you called."

"I don't know if you remember me, but we met at a conference about a year back. Identity scams. Anyway, I got something I want you to see. Not really sure what the hell it is, but figured if anyone knew, it'd be you."

"Sure, where do you want to meet?"

"I'm sitting outside your place right now," Brager said.

"The office?"

"No, your house. Winters said you were working from home today and gave me your address."

Appreciate Winters covering for me, he thought.

"I'm about six blocks from there right now. Hang tight and I'll be there soon." He double timed it up the hill and chuckled to himself, unemployed and in demand.

The four way stops at all intersections caused traffic to flow in herky jerky fashion through Georgetown. The fact that Sheriff Brager had found a parking spot was amazing. People circled these streets endlessly looking for an open spot. Nick swore some of these cars hadn't been moved since the Reagan Administration.

An Asian woman approached from half a block up the street. Three leashes were tethered to a dachshund, a cocker spaniel, and a black Labrador. The dogs sniffed at the base of trees, brick stoops, and patches of grass as the woman yanked and kept them moving in her general descent down the hill. The combined weight of the dogs was more than the woman, but the dogs scurried forward happy to be in the open air. Well, all happy but the Asian woman.

Wonder what that jobs pays?

The dachshund tugged toward Nick, sniffing at his shoes as they passed on the narrow sidewalk. Nick smiled at the woman. She yanked on the leashes and kept moving.

Nick crossed Dumbarton and turned left. His house was two blocks up the street. He scanned ahead and spotted the West Virginia sheriff's car across the street facing toward him. Nick checked for traffic and moved into the street toward the car. Brager's arm hung out the window, and he looked like he was catching a few winks.

"Hey, Sheriff, come on in and I'll make you a cup of coffee."

Brager didn't respond. As Nick drew closer he realized why.

The sheriff had a bullet hole in the middle of his forehead.

Chapter 11

Washington DC was an illusion.

The limestone and marble were real. The community was merely a proxy for reality. People came here to change the world, Haden knew. Instead, the city changed them.

Idealism and belief drew them to DC like moths to an unrequited flame. Motivations were converted by expediency. Thirst for power consumed its victims. The sequence was uniform. Unwilling and resistant at first, in denial for some period of time, then, unapologetically changed. Few survived the siren's song of Washington, DC.

Interns were scorned by the powerful, but still held sway over the morons called constituents. Eventually the intern's growth channel defined itself, sometimes within a congressional office, sometimes in an office of the executive branch, sometimes in the lobbying shops of K Street. Power created privilege, privilege begat authority, and authority was the only justification needed for any action in this town.

No one was from here. Community was collective necessity, not culturally driven nor nurtured. The long-term view in this town meant through the next election. Those who executed the real work of the government resented the appointed leadership, but marched in time like good soldiers.

All growth was centered on the federal machine. If the machine grew, times were good. With rare exception, the machine always grew. Expectation of growth dulled service quality and incentive. It was a self-fulfilling cycle. One fed the other and, with the power to levy taxes, the party would never end.

The change in behavior happened innocently enough; not an overt act, but something simpler, more gradual.

It paid to look the other way in this town. It wasn't wrong; it was just allowing what would be to be, all the while getting paid for it.

Gatekeepers made serious money in the city of a billion gates. At first the toll was free, but eventually it made no sense to remain free. Information was a commodity to be traded and exploited. Access to power was the toughest gate to pass. Many paid the gatekeeper in the hope it would get them closer to what was behind the gate.

Sometimes it was money, a steak dinner, a bottle of champagne, sports tickets, golf outings. The road steeply descended, and soon the wheels were off. Favors weren't innocently offered, but were casually received. This town ate good intentions like hyenas tearing into a bloody carcass.

Keeping perspective was a struggle in this town. Soon jaded or co-opted, only the rare human could evade the centrifugal pull of this town.

Haden Maxwell had fought the demons to a draw for most of his career, but little by little the envy grew, the cynicism festered. He watched the undeserving win promotions. Politics defeated merit. He watched the corrupt get wealthy. Connections trumped talent. He grew angry and impatient.

But there were benefits. A trained chimp could do most of his job. After a while it was all second nature. The trick was fooling the leaders that what he did required experience. The top officials in the agencies, the political appointees, turned over as frequently as sunbathers on Ocean City beaches. They were never around long enough to understand what purpose the agency even served. The non-politicos, the leadership among the agency lifers knew the game because they played it, too.

The exact time when Haden flipped couldn't be determined. It wasn't as simple as an event or a point in time; it was more like the pounding waves eventually causing the cliff to come crashing into the ocean. Once that happened, only God could put it back, and God didn't perform many miracles in Washington, DC.

The plan laid out for Haden Maxwell was simple. When the opportunity was offered, he jumped at it before it was even out of his friend's mouth.

It was like jujitsu or karate. Use the force of the system to flip his mark. There was no need to create a new system or hatch a unique idea. Money was available for helping people who might win anyway. It was common in this city. People were willing to pay for a known result, even if the payment didn't actually cause the result. It was insurance money. It was how lobbyists got rich in this town.

If there was a need, he could provide the solution. The more money available, the faster the solution would arrive.

They'd practiced the conversation in his apartment. They'd picked his mark. The mark was all-important. They needed someone like him, angry and impatient. They needed someone driven and motivated. He needed to have a relationship, however shallow, with the person, and needed to promise that they could achieve the result.

News of the cancellation of Center Tech's DOMTER contract was like manna from heaven; big money contract, an arrogant asshole like Elliott Galbert, and the ability to touch off a firestorm for reasons Haden didn't give a damn about.

The DOMTER contract was T for C'd or terminated for convenience. It was a fancy government expression meaning "we ain't living up to the contract we signed, fellas." All government contracts gave the fed the authority to simply walk away or terminate for convenience. Sometimes it meant the contractor was one inch from being terminated for cause; sometimes it meant the project was disfavored by political winds; sometimes it meant that funding needed to be redirected.

It didn't matter to Haden. It was just the opportunity. It was time for the town to pay him back. It was his turn at the trough.

If he'd known it was this easy, he would have started much earlier. Galbert was noticeably suspicious, but Haden played him perfectly. He could help re-prioritize things within the government. He'd be Galbert's eyes and ears. He could influence decision-makers. Hell, he could influence those who influenced the decision-makers.

The agency would come on bended knee, begging Center Tech to come back. The contract would be extended; heck, it would likely be increased. The money was a down payment, a pittance, something to prime the pump. And if Galbert was in negotiations to sell the company, having this contract in his satchel would be worth many times the face value of the contract.

Haden knew Galbert would hesitate. He didn't get rich by behaving irrationally or without protecting his flank. Haden was content to slow play him. Three days later the call came from Galbert. The meeting was set for the atrium of the Portrait Gallery.

Nice pick, Haden thought, public, yet private. Galbert wouldn't risk something showy like cocktails at the Four Seasons or lunch in a posh, five star restaurant. Galbert was smart. There were too many ethical rules, too many eyes, too many ears.

In the Portrait Gallery it was just two suits observing artwork. Just as he'd hoped, Galbert didn't want the details—plausible deniability, the cornerstone of this town. Haden yanked hard on the rod and set the hook deeply into the marlin's jaw. He'd give the fish some slack; let him run some to think he had a chance. Eventually, Haden would reel him in.

Haden quickly learned the cardinal rule of extortion. Once the bond was formed, the mark never got out alive.

Finally, it was Haden Maxwell's turn to score.

Chapter 12

Nick leapt away from the car. The front door to his house was ajar. He couldn't see any movement inside.

Am I being watched right now?

His head snapped side to side as he checked the street. No movement anywhere. Whoever shot Sheriff Brager was either long gone or hiding inside Nick's house. But why would he leave the front door open?

Then he spotted it.

There was no one in his house; not now anyway.

In the lap of the dead sheriff was Nick's gun. It was a nickel-plated Smith and Wesson, nine millimeter, with a black grip. Could be someone else's gun that looked identical to the one Nick stored in his cigar box, but what were the chances?

Whoever shot Brager was intent on setting him up. How would anyone know that Brager was here? Only Winters knew that Brager was looking for him. Winters couldn't have done it. Heck, he wouldn't cross the street against a red light, but who could he have told about Brager? Who had Brager told?

On the seat next to Brager was a manila envelope. That must be what Brager meant to show him. Nick raced around to the other side and, using his shirt tail, opened the passenger door. As he grabbed the envelope, a billfold rolled off the envelope onto the seat. Brager's? No chance this was a robbery. The last thing he wanted was Brager's wallet. He slammed the door shut, careful not to leave a fingerprint.

His heart was hammering against his rib cage, and he struggled to swallow. Should he call it in? What would he say?

A siren signaled the approach of DC's finest. How the hell could they be on this so quickly? It made no sense.

Up the sidewalk a slender middle aged woman in a black and yellow track suit walked toward him, shadowing a French poodle. He didn't know her, but there were hundreds of women like that in Georgetown. Women of wealth, who walked the dog, had an expensive lunch, hit the spa, got some shopping in, and made it home in time to be taken to the latest chic restaurant. It was a burden, but some women were able to adapt to that lifestyle.

Their eyes locked as she was approximately thirty feet away. She would easily ID him. He smiled, turned around, and began walking briskly up Volta Street toward Georgetown University campus. The siren pounded out its song, growing louder as it neared from behind him. Maybe she wouldn't notice the man in the car. Maybe she would walk right past.

A frantic scream pierced the air. He got his answer; no such luck.

Nick sprinted to the corner of 35th, turned left, and kept running.

At O Street, Nick took a right and sprinted through the brick-arched entrance to Georgetown campus. In his attire he quickly blended in with a typical college student. He ran to Healy Hall, taking the stairs two at a time, and ducked into an empty classroom.

Puffing loudly, he inhaled deeply and tried to get his breathing under control. Sweat ran down his forehead.

59

He peered out the window, in the early spring budding season; he was able to see through the trees back toward Volta Street. He couldn't see the scene, but could imagine it crawling with police and soon forensic officers. The woman and the poodle would still be there, throwing her cultured day into havoc.

Nick pulled out his cell phone and shut it off. When they started turning the screws to find him, the cell phone would be a homing device. He couldn't take the chance that one of his pals would throw a call into him when he least needed it.

Who was doing this?

Why were they working so damn hard to pin this on me?

The call to the police had to be seconds after the shooting. His arrival to meet Brager was just too convenient.

With an eyewitness, not to mention his gun possibly the murder weapon, Nick needed to get out of DC. Running was the last thing he wanted to do. He'd rather tell the truth and work with authorities to find the real killer, but in this charged environment, he knew he wouldn't have a chance.

Someone had gone to great lengths to make it appear as though he was the killer. Worst of all, they had access to information only known within the government. Whoever was involved either got their information from the government that was supposed to protect Nick, or they were able to tap his calls. Or had Brager simply been followed?

It didn't matter; he was fighting an enemy he couldn't identify and one with access to unlimited resources.

Without warning, the thought crashed into his mind.

What would dad do now?

For his adult life, he'd fought the thought. He worked to keep it segregated, compartmentalized. He kept it in a nondescript shoebox, high on a dusty shelf in the garage of his mind.

It wasn't that he didn't need sage advice or insight right now. The thought was a path that he refused to permit his mind to follow. He fought the notion. He blocked it out.

He walked to the door and scanned the hallway. All quiet. Nick turned the envelope in his hand. No markings, just a plain sealed envelope. Nick took two deep breaths, wiped the sweat off his forehead, ripped it open, and peered inside.

Careful not to leave any prints, he poured the contents onto the table. A cellophane evidence bag tumbled out. Nick picked it up and gingerly studied both sides of the document. A yellow sticker was attached to the upper corner. On it someone had recorded the date of collection, location, and relevant witnesses. Also listed was Sheriff Brager's name. Nick considered it for a long moment.

He instantly recognized the document in the cellophane evidence bag.

If this had anything to do with Justice Caprelli's kidnapping, it wasn't the work of an international terror organization—not a chance.

Chapter 13

Thirty minutes later Nick slipped out the door of McDonough Gymnasium and punched the speed dial on his phone. He moved away from the main campus and found a quiet spot on the far side of the building. The lost and found basket in the men's locker room had provided him with a blue hooded sweatshirt and black stocking cap, all without actually interacting with anyone.

It wasn't a perfect disguise, but enough to get lost in a crowd and cover the checkered red corduroy shirt that would accompany his description.

"Where are you, man? The shit is coming down on you," said Winters.

"What do you mean?"

"Dude, there's an APB out on you. What did you do?"

"APB? What the hell? What for?"

"You've been named a person of interest in the Caprelli kidnapping."

"*What?*" Nick shouted.

"I don't know, man, but they're lighting up the system on you. Some blogger broke the news of the APB. Beats me how these guys can get information so fast."

"It's a set-up, Dave." Nick walked in a tight circle with one hand on his forehead. "You know I don't have anything to do with that."

"Where are you?"

"Dave, you know it's not me."

Silence. Nick stopped suddenly. Winters had been like a father figure to him, or at least the closest thing to it. What was causing him to freeze up?

"I gotta ask you, Dave. Who did you tell about Sheriff Brager?"

"I'm sorry, Nick. You know I'm a—"

"Just tell me."

"I'm a short-timer. I can't put my pension at risk."

"Who did you tell?" Nick demanded.

"The task force. Man, I'm under orders to pass everything to them. I had to tell them you called asking about the DOMTER files. Nick, I had to. I'm sorry."

Don't burn a bridge here, Nick thought. He exhaled loudly and rubbed his neck. "It's okay. Just needed to know."

"Boys from the FBI came in about ten minutes ago. Cleared out your office, computer, files, everything. Got yellow tape over the door, but it doesn't matter; they took everything. I have to write up a full detail on you, soup to nuts. These guys aren't joking around. You're in a heap of shit right now. Where are you?"

"Brager called me. Told me he was outside my house. I get there and he's dead. Somebody broke into my place. Think they may have used my gun. Here's what I need you to do."

"Nick, you know I can't. I gotta follow orders; sorry."

"It's okay. Here's what you need to do. Tell Lozano I'm going to call him within the hour. He's got to take my call. Not some flunky. Got it."

"Sure, I can do that. Just don't get me involved."

"You're not involved. I just need to talk to him, that's it."

"You got it. Hey, watch your back, man. The dogs are out."

"I don't know what's going on, but save yourself, Dave. Whatever you gotta do, I understand. See you."

Chapter 14

Nick made himself virtually invisible. His hair was mussed and stuck out in odd directions from under the worn stocking cap. The hooded sweatshirt hung from his frame like the covering on a scarecrow. Grease smudges covered his face. His shirt was partially untucked with buttons unevenly fastened. He limped with slumped shoulders through the train station with a stained and beaten backpack strapped to him like a parasite.

Homeless people were all too familiar to those who frequented Union Station. The one thing they had in common was travelers rarely made eye contact with them. When a homeless person came within peripheral vision, eyes were averted. Most pretended they weren't there. That's what Nick was counting on.

Union Station was a majestic building with ornate carved and painted ceilings, high end boutiques, trendy bars, and fashionable dining establishments. However, as a public building, the homeless were as welcome as the first class travelers. It provided a sanctuary from the heat, cold, rain, or sleet that beat down many of the city's homeless population.

Nick grabbed the pay phone, a relic from the far away past. In the train station, it remained a staple even if rarely used. He punched in the number, turned his back to the phone, and scanned the area. Just bored travelers shuffled about.

"Special Agent Lozano, Nick James calling." He knew he had to be quick. Ten minutes before he'd used his credit card to buy a one-way ticket on the Northeast Regional headed to New York. Be fast.

~

"Hello, Nick."

"Lozano?"

"Where are you, Nick?" Javier held up his hand to signal he had him on the line. Scottie Palmer scanned his computer, getting a location on the call.

"You the OIC on the Caprelli kidnapping?"

"Yes, I am, Nick, but I need to know where you are. We need to sit down and talk."

"We'll talk right now," said Nick. "Look, I got nothing to do with Brager. It's a set up. I don't know what you've heard."

"I know a few things."

Scottie signaled Javier to stretch it out. He was getting close.

"I know I need to talk with you," said Javier. "Just tell me where you are and we'll bring you in for a conversation, get all this straightened out."

"No. Here's the deal," Nick said, speaking quickly. "There's a Kinko's down the block from you. There's a package with your name on it. Get it, then we'll talk more."

"Nick, we need to talk now. Just tell me where you are."

Palmer gave him thumbs up and whispered, "Union station, second floor. Payphone. What an idiot."

"Get the package," Nick said. "Then I'll call you again."

~

Nick hung up and moved quickly away from the phone. A police officer with a sniffer dog stood at the end of the walkway.

65

Several people were lining up for impending announcement of the next Amtrak train. Nick ducked his head and moved past the officer. He exited the hallway, turned right, and shot down the escalator and into the metro station.

~

Javier slammed the phone down. "Shit. Get him," he shouted.

Scottie tapped more keys on his computer. "What a dope. We got a hit on his credit card. Guy bought a one way to New York. Amtrak 134. Leaves in..." A few more clicks. "Damn it... right now, 12:10."

"Stop the damn train," Javier screamed. "Get Amtrak on the horn. We need to search that train. Don't let that fucking thing leave the station. Right now. Let's move."

Phones were dialed, buttons punched in a flurry of response. Shouts of instruction were blown into the equipment. Javier crossed his arms and stared toward the ceiling.

Scottie piped up again. "He hit an ATM fifteen minutes before he bought the train ticket. PNC bank, 13th and H Street."

"Metro Center," Javier said. Metro Center was a major subway station where the red line and blue line intersected.

The only person who hadn't moved was Kate. She sat quietly at the table, her legs crossed, leaning back slightly. Eventually, Javier looked at her, then looked down.

"It's too obvious, isn't it?" Javier mumbled. "Guy gets cash at an ATM, then buys a ticket with his credit card?" He turned toward Kate. "He's not on that train, is he?"

Kate closed her eyes and shook her head.

Chapter 15

Kate pinched the bridge of her nose, squinted, then looked Javier straight in the eyes. There's no hiding it, she thought. "We need to talk."

Javier pointed firmly out the doorway. Knowing what was coming, she appreciated the courtesy. Kate rose and crossed out of the room, following Javier into a smaller conference room across the hall. She took a seat behind the round table. Wesley snuck in just as Javier shut the door.

"You know this guy?" Javier asked.

She nodded.

"How well?"

"We dated for a while," she said, looking away from them.

"You *dated?*" Wesley screamed.

Javier motioned for him to be quiet. Kate glared at Wesley, but remained silent.

"Gotta ask you, Kate," Javier said. "Why didn't you say anything when the APB went out?"

"No kidding!" Wesley threw out sarcastically.

She knew they were both thinking the same thing. Did she have to come off the task force? This was as high profile a matter as she'd ever worked on. This was the hottest matter in the country. She'd worked too damn hard to get to this point.

From valedictorian as an undergrad to law review at UVA, her career knew only one direction—up. And she only knew one speed—mach one. Getting tossed from the task force would raise questions—questions about her femininity—that she couldn't cut it in a man's world. She'd fought that for years at every level. She couldn't take a setback. No one was allowed to question her ability.

"Were you—um." Javier stopped mid-sentence.

Don't go there, Kate thought, quickly glaring at Wesley who appeared to be enjoying this despite his mock outrage.

"Never mind," Javier finally blurted out. "Why didn't you say something?"

"It wasn't relevant," she said.

"Wasn't relevant?" Wesley shouted. "How could it not be relevant? You dated a guy who's being investigated by this task force? Jesus."

"Wesley," Javier said calmly, turning toward him. "This is the last time I'm going to say it. Either shut up or get out of the room."

"How long ago?" Javier asked with a pained expression.

"I haven't seen him in three months," she said defiantly.

Javier rubbed his face. He's got to call the shot right here, Kate thought. He crossed his arms and stared out the window. Javier inhaled deeply, then blew it out.

"Okay." Javier paused, then stood straight. "You're too damn valuable. I can't afford to lose time bringing someone up to speed."

Wesley rolled his eyes.

She was staying.

Javier continued. "I need you to write down everything. Every person he knows, every place you ever went, every friend he introduced you to, every neighbor, every relative, every hobby, interest. I want to know every freaking book he read. Got it?"

She nodded.

"God," he mumbled to himself. "And one other thing. Don't ever. And I mean ever, hold back information that could be the slightest bit important. I can handle the media, but if they broke this without me knowing or surprised me with it..." His statement hung heavily in the air.

"Understood," she said.

Javier turned to leave. Wesley grabbed his bicep. "Seriously, we've got the guy's girlfriend on the task force. Are you kidding me? The media's going to crucify us." He lowered his voice to a whisper. "How do you know we can trust her with information?"

Javier pulled his arm loose. "It's my call. I've made it. You got a problem with that? Take it upstairs." He stormed from the room.

Wesley turned back to Kate. She stood behind the table.

"Nick's not part of whatever's going on with Judge Caprelli."

"You're wrong," Wesley said. "Guy's got motive, opportunity."

"Motive? What motive?"

"He lost his job. Do we have to watch a guy go in with a gun and shoot co-workers before we acknowledge the impact of job loss on some people?"

"That's crazy," she said. "He loses his job, then decides to kidnap a Supreme Court Justice, then kill a sheriff? It makes no sense."

"He knew he was going to lose his job. Or at least he should have. When Center Tech had the DOMTER contract de-funded, everyone knew the writing was on the wall."

"Look, I know this guy—"

"Yeah, I heard," he said, dripping with sarcasm.

"I know he had nothing to do with Caprelli."

"You're wrong," he said, pointing at her. "How do you explain Brager? Guy is killed with James' gun, in front of James' house, after calling to schedule a meeting with James. James is seen fleeing the scene. Going to tell me it's all some kind of misunderstanding?"

"He said he's been set up."

"And you believe him?" He threw his hands in the air. "Jesus."

"He's entitled to the opportunity to explain his side."

"His side?" Wesley chided, throwing his arms out. "Who explains Brager's side? Who explains Caprelli's side?"

"You don't know him. You don't know anything about him."

"I know plenty about him and his kind."

"What do you mean, *his kind?*" she said forcefully.

"Your problem, little miss prosecutor, is that you've lost your objectivity. You ever think he dated you to learn about the department? To learn about how the agency responds in a crisis?"

Call me little miss again and I'll rip your throat out. She opted for, "that's crazy."

"No," he said, pointing at her. "What's crazy is a Supreme Court Justice got nabbed. This guy's our best lead, and because he was lover boy at one time, you want to defend him. Start defending your country. That's what you swore an oath to do."

That's so trite. Is he that stupid? "My oath is to pursue the truth," she said. "So's yours. We don't know what the truth is. What I know is that your theory about James and Caprelli is weak. It's ridiculously weak. Even if I didn't know him, I wouldn't buy your theory. Knowing him, it's just plain nuts. Regarding Brager, we don't know enough. You've got the guy convicted. Would be good to hear his side of it before we execute him, if that's not too much trouble for you."

"If he's innocent, why is he running? Why doesn't he come in and explain it to us? I'll tell you why. 'Cause he's guilty. He's running 'cause he did it."

She shook her head. "I'm not buying it. Don't be so sure he's running from us. He may be trying to do what we haven't been able to. And if he is involved with Caprelli, where the hell is the justice? How's that fit into your half-baked master plan?" She moved toward the door. He backed up to let her pass.

"He's got a team," Wesley said.

She laughed. "Got a team. Right. That's a lot of assumptions. We need to bring him in to learn what he knows, but pinning this all on him just doesn't square with reality." She moved past him into the hallway.

"I'm watching you," he said after her.

"Whatever."

Chapter 16

Young boys were highly impressionable, especially when the father provided the impression. Children didn't learn as much as they absorbed. Wolfe's father was a proud man. It was a trait with which he'd stamped his get.

Carlton Wolfe owned the implement dealership in Washburn, WI. He left school at fourteen and started working in the back shop of Grissom's tractor. Driven, devoted, and quick smiling, Wolfe soon became the favorite of the owner, Woody Grissom.

Carlton worked six days a week when the dealership was open. On Sunday, he could be seen hanging around, sometimes working on his car or learning the ins and outs of heavy equipment. Oddly enough, he never worked enough hours that he turned in overtime.

Grissom's only child, a daughter, had moved to Kansas City and married a pediatrician. Carlton became the son Grissom never had. At twenty-one Grissom moved Carlton into the front office. He'd already mastered every part, model, service plan, and mechanical trick from the shop. In the front office, he was on a crash course, accounting, inventory control, finance, and sales.

Quickly adept in all fields, Carlton found his niche in sales. He was born with the gift of gab, but better yet, he could read a prospect and knew when to ask for the order. Grissom's Tractor expanded under the new sales leadership of Carlton Wolfe.

Redemption Day

He married Connie Havalka and little David arrived shortly thereafter. As a toddler, David grew up in the office. On Saturday afternoon and Sundays it was just the two of them in the office.

It was on a Sunday that the call came in. Old Man Grissom had suffered a stroke. Carlton and son arrived at the hospital in time to see the doctor leave the room and shake his head, signaling the permanence of the result to the new widow.

Following a flurry of meetings with bankers, lawyers, and product representatives, Carlton was able to patch together a plan to buy the dealership. Wolfe Implement was born. The bank loans were heavy in the early years, but Carlton ground out an existence and slowly built up the business. In Washburn, non-profits, Little Leagues, Girl Scouts, high school trips all came to depend on Wolfe Implement to provide a helping hand.

The business provided a handsome living for the Wolfe family, and they held a place of prestige among the local community.

That was until the farm crisis hit.

Wolfe Implement had just completed a major renovation and upgrade to the mechanical shop. Twenty-two consecutive quarters of profit and increasing revenue made the new loan deal look like a slam dunk.

And it would have been a slam dunk if the farm economy hadn't fallen off the face of the earth. David was seventeen and entering his second season as starting quarterback at Washburn High. As a sophomore he'd been named all-conference in three sports. With chiseled good looks, a wicked sense of humor, and alpha male traits, David Allen Wolfe was the prince of Washburn.

But he noticed his father's mood change. Carlton Wolfe became quick to lose his temper. He frequently rubbed his face and mumbled. He argued with Connie. It was several weeks later that David learned what had caused the change of behavior. Following the funeral, the banks foreclosed on the business.

David and his mother were left with nothing. Carlton had poured everything into the business. He always thought he could pull through, just a few more months. It would turn around—just be positive and believe. The heart attack came before the turnaround.

The fall was swift and unforgiving. David couldn't understand why the community didn't help. He didn't understand why the bank took everything. Years of paying bank loans, mountains of interest, and every bake sale, uniform purchase, and band trip funded by Wolfe Implement, but when his family needed help, there was none available.

David lost interest in school, sports, and activities. Truth known, he was too embarrassed to show up. He took an interest in firearms and weapons. At a gun show outside Madison he learned about a group called the Montana Brotherhood.

Their view of the world wouldn't bring his dad back, but they made extracting vengeance seem noble. David was drawn to that. The enemy wasn't the local bank. They were thieves, of course, but the enemy was much bigger. As a result it was easy to attack, but hard to kill.

It was a struggle to which David Allen Wolfe had quickly dedicated his life.

Chapter 17

The Metrorail accelerated sharply as it moved from Union Station toward Gallery Place. Nick lurched forward as he stood holding the railing. He kept his head down. He didn't know how much time he had.

They would quickly figure out that he wasn't on the Amtrak to New York, and logic would say the metro was how he escaped Union Station. The metro would be crawling with cops, and they likely would start searching the subway trains first.

The plan was to get off at Gallery Place and make way across town above ground. The train eased into the station, the doors opened, and Nick shuffled off onto the station platform.

He worked his way through the oncoming traffic of commuters toward the 9th Street exit. As he broke into an opening in the humanity, he noticed two police officers coming down the escalator. Nick ducked his head down.

Was one of them looking at me?

He continued in his role as a street bum. The escalator crept forward. Nick shifted to the left so he could get around the down escalator to the one beyond that would take him up to the first level of the station above the tracks.

He couldn't resist; at the bottom of the escalator, he turned his head to look at the cops. The bigger of the two, nearer Nick, made eye contact. Nick noticed the flash of recognition in his eyes. He'd been made.

"Hey, you. *Stop*," the cop shouted.

Nick's head snapped forward, and he moved quickly toward the up escalator about thirty feet away. Maybe the cop was yelling at someone else. When he got to the base of the up escalator he looked back. The cops were coming straight for him. No question what they were doing.

"You," he shouted again. "In the blue sweatshirt, stop."

Nick looked up the escalator. He'd have to outrun them, and there was a good chance they had assistance up there or someone who would try and stop him. Three dings came from the train, indicating that the doors were about to shut. If he jumped back on the subway, he was trapped. The cops were moving quickly, closing in. One had his hand resting on his holstered gun.

Nick bolted, running to the end of the station. There was no escape, and clearly the cops knew that.

The officers slowed and secured the area, making sure others were out of that section of the platform. There was about a twenty foot gap between the front of the metro train and the beginning of the tunnel toward Metro Center. The gap was narrowing as the train's brakes had been released.

It slowly rolled toward the tunnel.

Now or never.

Without breaking stride, Nick jumped from the platform onto the tracks and scampered into the tunnel. The metro engineer must have seen him on the tracks and locked up the emergency brakes, causing the train to lurch and slide as the first four feet of the metro car entered the tunnel.

The full beam of the train's headlight illuminated the tunnel as Nick raced away. Rats scurried along the edge of the tunnel, their fleshy tails dragging behind them like rubber hoses. The smell of burned rubber filled his nostrils. The trains were powered by electricity, but the brakes were still metal on rubber, the residue of which hung in the air, particularly in the dank tunnel between stations. Ahead, the tunnel veered to the right as it lined up for the approach to Metro Center station.

Panting hard as he stumbled forward, now covered by darkness, he considered his options. The train from Gallery Place would sit tight, not risking running down a vagrant on the tracks. Cops would be alerted in the Metro Center station, so he was trapped like his friends, the rats.

A quick glance over his shoulder revealed lights bouncing up and down. The cops were on the tracks to flush him out to the other side.

The tunnel was divided into two sections, one for each direction of track. Concrete pillars were spaced approximately every twenty feet supporting the tunnel. Between the pillars were cement stanchions about three feet high. These stanchions were the last line of defense in preventing a derailed train from crossing over into oncoming trains.

Nick could see the illumination from Metro Center as he neared. The headlight from an oncoming train splashed light and approached where Nick stood. There was likely someone walking toward him in a squeeze play with the cops behind. Whoever was walking that way would have a gun, and the headlight would reveal Nick, making him an easy target. He ducked down along the cement stanchion as the light neared. He was running out of options and space.

There was no way out.

Chapter 18

Stirring inside the cabin caused Wolfe to turn.

"How's our boy doing?" Wolfe asked.

Gibson was in mid sip of his coffee and leaned forward to avoid spilling. The steam from the coffee fogged his eyeglasses. "He's a tough old coot, but he's coming along."

"Do you have the camera set? Lights? Everything?"

"Yep," said Gibson. "We're good to go. Oliver Stone would be impressed."

Wolfe ignored the comment, gazing out toward the highway far below. After a moment of contemplation, he said, "Get Landers and let's go."

Wolfe stepped off the porch and headed around the cabin. The entrance to the shaft was nearly a quarter of a mile back up the mountain. The mine had last been operational in the 1930's when horse-drawn equipment was all that could reach this point. As a result there were no roads indicating anything beyond the cabin other than mountain. Wolfe had used an ATV to get the equipment and Caprelli to the location.

Wolfe had instructed them not to take the same path twice, so that any kind of pattern or roadway could be discerned. The mine shaft was a bonus for Wolfe. The land was all he needed, but upon hiking the metes and bounds of his newly acquired domain, he stumbled upon the abandoned mine. The shaft traveled about seventy yards into the mountain, and a good sized room had been carved just beyond the narrow confines of the opening.

Landers and Gibson had hauled lumber and white wash to build the interior Wolfe wanted. Once the set had been built and the coffin and hostage were sealed away, Landers dug up a six foot pine tree and planted it in the doorway. He also spent several hours moving dirt to build up a berm along the ridge line. The entrance to the shaft was difficult to spot under normal conditions; with the pine tree and berm, it became nearly impossible for anyone to detect.

A padlock secured a reinforced wooden door. The padlock was hardly necessary, as the person inside the mine wasn't going anywhere.

Wolfe worked up a good sweat climbing to the shaft. The sun blazed fully in the sky, and warmer than normal temperatures contributed to the cardiovascular exercise. He spun the combination lock and quickly snapped it open. The air inside was dank and smelled of human feces and urine.

He left the doorway open. Inside, he flicked on one of the stage lights, and it illuminated the refurbished room. The coffin rested along the opposite wall and was framed by decades old piling and pillars from the original mine.

With one hand Wolfe opened the heavy casket. The man quickly raised his bound hands and covered his eyes.

"Wha—What?" said the naked man.

"Good morning, Mr. Justice," Wolfe said. He reached down, grabbed the elderly man's arm, and lifted him into a seated position.

Wolfe's days in Afghanistan had taught him a few things about hostages. Softening someone up was psychological, not so much physical. What they needed psychologically, they were denied. The barest of necessities for physical comfort were allowed, but keeping the subject off balance was the top priority.

The justice glared at Wolfe, but didn't speak. He had struggled, argued, screamed, and yelled in prior visits. None of it fazed Wolfe.

Taking a hostage's clothing was one of the first rules. Not because a naked escaped hostage was less effective than a clothed one. Risk of escape was never a concern. A man without clothes was a man without dignity. Wolfe's first rule was to strip the subject of dignity.

Next was confusion. This involved waking the hostage every two hours. The first six hours didn't matter because they were so scared they couldn't sleep anyway, but once they became exhausted, the trick was to never allow them to achieve REM sleep. Keeping the hostage disoriented was critical to breaking them.

Finally, he made the subject dependent. If he requested something, it was always denied. Any positive modification came at the suggestion of the captor. It wasn't unlike training a puppy, denial and repeated reinforcement of superiority. Eventually the hostage softened.

Wolfe had given this subject particular attention because he needed him softened quickly. Time was short, and he couldn't lose days because of a reluctant hostage.

Caprelli rubbed his eyes and his face.

"Hungry?" Wolfe asked.

Caprelli nodded.

Gibson began setting up a tripod with a digital camera secured to it.

"Got a nice meal for you, but we have to do some work first," Wolfe said. He unbound the justice's hands and thrust two typewritten pages toward Caprelli with one hand and held Caprelli's eyeglasses with the other.

Caprelli shook as he struggled to get his glasses over his

ears. He stared at the first page, then the second and back to the first. He swung his head side to side. "I can't do this," Caprelli said. "It's—it's not true. It doesn't mean that."

Wolfe shook his head and made a disappointed "tsk tsk" sound. "But it is true," he said calmly. "It is the only thing that is true."

Wolfe's voice was steady and without inflection. He wasn't threatening; it was more like he was counseling the justice.

"I can't do this," said Caprelli, then finding his courage, "*I won't.*"

Lander snickered. Wolfe shot him a glance. Gibson went back to setting lights in front of the set. Wolfe kept his eyes on Landers and spoke in the same calm voice. "Brother, please come here and help Mr. Justice onto a chair."

Once the naked justice was settled onto the wooden chair, Wolfe leaned in close. "I'm going to ask you again. Please read what's on the pages."

Caprelli shook his head, not speaking.

"You are going to do this," Wolfe said. "The only question is whether you'll do it now or a few excruciating minutes from now."

Caprelli stared at the ground.

He won't look at me. That's good, Wolfe thought. He's getting close.

Chapter 19

Wind whipped Nick's sweatshirt. The roar from the oncoming train deafened him. The first subway car sped by, simulating a sideways movie, each frame, people standing and sitting on their way to work. If he stayed put, he was as good as captured. Realizing his only option, Nick climbed onto the cement stanchion; the train was slowing, which gave him his only chance.

He timed his jump and leapt. His hands scurried for any purchase as the train slid by. He found the grab iron on the back of the next to last rail car and held on. He screamed out in agony as his fingers struggled to hold onto the hand hold. His fingers might be bloodied and broken, but he knew if he let go, he was sushi on the train tracks below.

His feet scrambled to find anything to support his weight. His legs swung back and were able to reach the following train car. This allowed him to press forward with his shoulder against the end of the car. He still gripped the grab iron with all the strength he could muster.

The train burst into the Gallery Place station and began decelerating sharply. The original train was still parked on the adjoining track. Because of the emergency, the train had been evacuated. The empty train on the adjoining track provided some cover for him as his train slid to a halt.

Being pinned between the fifth and sixth rail cars meant that no one could see him from either car of the train. He was in a compartment visible only to those above him, which was a concern. Those on the station platform might spot him.

The train ground to a stop. Nick reached down with his feet and found the turnbuckle connecting the two cars. He leapt from the turnbuckle onto the platform, nearly knocking down an elderly lady.

"Hey, watch it, buddy," one man said.

"What the hell?" another shouted.

Nick didn't waste time. He bolted down the platform away from the 9th Street exit and back toward the center of the platform. The yellow line trains ran perpendicular to the red line metro trains, one level below.

He scurried down the escalator, taking two and three steps at a time, bumping and jostling other commuters who stood on the right side of the escalator steps.

A bell dinged three times as Nick flew onto the lower platform. He raced to beat the closing doors of the yellow line train. It didn't matter which way the train was going; he just needed to get out of the station. He slid sideways through the closing doors and swung into a seat, winded and soaked in sweat. He unfolded a disowned newspaper lying beside him and shoved his face into it.

His breathing came in huge gulps, and he had to press one hand against the window to keep at least one of his hands from shaking noticeably. Blood dripped from the damaged knuckles of his right hand down the metro car window. The train slowly started rolling.

Chapter 20

Wolfe placed his hand on Landers' shoulder. "Brother, please bring over the magneto device. Mr. Justice requires some additional motivation before we begin."

From a darkened corner of the cave, Landers brought over an instrument the size of a toaster with a wooden handled crank on the side. Two electrical cords hung from the front of the contraption.

"Do you know what this is, Mr. Justice?" Wolfe asked.

Caprelli looked up, then quickly down and shook his head.

"Oh, you know what this is. You probably used one in your youth." Wolfe paused, waiting for Caprelli to look up. He didn't. "This is a multipurpose device. Handy little devil. A few decades ago folks used it to create electricity, before the power grid connected everyone. I have to tell you, it can create quite an electrical current. I'd like to ask if you've reconsidered your decision Mr. Justice?"

Caprelli remained silent, shivering.

"Brother," Wolfe said. "Please secure the Justice, so that we may proceed."

Landers bound Caprelli's ankles to the wooden chair with duct tape. Next he secured the man's upper calves to the frame of the chair just below the seat.

Caprelli struggled, but he was all but locked to the chair. Wolfe held the two electrical leads in one hand. They were positioned about an inch and a half from one another. He slowly cranked the generator with the other hand and sparks crackled between the two wires.

"You know what I like about this crank generator, Mr. Justice?" Wolfe said, eyeing the electrical charge. "It's a symbol of all that was once right about this country." He paused, smiling. "Not too long ago, people were responsible for themselves. There was no big brother government that would come along and wipe your ass for you. Nope, we were on our own. If we wanted electricity, we had devices like this and created what we needed. If people were too lazy, they were just out of luck. But then someone decided that it wasn't fair. That lazy people shouldn't suffer the consequences of their laziness."

He moved the electrodes toward Caprelli's face. The justice recoiled. "Yes, sir, this contraption is a symbol of our freedom and independence. And now these sit in museums, and power is controlled by the government. Electrical power, that is. But all that will change. People will realize that their liberties have been stolen. They can take it back if they want. And they will." Wolfe stopped cranking and dropped the electrodes. "And that's where you come in, Mr. Justice."

Turning to Landers, Wolfe said. "Brother, please help the justice see the light."

Landers knelt in front of Caprelli and with the assistance of small pieces of duct tape, fastened the electrodes on either side of Caprelli's testicles.

He squirmed, but it was useless. "What are you—" Then looking up to Wolfe, he pleaded, "Why are you doing this? Why are you—"

Wolfe gave the generator a quick half turn.

Caprelli lurched forward at the waist and howled in pain. He panted and tried to speak, but no words came out.

"You see, Mr. Justice," Wolfe said. "When I ask you to do something, you need to do it. You will learn. You will learn."

Wolfe cranked the generator several times. Caprelli curled forward and shook. His eyes bugged out. He screamed twice before he vomited. After two more cranks, the body slumped forward, his head hung down.

He was out.

Chapter 21

Scottie Palmer signaled Javier a split second before the phone rang. Javier snapped it up. "Nick, where are you? You need to come in right now."

"Did you get the package?"

"Yes, I sent an officer over to bring it back. We've been studying it here internally. I have to ask you what the heck is it?"

"It's a fractional reserve note."

"I gathered that much. That's what it says. But what is it?"

He's stalling, Nick thought. "I know who did it," he said quickly.

"Did what? Kill Sheriff Brager?"

"No, Caprelli."

Palmer signaled thumbs up. He had the location. Javier made a circling gesture with his finger to say round him up. Officers picked up phones and punched furiously. Three on cell phones raced out of the room raising their voices as they exited.

"I want to talk to you about Caprelli and Brager," Javier said, jumping to his feet.

"I had nothing to do with either one," Nick said as he scanned the up and down the street.

"Nick, we've got the gun registered to you, your prints on it." Javier slowed the pace of the conversation noticeably.

"He was killed in front of your house, the last phone call Brager got was from you. We have a positive ID of you running from the scene, and you took something from Brager's car. Yeah, I guess there could be reasonable doubt."

Palmer handed him a note. Javier gestured hurry up.

"I didn't do it," Nick said. He ran his hand up his face and over his head. "He was already dead when I got there."

"You know we're going to find you, and this will go better if you give yourself up. Who are you working with?"

"I don't know what the hell's going on with Brager, but I know who has Caprelli, or who took him anyway. What I don't know is who made me a person of interest in Caprelli? Where did that come from?"

"That's why we need to talk. I can explain it all."

"You have my location yet?" Nick asked.

"What?"

"I know you're tracking the call. Do you have my location yet?"

"Yeah," said Javier, glancing at the note in his hand. "Pay phone, Wisconsin and M Street in Georgetown. Stay right there."

"There's a garbage can on the southeast corner. I have another package for you. I'll call when I know more."

The phone went dead.

"Get him," Javier shouted. "Guy's starting to piss me off." He slammed the phone down. "Standing in the busiest intersection in town. Shit. Somebody get that guy."

Chapter 22

Caprelli's head started to nod and roll. He was coming to.

The hand generator had been put away. Gibson had completed arranging the camera and lighting. They were ready for the taping.

"Clean him up and get him dressed," Wolfe said.

"You think he's ready to cooperate?" Landers asked.

Wolfe chuckled. "Yeah, he's plenty ready. I don't think we'll have to worry about his cooperation going forward. We make the slightest move toward the magneto and he'll be singing his head off."

Landers tapped Caprelli on the side of his face. His head bobbed twice, then his neck muscles caught hold. His eyelids creased, then slowly rose to half mast. Caprelli looked straight ahead, his eyes like a blank slate. His brain suddenly engaged, and his eyes shot open fully. His back hit the frame of the wooden chair, and his eyes scanned left and right.

"Nice to have you back," Wolfe said.

Caprelli just blinked and looked at Wolfe's feet.

"Now that you've been properly motivated for the next task, Brother Landers is going to place you on the set, get you dressed, and all prettied up for the camera."

Fifteen minutes later Caprelli was seated behind a large wooden bench. Gibson had done a good job brushing the justice's hair and shaving his face. They weren't about to

Steve O'Brien

trust the guy with a razor. Gibson had applied some makeup to brighten the bags under Caprelli's eyes and to give him a camera-ready sheen. By all appearances, it was just another day on the bench for Justice Silvio Caprelli.

A nameplate sat before him, and a large seal graced the back wall. Gibson had ably replicated an appellate courtroom. Although most appeals were heard by a minimum of three justices, Caprelli had this bench all to himself.

Caprelli turned and looked at the seal. "What the heck is that?"

"Don't you worry about it," Wolfe said. "You just read. With conviction. If everything goes well, you'll get the rest of the day off. Get it right the first time and we'll be out of here. Mess around and I'll have to see if we can add a little spark to your presentation."

The justice scanned the pages in front of him. He shook his head ever so slightly, as if he didn't want to signal a lack of cooperation. "It's just not true."

"You don't decide what is and what is not true," Wolfe shouted. "Your truth has been a fiction that has destroyed this country. You've fought the real truth. You've choked the real truth every place it has sprouted up. Your truth has placed this country's people back in slavery. This country's had enough of your truth."

Capprelli's head stayed down, focused on the pages in front of him. Fear or submission? Wolfe thought. Didn't matter. He'd broken the man. That was the plan.

Wolfe turned to Gibson, who was busy doing final adjustments on the lighting. "We ready?"

"Quiet on the set," Gibson shouted as he moved away from the bench and leaned in behind the camera.

Wolfe and Caprelli locked eyes. The captor's glare said, I own you. Caprelli's eyes were vacant, as if Wolfe was a fuzzy math problem on a blackboard. Caprelli's face sought answers. He wasn't going to get any—not from Wolfe.

The captor moved a half step closer to the set. His lips spread into a flat grin. He folded his arms, without breaking his stare with the justice.

Wolfe said, "Action."

Chapter 23

The April sun pressed through the clouds and brought the temperature into the seventies. Visitors milled about on the National Mall, pushing strollers or pointing into the distance as they moved from monument to monument.

A prolonged arctic wave had created the coldest DC winter in decades. Even the staunchest of global warming advocates had begun to scratch their heads and pray for spring. Even though several weeks late, spring had finally arrived, and the tourists flooded the Mall to witness the late blooming Cherry Blossoms.

The Cherry Blossom trees were originally gifts to the capitol city from Japan. During two weeks each spring, the blossoms burst forth. And like lemmings, people visited. They clogged the streets along the Mall. Intersections were flooded with humanity, and cars stood emitting exhaust.

Strollers, walkers, kids on leashes; all manner of transportation and child management were visible. The visitors shuffled in one continuous mass of people. They wound around the Jefferson Memorial, past Independence Avenue, and along Park Drive nearest the Potomac. Crowds swelled around the World War II memorial and spilled out like smoke onto the grounds of the Washington Monument to the east and the reflecting pool to the west.

As people shuffled, traffic snarled. It was part of the charm of the city.

Redemption Day

Millions of visitors descended on the nation's capital each year, and the proximity of the attractions to downtown Washington and government agencies meant commuters were late, appointments were delayed, and frustration ensued. Cherry Blossom season, national holidays, inaugurations, and the routine presidential motorcades built twenty-minute drives into hour long adventures.

It was an anthropologist's dream—fat people, skinny people, old people, babies, kids, Caucasians, Blacks, Asians, Hispanics, Indians, native and otherwise, all slogging along the Cherry Blossom march.

For the visitors, pink and white were the colors of the day. For DC natives, they were dusty grey and outward evidence of the bombardment of pollen in the air. Barring a windstorm or heavy rain, the blossoms would last about ten days. Then the flowers would blow into the Potomac, the tidal basin, and onto the mall. The city would empty out, awaiting high school field trips and the next national holiday.

Nick crossed 16th Street at the crosswalk, headed east toward the Washington Monument. From this distance he could see the different shade of marble in the lower half of the monument. The Civil War and budget constraints had imposed a twenty year interruption in the construction of the monument. In the right light, curious spectators could identify the darker colored base. When finally opened to the public, the monument was the tallest structure in the world, only to be eclipsed by the Eiffel Tower a few months later.

He still had his homeless man disguise on, and the rising heat was causing him to sweat under the hoodie. As he approached his destination, he would have to upgrade his appearance, but for now, since he was in the open, the disguise remained crucial.

Nick patted his back pocket to ensure the evidence pack was still with him. He'd taken the contents of Brager's evidence envelope and repackaged it for Agent Lozano. Nick retained the outer wrapper, which had the location from which the evidence was gathered as well as the names of witnesses. That information was something Nick wasn't prepared to share at this point. He only hoped that Brager hadn't talked to someone on the task force.

Brager was the wild card. Was it even connected to Caprelli? What was the link? The fractional reserve note in the evidence pack confirmed Nick's gut reaction to the kidnapping, but was there a connection?

Also who had Brager talked to? Who else knew what Nick knew? There was no easy way to find out. He could surrender. That thought was quickly dashed.

If he could tie Brager's evidence to Caprelli, it wouldn't just clear his name, it might save a Supreme Court Justice.

It was critical to Nick that he not break any laws if at all possible. Being on the lam was one thing. He needed to figure out who had framed him, but he didn't want to rack up misdemeanors and felonies in the meantime. He would turn over the evidence pack at the appropriate time. But for now he needed the head start that the information would provide.

The APB meant that the train station, the airports, rental car agencies, bus terminals, everything would be on alert. He had to find a way out of the city. The traditional methods were foreclosed. The FBI would be pressing any acquaintances in the region. Favors from friends were out of the question.

Nick passed the base of the Washington Monument. Dozens of folks stood taking pictures of an object that appeared in any American history book. Hundreds of shots snapped per hour of the same obelisk from the same repeated angles. All attention was on the object, so Nick slid by without notice. He strode to the southeast as the sidewalk separated and continued east on Independence Avenue.

Keeping an eye on the street, he cruised past the Smithsonian Castle and crossed the mall toward the National Museum of Natural History. His destination was the northwest corner of 9th and Constitution.

One city block away stood the FBI building where a task force toiled to bring him in. Being this close was nerve-racking, but the corner was his best shot. He imagined them looking out the window and watching him stand on the street corner under the mushroom cloud of their efforts.

Since the kidnapping, the police presence in the city was constant, though not readily apparent. Like the duck moving across the pond, underneath the effort was swift and furious. Above water, all was calm and serene. This was Washington, DC. While agents worked nonstop to solve a grisly kidnapping, no one wanted to frighten the steady stream of tourists who came through town. Law enforcement was there on the National Mall, though, and he could feel their presence. He had to move quickly.

Behind the Natural History Museum Nick found a water fountain. He splashed his face and scrubbed it as clean as possible. He also doused his hair and finger combed his wet mop to a suitable style. He ditched the blue hoodie and tucked his shirt, making himself as presentable as possible, given the circumstances.

The light flashed red and the pre-rush hour traffic along 9th Street shrugged to a halt. Nick scanned the cars for passengers. The first car had two people in it, so he moved up the street. The next car had a single. Nick pointed at the driver, but the man waved him off. The next car had three passengers, so he quickly moved along the sidewalk up

9th Street. The fourth car was also a single. Nick pointed at the driver. The passenger window went down.

"How far you going?" the man asked, leaning over.

"Woodbridge," Nick said.

The driver waved him forward. "Hop in. Going to Dale City, but I can drop you."

Nick jumped in the car. "Thanks, man."

In DC they were known as slugs. In other parts of the world they would be called hitchhikers. However, rather than relying on the kindness of strangers, slugs in DC had leverage. To access the HOV lanes, single drivers needed a passenger. For longer commutes the difference between having a slug and driving alone in the non-HOV lanes could be an over an hour. Slugs were valuable. They bought drivers time.

The car drove through the 9th Street tunnel, merged onto I-395 southbound into Virginia, and slipped over to the HOV lane. Nick leaned back on the headrest and blew out a deep breath. He was out of the city.

"Thanks, man," Nick said. "You're a real lifesaver."

Chapter 24

The air whipped Nick's face as he sped westward along Highway 211. The road eased downward. He pulled the clutch and coasted, careful to keep a fair distance from the eighteen-wheeler ahead of him. The headlight had been on since he'd motored out of Woodbridge an hour before, but dusk was now casting shadows, and the illumination was beginning to pierce the night.

Of the four people he knew in Woodbridge, there was only one he could trust. Tim Redfield was a former Center Tech employee. He'd been fired nine months before when he had a meltdown with an HHS contracting officer.

Redfield was the project director on the new Health Screen initiative at HHS. He'd received verbal assurance that a contract modification was to be signed. In reliance on that representation, Tim authorized the purchase of fifty laptop computers to monitor communications on the HHS Health Screen contract. The mod never came through. The contracting officer denied making the representation, and Tim was left hanging out to dry.

It was common to get verbals from contracting officers, but the rulebook said until he held a signed contract in his hand, everything was theoretical. Tim compounded the problem by phoning the contracting officer and blasting him.

Expending money on behalf of Center Tech was bad enough, but verbally abusing a contracting officer was an unforgivable sin. He was summarily fired. Tim wasn't one to easily move on from a setback like that. He carried a supersized grudge along with his personal items when he left the office.

When Nick called from Park Plaza Mall, he opened with the fact that he'd recently been fired from Center Tech. This made them blood brothers, and twenty minutes later they were slugging down beers and bad mouthing Galbert and other Center Tech execs.

By the look of Tim's apartment, he had unplugged from the civilized world—no television, no newspapers, no computer. There was just a kitchen table and a worn couch in the main room with paperback books scattered.

Tim shrugged and said he'd been catching up on his reading. And drinking, Nick thought.

When the need for wheels came up, Tim couldn't part with his Jeep Wrangler, but he had a Kawasaki he'd rebuilt, and Nick could borrow that. Realizing he had to take a chance, Nick told him about Brager and the FBI and that they would probably contact him if they hadn't already.

Tim smiled, grabbed Nick's hand and pulled him in for a bro hug. His hatred for the government and Center Tech ensured that Nick's trail wouldn't be followed. They were the last people on earth Redfield would want to help.

It had been two years since Nick last rode a motorcycle. He was able to get away from Tim's place without grinding gears and mistakenly downshifting. He provided entertainment at the first two stop lights, killing the engine once and jerking through an intersection in second gear. By the time he made it outside town, he was able to compensate and was now actually enjoying the ride as he cruised through Warrentown, VA.

Nick wore the required head protection, but true to Tim's rebellious side, there was no face protector on the head gear. Not wanting to lose a tooth or an eye, Nick stayed back from the vehicles ahead of him to minimize the chance of being hit by a stray rock.

Twenty minutes later he stopped to top off the gas tank in Washington, VA, better known as "Little Washington." Down the street from the station was the last place he and Kate had dinner, The Inn At Little Washington. The restaurant was world famous for some of the finest cuisine, along with a classic and romantic decor.

Rather than take one of the bed and breakfast rooms at the Inn, Nick had sprung for a sedan and driver to bring them to the restaurant and back home. The seventy miles back to the big Washington was more than he needed after a big meal, cocktails and wine.

The place looked different this night, more lonely with few cars moving along the streets of the village and even less foot traffic. It was a throwback to a quieter time, more civilized and refined.

He remembered Kate's sheepish smile and laugh over the candlelight as he told her about having his car stolen two weeks after moving to Washington. She rolled her eyes as he described the boredom in the police force when he'd reported it. He was just a punk from the Midwest who thought his was the only car ever stolen in the metro area. Why weren't they out looking for it?

The candle's reflection danced in her eyes. Soft curls shook as she laughed. Her smile revealed all as she shifted between amusement and embarrassment for Nick's predicament.

The levity was such a contrast from the driven, high competition persona that she demonstrated in her work. Maybe if he'd gotten away with her more, gotten that innocent, gentle side to come out more, things would've been different. Too many "maybes," that was always the problem.

He called her twice after dinner at the Inn. She was in the middle of a high profile criminal trial, and her game face was on constantly. She called him a week later. Nick let it go to voicemail and didn't call her back.

He stood shivering at the gas pump.

Maybe she could help him. He didn't want to get her involved, but she would know he couldn't kill someone, that he couldn't be involved in something like this. Would she even take his call?He paid cash for the gas, kick-started the Kawasaki, and headed down the road, toward West Virginia, toward Yellow Spring.

Two miles from the gas station, Nick cruised over a hill to discover red and blue flashing lights. A state patrol car was pulled onto the highway, blocking Nick's lane. The trooper was outside the vehicle, standing with hands on hips as though he'd been waiting for a late arrival.

Chapter 25

Kate Buchanan scanned her already opened emails, but mostly she just stared at her Blackberry and twiddled with it. She regretted being here. Her Grey Goose and soda lacked one sip as it sat on the lounge table in front of her. That idiot Wesley thumbed out an email across from her. She was content to ignore him until Javier returned.

He was standing in the alcove of the Bombay Club nodding and listening on his cell phone. When Javier invited what was left of the team at eight o'clock that night, it seemed like a good idea. She'd be happy to spend time with him reviewing their progress and strategy. Had she known Wesley was coming, she'd have bagged. Wesley had already pounded down one scotch and was signaling the waitress for a refill. She felt like a prisoner and wished for an emergency email that would require her to politely excuse herself.

Javier's shoulders slumped as he returned to his seat and poured his phone into his jacket pocket.

"That was Schaeffer," he said, referring to Executive Director Matthew Schaeffer, the FBI special investigation's head. He gave a mocking grin. "Wants to meet tomorrow at 7:30 to discuss progress."

"I'm available," Wesley said, like an untrained Labrador pup.

"Kate and I will take the meeting," Javier said. "I need

you to get that team of agents on the pavement, interviewing all of James' contacts."

Wesley gave Kate a grim face.

Moron, she thought. "Where's the meeting?" she said.

"His office," said Javier, taking a pull on his drink. "Probably going to have someone from the White House. Wouldn't surprise me if Jannsen was there, too."

"If it was Jannsen, wouldn't we meet in his office?" Kate asked. The FBI Director didn't need to take meetings in an underling's office, she thought.

"You'd think so," Javier said. "Just don't be surprised. The international leads are crap. We've had four groups take credit. Damn Muslim Militia takes credit for every loud noise in the night. We've gotten a hundred and fifty calls, but most are just whack jobs looking for payback for Arab terrorists. Nobody's got anything solid." He scanned his email messages.

"It's not a foreign group, Javier," Wesley said. "It's Nick James and whoever the hell he's working with." He gave Kate a glance to emphasize the point.

She wanted to ignore him, but couldn't. "Get off it. We've been through that."

"He's the only thing that makes sense. He's studied terrorists. That was his job," Wesley said.

"I studied Criminal Law; that doesn't make me a criminal," she fired back.

"We're on James," Javier said. "But I'm with Kate. It doesn't make sense, but we'll track it down anyway. Right now, it's the only solid thing we have to go on."

Kate sat back and looked toward the street. She knew it wasn't Nick, but it didn't help matters that he was being uncooperative. He needed to come in and explain what happened. In the vacuum, Wesley was painting him as a crazed terrorist. She'd tried his cell phone three times that day, but he didn't pick up. She didn't leave a message because Wesley would invent a way to tie her to the plot. She also wasn't sure what she would say to him, other than come in and talk.

She knew he owned a gun, as they had been to the range in Alexandria to fire it soon after he bought it. The Supreme Court case in District of Columbia versus Heller, allowing gun ownership for DC residents had spurred his purchase—that and the increasing danger on DC streets. Under the decision, residents could own weapons to protect themselves and their property, but couldn't legally carry the weapon outside the home unless it was locked.

As Nick told her, area thugs had realized that DC natives were unarmed—in fact, it was illegal to be armed. That made the thug's job safer and easier. The thought that Nick would pull the gun and kill a sheriff made no sense at all. None.

"We're wasting our time and resources on James," she said. "What. He's running around the city—at the train station, on the metro, in Georgetown, and we're supposed to believe he's got a Supreme Court Justice in his pocket or something? It's a red herring or at best unrelated."

"Explain how Caprelli's wallet got in the sheriff's car." Wesley challenged. "How's that unrelated?" He reached out and took the fresh glass of scotch from the waitress.

Kate paused until the waitress moved away. "We don't know how his wallet got into the car," she said flatly. "That doesn't put it in Nick's hands."

"Still protecting lover boy? When you going to give that up?"

She shot forward, glaring at Wesley.

"Alright, enough," said Javier, raising a hand between them. "We don't know. Okay? Shit, I can't even write down all the crap we don't know. We've got forensics on all that.

We've got other leads we need to track. I don't like going into Schaeffer's office with a bunch of speculation."

"We've got a description of the vehicles," Javier continued. "But that's like a million to one. Two nondescript vans. Hell, for all we know, the poor bastard's been flown out of the country. Trying to get information on private aircraft is like finding an oyster in the desert. That's if we had access to all the private flights in the country. There are ten times as many private airstrips as commercial airports, and that's just counting the legal ones. Private flights are so damn secretive anyway. Pilots aren't required to list the names of passengers or even number of passengers. We don't know if Caprelli's next door or in Katmandu, for Christ sakes."

Kate calmed herself and turned to Javier. "You've set up and covered ground better than anyone. We've got agents out scouring and hitting all the right buttons. With no communication from the kidnappers, I don't know what Schaeffer can expect," Kate said.

Javier nodded. "Just not very comforting right now."

"Next time James turns on his phone or tries to send an email, we're going to jump the guy," Wesley said. "That'll please Schaeffer. May have him by your 7:30 meeting."

"How were you able to log his cell phone and personal email so quickly? His calls to Javier were made on pay phones, and I sure as heck wasn't asked to get a subpoena," Kate said.

Wesley smiled. "Same phone he used at Homeland. Had to be registered for email. Once he got canned, the email access was shut down, but he's still carrying the same phone. Next time he turns it on, he'll be face down on the pavement."

Kate skimmed her email—only a blast message about a sale at Barnes and Noble. She clicked it and gave a puzzled look. "Oh, crap. Got to go. Sorry. You guys go ahead and have dinner. I've got something I need to take care of." She swept up her purse and moved to the door. Looking over her shoulder at Javier she said, "I'll be online tonight. We can meet at seven and prep."

She stepped onto the sidewalk and took a deep breath. *What was Wesley's problem?*

With three older brothers and four years of Division I lacrosse, she'd learned how to deliver a few elbows. She also knew how to maintain her composure under stress. But if Wesley keeps it up, the guy's going to lose a few teeth.

Chapter 26

The fight or flee adrenaline flashed through Nick. He could skirt around the patrol car and outrun him. These Virginia patrol cars had souped up engines and could flat-out fly. Nick was competent on a motorcycle, but a high speed chase was asking more than he could deliver. He could off road and lose his pursuer. The motorcycle gave him an advantage, especially in this wooded, rural part of Virginia.

Headlights poured over Nick from behind. Another vehicle was approaching. Nick turned to look, but all he could see were two blinding spotlights. He couldn't make out the type of vehicle. Could be another patrol car. Nick downshifted, pulled the clutch, and coasted toward the stopped vehicle.

The patrolman casually walked to the side of Nick's motorcycle, checking out the bike. He was about Nick's age and cut like an NFL linebacker. His hair was cropped in a Marine style, high and tight.

He's probably comparing the bike to the information on the report and APB, Nick thought. Sure as hell, Tim had given him up. Nick ginned up his courage and looked the patrolman in the eyes.

"Evening Officer," Nick offered up. Be polite, show respect, Nick said to himself.

"Eighty-seven?" the patrolman asked, nodding.

"Huh?" Is he saying he clocked me at eighty seven miles per hour? No chance I was going over sixty. Great, after he holds me for a bogus speeding infraction, he'll figure out who I am. He'll run my driver's license and I'll be busted. Just my luck, I get caught here in nowhere Virginia all due to a malfunctioning speed gun.

"Looks like eighty-seven, but could be eighty-eight."

"I'm sorry, sir. Are you saying I was driving that fast?"

The patrolman looked at Nick, then back down at the bike. "The muffler, engine, and gas tank all say eighty-seven, but the headlight is definitely eighty-eight."

"Oh," Nick laughed out of relief. "Yeah, it's a bit of both."

"Got one back home I'm re-building. First bike I ever owned. Hard to get original parts for the damn thing."

"Sure is," Nick said. Why the heck did he stop me? Nick shot a glance over his shoulder, and three cars were stopped behind him, none of them police vehicles as far as he could tell. He didn't want to say too much, first, because he didn't know the first thing about motorcycles and, second, he didn't want to offer up that it wasn't his bike.

Looking up the highway to the other vehicles stopped behind Nick, the officer snapped into patrolman mode.

"Sir, the reason we stopped you this evening is we're doing a random impaired driving check." Nick exhaled deeply. His chest felt like he'd held his breath for ten minutes. "Gotta ask you. Have you been drinking tonight?"

"No, sir. I haven't," said Nick. Wasn't completely true, since he'd had half a beer with Tim about three hours before. Nick confidently stared into the eyes of the officer. He knew the officer was looking for signs of intoxication.

After a pause, the officer directed him around the police car. "You have a nice night. Take care of that bike. She's a beauty."

Nick's reply was drowned out by the bike as he swerved around the police car and accelerated down the highway.

Chapter 27

Shadows grew longer and the wind picked up its pace. The sky blackened, but no rain would come. The rust-colored pickup edged through the trees farther and farther from the main road. A sharp veer to the left brought the shack into view.

Smoke filtered from the chimney as it rose and disappeared into the branches of the barren trees. Wolfe honked twice to give the "all clear," and a man stepped from the shack onto the withering porch.

"Brother Jackson," Wolfe shouted as he exited the truck. Gibson and Landers trudged behind him.

"Brother Wolfe, good to see you," Jackson said, stepping from the porch and embracing Wolfe in a bear hug. They slapped backs.

"Boys all here?" Wolfe asked.

"Inside," said Jackson. He nodded in the direction of the other two. "Package all secure?"

"All good, Frank," said Wolfe. "Like a charm."

Inside, three men sat around a wooden table. They nodded, but none rose as the newcomers entered. A fire burned in the hearth, and a man tossed two more logs on the fire.

"Brother Wolfe, you know Mitch and Tommy," Jackson said waving toward two men at the table. Mitch's long blond hair was tucked under a faded red cap. Danny ran his hand over his bald head and nodded to the newcomers.

"Appreciate your help, boys. You were the driver?" Wolfe stated to Danny, which drew another nod.

"Nice work, Brother," Wolfe said.

Jackson continued the introductions. "This is Kirby," he said, gesturing to a kid whose fingers nervously tapped the table. "Kirby was in Irbil with me. He's a demo guy. Damn good one." He turned toward the fireplace. "And you know my brother Willie."

Willie walked over and shook Wolfe's hand. "Nice to see you, Brother."

Wolfe thumbed over his shoulder. "Landers and Gibson."

"Good to see you fellas." Frank turned and slapped Wolfe on the shoulder. "Wouldn't be here without this guy. Pulled me from a burned out building in Kabul." He laughed. "Bastards booby trapped the damn place. When that thing went off, I thought I was a goner. Wolfe carried me to the humvee, firing his M16 in the other arm. Like some damn Rambo." This drew a chuckle from Wolfe. "I owe this guy everything," Frank said. "He asked if I was up for a skirmish, I said 'I'm in.'"

"Time is short," Wolfe said, addressing the room. "Redemption day is coming," he shouted. "Redemption is upon us." This drew the attention of the group, and the men shouted in agreement.

Wolfe spread his arms. "This mission is the most important thing in your life right now. Anybody who wants out, the door's over there." None moved. "We need firepower. We need to hit these bastards with everything we've got. It's shock and awe time, baby," he said, smiling.

The men leaned closer, pulled by the power of Wolfe's conviction. "We may not all make it, but the mission comes first. Wolfe stepped to the table and laid out a rough diagram. The men huddled around. "These are the pressure points. We want to hit these four spots." He circled them with a pencil.

"You want them shut down?" Willie asked.

"I want them blown to shit. I want to lock the damn place down."

"What do you want?" Frank asked. "We gonna go ground or by water?"

"All of the above," said Wolfe, looking him in the eye. "I want all four of these taken out. These surgical hits will shut down the city. That'll give us what we need for the main event, which will be right here," Wolfe said, tapping on the center of the paper."

"Center of the star," Frank said.

"That's right, Brother. Center of the star," Wolfe repeated smiling.

Willie and Frank exchanged a glance and nodded.

"Piece of cake," said Frank. "We'll need help with resources."

Wolfe turned to Gibson and nodded. Gibson reached under his shirt and tossed an envelope onto the table. Greenbacks slid out onto the table.

"There's your resources," Gibson said, bringing laughter to the room.

Frank picked up the envelope and thumbed the bills. "Where's the money coming from?"

"Don't you worry. I've got that covered," Wolfe said. "If you knew, you'd laugh your ass off. Believe me. Just let me know if you need more."

"This should get us what we need," Frank said.

"What are you going to use? PCT, fertilizer, clay?" asked Wolfe.

"All of the above," Frank said, chuckling. "Plus more. Gotta load of clay on the way. Be here tomorrow."

"I've been to every damn feed store and home and

garden in a three hundred mile radius," Willie said. "Dumb shits will sell anything around here. We'll have plenty of boom."

Frank leaned into the table. "If we go above ground, I got an idea for that."

"Small pop is all we'll need to shut this down," Kirby said. "Confined space. Child's play."

Frank pointed at the chart. "Willie, you take that one." Willie nodded in response.

"Lotta good men have died in this cause," Wolfe said. "This is for them. We're gonna bring the bastards to their knees and take back our country."

"We took back some countries for a bunch of pussy towel heads," Frank said, crossing his arms. "It's about time we took back this one."

An hour later, the rust-colored truck rolled away from the shack.

"You trust these guys?" Landers asked.

"Jackson?" said Wolfe. "Trust the guy with my life. He can bring down a whole damn city by himself. Hell, I seen him do it."

"Are they in it for the cause?" Landers continued.

Wolfe gave him a long stare, then turned back to the road. "He knows what center of the star is." They drove in silence for a moment. "Frank and Willie had an older brother. Lost him at Foster's Glen." Wolfe paused and reflected. "He wasn't just killed by the FBI; it was an execution. Stone cold murder. One of theirs got shot, so they had to take one of ours. Guy wasn't even armed. They shot him in the back, shot him anyway. Cowards. Made up some bullshit story about automatic weapon fire and landmines. Guy didn't even have a gun. Then they pinned the fibbie's killing on Earl Baker. Hell, Earl wasn't even there. They wanted to take him down. Bad. Bunch of lying bastards."

Wolfe turned onto the highway and accelerated. "If you been shit on like they have, you'd know. They're in it for the cause. They want redemption day, just like you."

Chapter 28

West Virginia was a place where wealth came out of the ground.

Generation after generation of families sent their breadwinners into the coal mines. They squeezed out an existence for rural West Virginia, but sometimes paid the ultimate price for their selected occupation.

The primary wealth was buried deep. Other forms of honest wealth in the area were hard to come by. Fifty yards inward from any major roadway was as far as the money seeped. If off the beaten path, West Virginia rivaled the most poverty-stricken areas of the country.

The people were proud and steadfast. Strong values and close families held the communities firm. What they lacked in finances, they more than made up for in resolve. Ten years behind in economic development, but a generation ahead when it came to family values, or a generation behind, depending upon the view of progress. It wasn't a place where strangers sought fortune; it was a place to get lost.

Two and a half hours after his encounter with the Virginia State Patrol, Nick pulled into Yellow Spring. The town was three blocks long on the main drag. He'd kept his eyes peeled for Nelly's Tavern and hoped it was on the main street, perhaps on the other side of town.

The town was closed for the night. No one on the street, all the businesses closed down, no lights anywhere. It was like he'd driven onto a vacant movie lot for a film about 1950's Middle America.

He passed through and kept going for nearly a mile. Just as he was preparing to turn around and head back to town, he spotted the bar tucked back off the highway. He pulled into the gravel lot.

An ancient Subaru faced the wooden structure which itself defied gravity. The building listed to the left with uneven wood nailed vertically along the front. It looked like an opening to a mine shaft, which might have been what the designer was going for. But the lack of upkeep cancelled the thought that a designer was ever involved.

One large window provided the only opening other than the door. Light poured out the window which was covered with chicken wire. Nick had seen that before, and he was never sure of the exact purpose of the chicken wire, safety or security. It certainly wasn't aesthetic appeal.

Nick stretched his stiffened legs and ambled awkwardly toward the entrance just as the neon sign flickered twice and expired. It was as if the sign had grown tired and just gave up.

The last vestige of light was extinguished as the front door opened. Before Nick could speak, the voice said, "Sorry pal, we're closed."

"Are you Sarah?"

The woman turned from the door and squinted. Apparently thinking better of walking into the darkness with a stranger, she reached back inside and flipped on the lights.

"Who are you?" she said, her keys splayed between her fisted fingers in case she needed to land at least one good punch.

"I'm Nick James. Sheriff Brager's a friend of mine."

"Not anymore he ain't."

Nick stammered. "Yeah, yeah. He was a friend of mine. I just want to ask a few questions." Noticing her hesitancy he continued. "Drove all the way from DC tonight. Just need a minute of your time." Sarah pulled back from the door to let him in.

Nick walked past her into the establishment, which consisted of a short bar with three stools and what had to be a thirty-year-old RCA television occupying a chunk of the top of the bar. One wall supported a row of booths held together by duct tape. In the middle of the room stood a pool table with a gaping rip in the felt and a juke box that was dark. Even money it was broken rather than shut off.

Sarah stood with her arms crossed as if to say, let's move it along. I got places to go.

"Sheriff Brager came to see me," Nick said.

She stiffened suddenly. The news was everywhere, he thought. She'd spotted him from what he assumed were TV notices about the APB.

Nick held his hands toward her, palms out to calm her down. He stepped back slightly.

"Listen, he was a friend of mine. I had nothing to do with what happened to him. He was actually coming to visit me when he got shot. Please, I only want to ask a few questions. To see if I can figure out who did this."

She nodded slightly.

"Brager came to see me about the receipt you gave him. I work for Homeland Security; well, used to anyway. I gave lectures and spoke at conferences about redemption receipts and phony scrip. Brager came to one of my lectures, so he called to see what I thought about it. Before we could talk, he was killed. But I was able to get the receipt."

He noticed that she wasn't as tense. The more he talked, the better. "I gave the receipt to the FBI. The task force looking into Justice Caprelli's kidnapping." This boosted his credibility substantially. She nodded, acknowledging that she was on top of that news story, too.

116

Nick didn't tell her that he kept the evidence envelope holding the receipt which identified Sarah and Nelly's Tavern as the location where the scrip was passed.

"I want to ask about the person who gave it to you."

"Okay." She took a deep breath and swallowed hard. "Three guys. Real jerks. Well, at least one was. He was kind of the ring leader."

She uncrossed her arms, placing hands on hips. Progress, Nick thought, but she still appeared uneasy.

"What did he look like?"

"I don't know; tall. Six two maybe, muscular. Big guy." She cast her eyes upward as if she was trying to spot him on the ceiling.

"Caucasian?"

"Yeah, all of them, Sorry." Her eyes remained upward, as if trying to remember. "Short hair, blond or light brown. Had a kind of military vibe about him."

"What do you mean by that?"

"Oh, I don't know. Kinda walked like he was on the way to kick someone's ass. He was definitely the leader."

"Facial hair?"

"Yeah, mustache and couple days growth."

What about the other guys?"

"One was kinda puny, with glasses. Long black hair, with that hockey kinda haircut."

"A mullett?"

"Yeah, one of those. And the other guy was fit. Short hair; looked like he worked out alot." She moved away from the door, offering him one of the bar stools.

"The big guy; any tattoos, marks, scars, anything?"

"Not that I remember. He was kinda good looking—." Then as if catching herself, she said, "If he wasn't such a jerk."

"They been in here before?"

"I'm not here all the time, but Zeke," she paused. "The

owner, he seen them. Bout a week before. Paid for their beers that time," she said with an exaggerated tone.

"Anything unusual about them? What they said, how they looked?" Nick said.

Sarah considered this for a few moments, eyes again to the ceiling. "No, not really," she said, shaking her head slightly. "They ain't from around here, that's for sure."

"Why do you say that?"

"First off, I know everybody in the county and the counties around us. Small place, ya understand." She looked directly at Nick. "Somebody moves in or out, it's news. These guys were just passing through from who knows where or they just got to the area."

"Names? Do you recall? They call each other by any names, titles, anything?"

"Nah, not that I heard," she said, shaking her head.

"See what they were driving?"

"Yeah, they all piled into an orange or bronze colored GMC truck. Mustache man driving."

Leave it to a country girl to notice the make and make of a pickup truck, he thought. "Which way they go?"

Sarah pointed south.

"No chance you got a license plate number?" Nick asked, knowing it was a long shot.

"Couldn't." She moved toward the bar and began leaning against it. "Didn't have no tags. On the front anyway." She paused a moment, then looked up. "What the heck was that thing he gave me? What he tried to pay his bill with? Never seen nothing like it."

Before he could answer, red and blue flashing lights burst through the window and door. Nick could see the front half of a police vehicle pull alongside the bar with headlights on full beam.

Chapter 29

Galbert clenched the phone tightly as he shouted into it. "Everything's messed up. What the hell are you doing to me?"

"Like I said, I'm making you a wealthy man, my friend."

Galbert eyes rolled around his dark shelved library. Mahogany and burgundy were his wife's template for Galbert's self-defined man cave. Books lined the walls; books he'd never bothered to read, but that made him look like a man of letters. Framed historic maps covered bare spots in the walls. A green shaded desk lamp and two torche fixtures illuminated the room.

"I gave you a lot of fucking money—"

"You've given me enough money to get this started. Your payback will be in the millions. My help costs you chump change."

"You're not giving me anything. It's all screwed," Galbert said, waving his free hand.

"Look, Elliott, I've got this all wired. You have your objective, others have theirs. I'm like a—a hotel concierge." He paused and a small chuckle snuck through. "Or a lobbyist. I bring people together to achieve each party's objective."

"You make it sound so clinical."

"Clinical or cynical?" The man said, laughing.

"What's with the international terrorist bullshit? That wasn't our deal."

"I have this all under control. My client had to buy some time. Their priority trumped yours in the short-term. Everything will come together in due course."

Galbert rubbed his hand from his forehead up over his receding white scalp. He stood and turned, looking out his window at the backyard pool of his neighbor's McMansion. He took two deep breaths. The man on the phone remained silent, that bothered Galbert the most. He was accustomed to using awkward silence as a weapon. Now this punk was using it on him.

"Okay," said Galbert. "I don't like it, but I'm—"

"Doesn't matter if you like it. I'm in charge."

"Like hell you are," Galbert said. The line went quiet. Shit, he thought. The guy is using the silent treatment again.

Eventually, the man on the phone cleared his throat. "I suggest you have one of your attorneys look up 18 USC 2339A."

"What the hell is that?"

"It's the statute making aiding and abetting terrorist groups a felony."

"I didn't aid and abet terrorists. I bought a solution to a problem. What the hell are you doing?"

"Well, it's simple, Elliott. Our futures are intertwined. If something bad happens to me, something bad happens to you. Conversely, good things that happen to you will be good things that happen to me. And while we're having this little fireside chat, I want to remind you to make another retainer deposit against my future fees."

Galbert swallowed hard and worked his courage back up. "That sounds like extortion. Are you threatening me?"

"I'm merely helping you achieve the objective sought. We knew it would be expensive going in, but I think we can agree that the long-term benefit to you outweighs these short term costs."

"You fucking Weasel." Galbert spat the words.

"Elliott, Elliott. Have we now come to name calling? I thought our relationship was above all that. This is a business deal, plain and simple. There's no place for emotion and derision."

Galbert took several breaths. After another silent moment, he asked, "How much are we—"

"Seventy-five, my friend."

"What? Are you crazy?"

"I know it seems like a lot, but think of it as an investment. In the long term you get to keep that cozy house you have. What is that worth? And we both know that the business benefit will pay off for many years. It's a small price to pay."

"Listen, you little punk," Galbert said, thrusting his finger at an imaginary target. "I can go to the authorities and take you down. It's not just me who's at risk here."

"You certainly could. Wouldn't be a wise thing to do. Quite a gamble if you ask me. You see, you'll go down. That's a known fact. The only question is whether you can take me with you. Interesting gambit."

Silence ensued. Galbert sat down.

"But keep in mind," the voice on the phone continued. "I know how the bureaucratic and political jungle works. I'm part of that jungle; you're not. Funny things happen in the jungle. Avenues and options are open to those in the jungle who can damage others. You see, the more information you have, from whatever source, the greater your strength in the jungle. You could try and take me down. The only thing we know for sure is that you'll be blacklisted, lose your business, lose your house, your pretty wife, and get a million points in the federal prison frequent stayer program."

Galbert ground his teeth. He had no choice. "I want to know what's happening and when. You've kept me in the dark too long on this."

"Elliott, you don't have a need to know. Sometimes details can be messy, and I wouldn't want to bother you—"

"Bother me? I'm paying you."

"I wouldn't want to bother you with the details. Watch the news over the next few days. You'll see my fingerprints on the news as it breaks. When it breaks, I'm sure you'll see the benefit of your investment." A deathly pause, then Haden continued. "So shall we say tomorrow around noon for you to replenish your retainer account?"

"Golf range again?"

"No, tomorrow I'll just come to your office.

"My office? I thought—"

"Don't worry. It'll be official business. You'll see. Just have the cash ready."

Chapter 30

Nick brushed past Sarah, getting out of the line of sight through the door and window. He scanned the inside of the bar, hoping he'd see an exit that hadn't been there before. "There a back way out of here?"

Sarah waved him toward the bar. "No, that's the only door."

"Believe me, I had nothing to do with Brager, but I think the guys who were in here did. I think I know who they are, but I can't catch them if I get hauled in. I need your help."

Sarah pointed. "Get behind the bar and get down."

Nick raced around the bar and crawled into a fetal position. The bar was short. He didn't want to risk having his feet exposed, so he tucked them in. He was lying on a skiff of dirt that had been ground into the wood floor. The stench of stale beer, wood rot, and rancid water washed over him.

The door squeaked open, and two heavy footsteps entered.

"Sarah?"

"Evening, Rich."

"Everything okay? I was driving past and know you're closed by this time. Noticed the lights on and your car. Just wanted to make sure everything was okay."

It was silent for way too long. Is she giving me up? Nick thought. What's she doing? Is she pointing behind the bar where I'm hiding? Nick began extending his hands below him so he could push off. Who knew what he'd do or where he'd go, but he didn't want to be caught lying behind the bar.

"You gotta chill, Rich," Sarah said finally. "Seriously."

Nick was able to start breathing again.

Sarah continued. "I'm just cleaning up and getting ready to lock up. Everything's okay. You gotta cool out, man." Sarah was shuffling around, making noises like she was picking up and preparing to leave. "This is the third time this week you've stopped by at closing to see if I was okay. I'm okay. Okay?"

"I just want to make sure you're safe. Don't like the idea of a lady closing up a bar this time of night."

Nick smiled. The patrolman was hitting on her, pathetic though he may be, but he was definitely hitting on her.

"I appreciate the concern, but I'm okay."

The next remark wiped the smile off Nick's face.

"Whose motorcycle out there?"

"What are you talking about?"

"The motorcycle. Nobody here. Who left their bike outside?"

Nick could tell Sarah was getting flustered. "Beats me," she said. "We had a group of bikers come in earlier. Somebody probably had too much to drink and just left it."

"Bikers don't just leave their bikes." Another footstep came closer. Nick could sense Sarah moving to cut him off before the footsteps got to the bar.

"Who knows what those guys do," she said, trying to laugh it off.

"Kinda funny. Has Virginia tags. Who's gonna drive over from Virginia and leave their bike overnight? Outside this place?"

"You know we've had guys come in and have way too

much. They wander off into the woods to pee or puke and end up sleeping it off."

It didn't sound very convincing to Nick. He was sure it was less convincing to Rich. He started to turn quietly to get his feet and hands under him. He heard another step toward to the bar. He could sense Sarah scrambling to come up with something, but she was running out of time.

"Rich, ya know," she stammered. "Just wondering. I didn't get a dinner break tonight. I'm starved. I'm gonna go up to Turner's and get some food. I know it's kinda late, but I'd love the company."

Rich's voice perked up, and Nick could sense him puffing out his chest. "I s'pose I could take a little break." Right, Nick thought, as if maintaining law and order in the middle of the night in this nowhere West Virginia town required the man's constant vigilance.

Feet shuffled toward the door, the light went out, and the deadbolt clicked shut. Nick waited until he heard two cars fire up and roll away.

It was several minutes before Nick's heart rate returned to some semblance of normal. In that moment, fatigue overcame him.

He'd started the day unemployed and walking his neighborhood for a familiar cup of joe. In a few short hours he'd become an accused cop killer and the most wanted man on the East Coast.

Nick cautiously peered out the window. Darkness shrouded all. He wanted to lie down and rest, but adrenaline would defeat that goal. With Sarah sharing pancakes with what was likely the only lawman on duty within forty miles, now was the time to move.

After heading south eight miles on the highway, he pondered his plan. It wasn't like he would just roll up on an orange or bronze truck. He needed rest, and he needed daylight.

He eased the bike off the highway, killed the engine, and walked it fifty yards on a winding dirt road. There were no lights visible, only a full moon cutting through the trees. He eased the bike into a clearing and leaned it against a stump. After scanning his surroundings and deciding he was hidden as well as could be expected, he settled under a downed tree and closed his eyes.

In moments, he was out.

Chapter 31

Darkness and silence ground on him.

Every two hours the routine was repeated. A small plastic bowl with rice and raw vegetables was handed to him along with a fresh canister of water. A gun always present during these brief respites. At least he was allowed to sit up and stretch. He wasn't allowed to stand.

They never spoke.

Only the big guy spoke, and that was when all three were present.

He'd given up asking questions. It only prompted them to motion for him to hurry up. The first time he refused to lie down he got a back-handed slap. He'd given up resistance and merely tried to prolong the moments of freedom. Breathing in the rancid, but cool air of the cave was welcomed by his aged lungs.

The closing of the coffin and the grind of the hasps meant he'd be alone again—until the next time.

Though exhausted, he couldn't sleep.

His shoulders were pinned with only a few inches to spare on each side. He couldn't roll over or even onto his side. Cramps from his calves shot searing pain through his brain. Though bending his ankles and lifting his legs a few inches provided some relief, it was just a matter of moments when the pain returned.

His body was attacking him.

The stench in the coffin caused his eyes to tear. But he wouldn't cry.

He'd learned to fight the tears early in life. Spilling his milk, breaking a lamp, or failing to complete his chores brought his father with a leather belt. Not crying gave him honor as he endured his punishments. His father learned to respect that.

That document was disturbing.

What were they doing? Letting me see their faces?

It made no sense. None of it made sense. They misinterpreted history. They misrepresented history.

On the law it was just wrong, but on a base emotional level? It resonated. It tapped into liberty. To self determination. To personal responsibility. Core principles, though mangled beyond comprehension. Core principles that this country has lost. We've legislated common sense and individual dignity out of society. We've legislated behavior in pursuit of the collective, the collective's rights.

We've lost our way.

Common law was the backbone of American jurisprudence. What separated us from European legal systems. It was like that case argued last term.

Winfrey versus...Winstead versus...Fourth Amendment... Fourth...

He blinked his eyes, which made no difference given the lack of light.

What was I just thinking?

Can't remember.

Just now.

What was I thinking about?

The jurist squeezed his fists, and his eyes squinted in the blackness. His left leg shot out as a cramp seized up his calf.

I was thinking about...I didn't forget...I didn't forget... What was it? I was just thinking about...it's gone.

He took several deep breaths, flexing his ankle.

Wish they would just kill me.

Chapter 32

April 17

Nick's plan was no better a few hours later when he awoke. How was he going to find the truck and the three men? This was sparsely settled hill country. Homes, shacks, even businesses were tucked back into the woods, nearly invisible from the main roads.

He couldn't even be certain he was going the right direction. All he had was Sarah's indication that they headed south after leaving the bar. Who knew where they were going? He was running out of time. Being on the lam didn't help, and he had a serious shortage of evidence. If he was right, it was only a matter of days before all hell broke loose.

Nick coasted into a lit up filling station. He knew one thing. Vehicles needed gasoline, even orange or bronze colored trucks.

A white-haired man who looked to be in his eighties sat on a paint bucket near the station's front door. The wrinkles and stains in his coveralls looked to be the same age as the attendant. In the open overhead doorway to the shop, a young man, maybe twenty-five rubbed his hands with a reddish rag. He wore blue jeans and a gray work shirt.

"Morning," Nick said.

The man nodded and spit between his work boots. A stitched blue patch on his coveralls said Smitty.

"You Smitty?"

"Either that or I stole Smitty's clothes." The old man chuckled. The younger one, with a name tag that read Doug, gave a snort laugh. Nick smiled to show he was agreeable.

"You're out early," Smitty said. "Then you roll in on that rice burner. Probably don't need ten bucks to fill the damn thing."

"Well, that, and I could use a cup of coffee."

Smitty motioned over his shoulder. "Got a pot brewing. Oughta be bout done. Grab me a cup on your way back. Course you got problems the coffee won't fix."

Nick tensed and stared at the man. *How could he know?* Smitty looked out at the highway letting his remark hang in the air.

Finally, the old man spoke. "You got pine straw in your hair and mud all over your jeans. You either slept on the ground last night or you need to find a new housekeeper." Smitty and Doug belly laughed. Nick was able to exhale. He ambled into the grease-stained and dilapidated station in search of coffee.

Nick longed for Megan's special latte. Though barely twenty-four hours had passed, that cup of coffee seemed a generation ago.

Nick handed Smitty a Styrofoam cup with coffee that tasted like boiled dirt. He choked down a few swallows figuring there was caffeine in there somewhere. He sat on the curb across the open doorway as the rising sun gave definition to the town just up the highway.

"What brings you to Walterville?" said Smitty. "Kind of an odd place to visit on vacation." He cackled again.

"Looking for a friend."

"You need better friends if they let you sleep outside." More cackling. Doug joined in the laughter. "What's your friend's name? Probably know 'em."

"Yeah, I suppose you know everyone around here."

"Whether they like it or not," Doug chimed in.

"My friend drives an orange or bronze colored GMC pickup."

"Here's a little tip," said Smitty. "Might want to learn the names of your friends. Sometimes folks sell their cars. Damn hard for you to keep track of your friends by make and model. Names are better." He blew some steam off his coffee, smiling to himself. "You a cop?"

"Me? No."

"Didn't figure so," said Doug, snickering. "Like to bitch about the pay, but most can still pop for a hotel room."

"What makes you think I'm a cop?" Nick asked.

Smitty leaned forward and spat again. "The only folks who come around looking for someone they don't know, is cops. Less of course your givin away the publishers clearinghouse check, in which case, I'm your man."

"The guy I'm looking for might be new to the area."

"So you figure someone new around here might buy gas from ol' Smitty?"

"Yeah, something like that."

"Lots of gas stations around here," said Doug.

Smitty stared at Nick and was silent. Whatever wheels were turning in his head were taking time to rotate. Finally he said, "Come to think of it, there has been a truck like that I seen a few times."

Nick leaned forward.

"Started coming in here a few weeks ago. Big guy, looked like he could bite ten penny nails in half. Recently he started sending another guy in."

Doug disappeared into the mechanical shop.

"Go through a lot of gas?" Nick asked.

"Yeah, a little, but they also usually fill a few five gallon tanks," Smitty said.

Generators, Nick thought. He nodded for Smitty to continue. Doug entered the station through a side door and was pouring himself a cup of coffee.

"Course I seen the one guy with a white van also."

Nick shot upright.

"You sure it was the same guy?" Doug piped up, still within earshot of the conversation outside.

"I know it was the same guy," said Smitty. Then the old man turned his head and shouted into the station doorway, "What do you think I'm going senile?" Smitty gave Nick an eye roll, as if to say *kids these days.*

"How long ago?" Nick asked.

"Few days, I suppose."

"Any idea where the guy lives? What direction they come and go?" Nick asked.

"What do you think I run here, the Oprah show? Guys come in buy gas, and leave. I don't play twenty questions with them. Just want them to keep coming back, so I leave them alone. One thing for sure, we're probably the closest gas station to wherever your friend is."

"Why's that?"

"Unless he's a real penny pincher, you don't much care where you get the gas for your five gallon container. Guy usually just goes to the closest place. Unless you get a buzz from driving around with containers full of gas."

Nick topped off his gas tank, twelve bucks, and handed Smitty a twenty. He rolled out of the station with renewed confidence. His first plan was to find the nearest gas stations on either side of Smitty's to narrow the territory. Even then he had to wait. It wasn't like he could go knocking door to door to ask if they were housing a kidnapped Supreme Court Justice. The old mining roads that intersected with the main highway pushed into the mountains and heavily forested grounds. He was still trying to find a needle in a haystack. He'd just found a way to make the haystack into a hay bale.

~

The first few cars of the morning pulled into Smitty's. The early risers were anxious to get to their jobs or chores for the day. Smitty welcomed most by name, and a friendly banter ensued with all. Doug was working on Dallas Simpson's transmission. Today he'd yank that thing and see what he could make of it.

He stood out back of the mechanical shop and smoked a cigarette. After poking his head inside to ensure he wouldn't be interrupted, he pulled his cell phone and punched in numbers.

After several rings the line engaged. "Hey Brother Wolfe, it's Doug. Gotta guy poking around for you. Driving a Kawasaki and asking a bunch of questions. Young guy, working alone. Don't think he's the law, but figured you'd want to know."

Then he slapped the phone shut and took a deep drag on his cigarette.

Chapter 33

Stupid plan, thought Nick. *Let's see, I sit here by the roadside and hope like hell that the pickup I'm looking for just cruises by. Even if it does, what the hell do I do?* He leaned against the bike with his ankles crossed. The kickstand of the Kawasaki was down, and it was parked off the highway. He'd pulled into a shaded area about a mile and a half outside town.

Since Smitty's was the gas station preferred by the pickup matching the description and since another gas station was on the opposite end of town, all six blocks away, the place to be was on the highway north of town. With arms crossed, Nick ran down his options.

Without something substantial on the Caprelli kidnapping, all Nick had was, *I didn't do it,* with regard to Brager. That wasn't a game he wanted to play. Brager and Caprelli were somehow linked, there was no doubt in his mind, but if he couldn't prove the connection, he would continue to be a fugitive.

He pulled the phone from his jeans and stared at it. He hadn't turned it on since leaving Georgetown's campus the day before. From his work with Homeland he knew that his position could be tracked through a process known as multilateralization. Every active cell phone sent out a ping to find the nearest cell tower. Even without making a call, the feds could track his location by localizing the pings emitted from his phone and triangulating his position. That's why he not only kept it off, he'd pulled the battery.

Nick had few options.

He could continue to watch the highway and hope to get lucky, or he could call in some help. The second the phone lit up, he'd be marked. How long would it take to get to me? At best he figured he had a half hour. By the time the fibbies rallied forces in West Virginia and got someone to pursue, plenty of time would go by. They weren't that efficient. He hoped not anyway.

He could always shut down the phone and move, but one signal would narrow the search. Right now he was totally off the grid. In a matter of seconds, he'd be pinpointed.

A faded red pickup with a camper rushed past from the south. Several seconds passed, and a white Toyota spun by from the opposite direction. Silence ensued. He looked up and down the highway; nothing.

He punched the on button for his phone.

As the system booted up, he noticed that he had about a quarter of a charge, so despite the warning signal it sent to authorities, he had to limit his power usage if he wanted to continue using the phone.

Five missed calls. He clicked them open. One from Winters, one from Mrs. McKenzie, and three from Kate. Seeing her name on the caller ID gave him a rush. It was like old times. He'd forgotten that feeling of care and excitement. Maybe it was love; how could he be sure? But that emotional wave washed over him. Being as alone as he'd ever been the past day, he needed that. He just needed to know that she still cared. That someone did. He stared at the device in his hand. Finally, someone was on his side; someone he could talk to, someone who understood him.

She'd probably seen the APB and was reaching out. She could be his link, his contact to make them see that he was innocent. Kate could be his only salvation. Winters was supportive, but afraid. Fear wasn't an emotion in Kate's quiver.

Thirty email messages downloaded, but he didn't have time for those; probably useless junk anyway, and he didn't want to waste juice on them. Kate could help him; she could talk to folks on his behalf. They'd listen to her. He jabbed the phone and dialed her cell.

~

"We go with what we've got," Kate said.

"Problem is, we don't have shit." Javier and Kate were huddled in the hallway outside the war room. In five minutes Javier would present what he had to Jannsen and Schaeffer. Just for giggles, there was probably someone from the White House joining as well.

"It's only been two days; really, a day and a half. What can they expect?"

"The first forty-eight hours are critical. We got nothing," Javier fumed, arms crossed as he leaned against the wall. "Sixty agents out pounding the pavement, running down every call, forensics, lab analysis—"

"Lead with that," she said, interrupting. "We may not have the results we want, but procedurally, you've done everything possible."

"We've got nothing."

"Guys were pros."

"And they're making us look like amateurs."

Kate's phone rang, and she fished it from her purse. "Jesus, it's Nick." She hit the button connecting the call. "Nick, where are you?"

"Kate, I don't know what you've heard, but I didn't do it. It's all a set up. I don't know why."

"Where are you?"

"I'm in West Virginia. I need your—"

"Nick."

"—help, I need you to talk to someone and get—"

"Nick."

"—them to back—"

"Nick." The line went silent for a moment. "Nick, I need to tell you something. I'm part of the Caprelli task force." She could hear the air whistle past the voice piece as Nick exhaled loudly. "I'm here with Special Agent Javier Lozano. We need to talk."

"Kate, I—" The line went silent again. She could sense his discouragement.

She locked eyes with Javier and said, "I believe you Nick. I believe you. I don't think you killed Brager. I don't think you could kill anyone—not like that. I don't know what's going on, but we need to talk. I'm going to put you on speaker. I've got Special Agent Lozano here with me." She punched a button on her phone and held it up so they both could hear.

"Hi, Nick. It's Javier. Need to know what's going on."

"It's the Posse Comitatus. That's who has Caprelli."

"What are you talking about?"

"The Posse Com—"

"I heard you," Javier said. "That's nuts. They were a bunch of whacked out farmers in the Midwest. The group died out in the eighties."

"That's who it is. I haven't figured out exactly where they are, but that's who took Caprelli, and I think they're somewhere in eastern West Virginia. I'm probably close to where they are right now. Believe me, they damn well haven't died out. I've been following them for the last three years."

"That's crazy," Javier muttered.

"Nick, what do you have?" Kate asked. Her eyes met Javier's and her stern glance said, *give him a chance to explain.*

"The fractional reserve check. That's classic Posse. They invented that notion that their own paper money could replace the government's."

Javier rolled his eyes. Kate motioned for him to remain quiet.

"Brager was bringing the receipt to me because he'd learned about it in a seminar I gave last year. I was on my way to meet with him when he was killed."

"What's that got to do with Caprelli?" Kate asked. She was testing Nick to see if he knew about Caprelli's wallet being in Brager's car. That was the only piece of evidence that connected the two cases.

"I don't know yet, but this isn't some international group; this is home grown. Something's coming down. These guys start dropping redemption receipts in local establishments means that they're getting brazen. It's not just some coincidence."

"The Posse wasn't into kidnapping, Nick," Javier said. "They just wanted to avoid paying back money they'd borrowed. They were trying to dodge bankers and judges. That's what the Posse was all about."

"They killed plenty of law enforcement officers over the years. Taking a Supreme Court Justice isn't out of the realm for these guys. I need you to ge—"

Wesley burst out of the war room. "You're gonna want to see this. They released a video of Caprelli. God almighty, you gotta see this."

"Nick, hang on," said Kate.

Javier's head snapped between Wesley and Kate. Finally settling upon Kate, though his body moved toward the door of the war room, he pointed at Kate and whispered. "Keep talking, reel him in. I'm postponing the meeting."

She gave him a curious look.

"We've finally got something," he said. "We'll meet later today. Get him located, get him under control, get him in here, whatever you have to do." Then he shot into the war room.

Kate took the call off speaker and put a hand up to her other ear. Elevated noise from the war room poured out into the hallway. She concentrated on her call. "Nick, I know you didn't do it. I can help." There was no response on the line. She heard rushing noises and thuds.

She heard a voice. It wasn't Nick's. "Get the fucking phone."

"Nick!" she shouted. "Nick. Where—"

The line went dead.

Chapter 34

Kate ran into the war room. Javier and four others were crammed around a computer screen. She nudged forward and between Wesley and Dave Winter's shoulders where she could make out Justice Caprelli in a tight shot. Dressed in his black robe and positioned on the bench, it looked like stock footage from a reporter's coverage of the Supreme Court.

She heard his last line before the screen went blank. This was no stock footage. "Redemption Day approaches."

Javier grabbed his forehead. "What the hell was that?"

Others shook their heads. "Rerun it," Wesley said.

Gathering himself, Javier said, "I want forensics on this tape. I want every angle, every word, every symbol analyzed. I want the lighting guys to study the shadows, the sound guys to look for any ambient noise. Everything. How did we get this?"

"Came with an email. Just had the link to the video," said Maggie Dillman.

"I want to know everything about that email account. Kate, get on that. I want to know what server it's on, everything. I want this locked down—"

"Too late, boss," said Scottie, as he clicked keys on his desktop computer. "It's gone viral."

"What?"

"Just now checking, but the video's gone viral. It's on YouTube, VidonDemand, probably half a dozen sites—still checking. This thing is out there."

"Kate, get them shut down. I want that video off the air."

"Too late," said Wesley, surprisingly sticking up for Kate. He leaned over Scottie's shoulder reading the computer screen. "The hits on this video are through the roof, but by the time Kate could get a judge to take action, it'll have been viewed millions of times. Add to that, the video has already been picked up internationally, so we can't touch any servers overseas."

"We could, but what's the point?" said Kate. "By the time we get any response or cooperation internationally, this thing will be everywhere. Can't put the toothpaste back in the tube."

"Shit, we need to get in front of this. Maggie, get some comm staff up here. We need to prepare a statement. He looked around the room. All eyes were on him. "Move," he shouted.

Bodies flew in every direction, phones engaged, and keyboards clicked in a frenzy of activity. Kate tapped Javier's arm. "They got Nick," she whispered.

"What do you mean?"

"I was talking to him. Sounded like there was a fight. I could hear other voices. Someone said 'get the phone,' then the line went dead. Somebody's got him. If Nick's right, it could be the same people who have Caprelli."

Javier considered it for a moment, then tapped Wesley on the shoulder. He'd been hunched over Scottie's shoulder as they studied the Internet hit pattern of the justice's video. Wesley quickly joined them.

"Kate was just on the phone with Nick."

"What?" said Wesley. "Where is—"

"Hold on," Javier said, extending a hand. "He just called in. He's in West Virginia and thinks he's on the trail of whoever's got Caprelli."

Wesley snorted. "What's he running his own investigation? Man's got an APB out on him and he's out playing James Bond."

Kate gave him a tight-lipped stare.

Javier continued. "Look, he was on the phone, then something happened. Maybe he was abducted."

Wesley smiled and shook his head.

"Javier, I can't work with this guy," Kate said, gesturing to Wesley. "Guy's not only a jerk, he's lazy."

"Look, sweetheart, let's face facts—" Wesley started.

"I don't need this right now," Javier said to both of them. "Get a location on Nick," he said, pointing to Wesley. "If his phone is on, get his coordinates. Get those to Kate. If he's on private property, Kate, get a warrant. May not be completely necessary, but no reason to take a chance. Call the Winchester office and get a couple of agents ready to support. And keep trying his phone. Who knows, maybe he'll answer." He walked a few steps, then yelled, "Where are those damn comm folks? Get them in here now. Maggie, I want a draft and release plan in five minutes. Wesley, call Jannsen. I'm on my way up."

~

Nick's head rolled slightly to the left and one eye opened. He saw chipped plaster board. The light hurt his head. He squeezed his eyes shut hard. He had a massive headache. His mouth was dry and sticky as he swallowed slowly. Then he remembered. His eyes shot open. He raised his hand to shield the sun streaming through the window.

He was on some kind of military cot, canvas suspended by an aluminum metal frame. It smelled like it had been stockpiled since World War II. He was alone in a small room. The cot was the only furniture that graced the design. A paint-chipped, wood door stood sentry across from his bed. He couldn't hear anything except for the wind shooting through the trees and branches gently tapping the window and roof. Cobwebs adorned the window frame and connected it to the ceiling in a haze of white, just like his mind.

He started to sit up, then rolled back down as his head nearly exploded. He grabbed his forehead and squeezed as if that was going to help. *Who the heck were those guys?* He never saw them coming. They must have approached from behind as he was talking with Kate. He looked at his hands. They weren't bound. He kicked his feet; they were free as well.

Moving slowly, Nick was able to get into a sitting position. He rubbed his eyes and took several deep breaths. He reached for his pockets. Everything was gone—wallet, cell phone, keys. How long had he been out? Could have been a few minutes or a few hours. He was glad to see the sun, more than just for the estimate of time.

The last thing he remembered was the smell. It was a sweet, pungent odor. When he felt the cloth go over his nose and mouth, his first reaction what, who fights that way? With a handkerchief?

Before he figured it out, it didn't matter. These have to be the guys who have Caprelli. Who jumps people without warning? Could be some kook mountain men, but they'd just shout, point a gun, and say *get the hell off my property.* No, to jump someone and lock them up like this, these had to be the folks he was looking for.

Nick flexed his shoulder. That had been where he took the first hit. Guy blasted him from behind and smashed him to the ground like a backside hit on a quarterback. Knocked the wind out of him. Were it not for that, he might have held them off. Well, maybe not. There were two of them, but he definitely would have put up a better struggle.

143

Never get cornered. He'd learned that from his father. It was a lesson his father unknowingly taught, but one Nick was destined to carry. Never get boxed in physically or emotionally. He shook his head and squeezed his eyes tightly, using brute mental strength the push his father's image from his mind.

Never get cornered. Never get cornered.

He stretched his neck and reflected back on his conversation with Kate. Just my luck, he thought. When I need to reach out to her, I find out she's part of the investigation. Well, they certainly got a detailed briefing about the life and times of Nick James.

Can I catch a break here?

The door knob squeaked as it turned slightly and the door pushed open.

Chapter 35

Wolfe scratched the stubble on his chin and paced the floor. Who was this guy? He comes poking around on a motorcycle; not law enforcement, just some guy. Nick's wallet and cell phone were on the kitchen table, license and cards laid out in a perfect line. Something is wrong here, he thought. Lucky they didn't kill the guy. If Wolfe hadn't intervened, Landers would already have him in a shallow grave somewhere on the property.

Gibson sat and clicked the keys on his laptop. He smiled and shook his head. "This thing has gone everywhere. Magic of the Internet, I tell ya."

"Nothing links back here, right?" asked Wolfe.

"We're clean. Sent the file to Merton through a phony email account I set up on the library's computer. Our computers can't be traced to it. Mert must have a thousand phony email accounts. He uploaded the file to his page, but also shot it around to all the file sharing sites and linked the damn thing to a bunch of emails lists and chat rooms that understand the fight. That video's the hottest thing on the Internet right now."

"Everything's traceable."

"First they've got to crack Mert," Gibson said, without removing his eyes from the computer screen. "Reconstruct his deleted files, hope they come together well enough to identify his incoming emails with metadata intact, trace them back to their origin. In which case, if they're incredibly lucky, they'll find one sent from the Hampshire County Public Library. From that machine, they could figure out that a thumb drive was used to upload the video. Without the thumb drive, they're screwed. And since I crushed the thumb drive with a hammer and scattered it all along state Highway 259, they're doubly screwed. Even if they got that all figured out, lined up all the freakin' stars perfectly, it won't matter, because it'll all be over by then."

Landers came through the door and headed to the coffee pot. Wolfe stared at him.

"I told you I was sorry, Wolfe."

"Use your head. We can't let little things interfere with the mission. The mission comes first," said Wolfe. "How long's he gonna be out?"

Landers checked his watch. "Gave him a pretty good blast of that juice. He'll be out another ten minutes or so."

"We need to fix this," Wolfe said. "Can't have a detail like this unravel what we've worked on."

"You tell Jackson about this?" Gibson asked.

"Jackson don't need to know. He's got his part, we've got ours. It'll all come together just as planned," said Wolfe.

Wolfe's cell phone rang, and he yanked it from his jeans. He looked at the incoming number and punched the line open.

"Yeah?" Wolfe listened and continued pacing. "Who? How long?" Several more seconds passed. "A bird? What are you talking about?" He moved toward the window, pulling back the dusty shade, and looked to the sky. "What can they get from that?" He listened, letting the shade back down. "Thermo-what? Oh, gotcha, just like in Afghanistan. What else?" He walked to the table focused on the conversation. "When?"

Gibson stopped typing and watched Wolfe, then stole a glance at Landers, who just shrugged.

"Okay," Wolfe said. "Thanks, brother. Hey, we're gonna need more cash." He nodded. "Right, I'll have Landers pick it up like last time. Tonight. Good. Thanks."

"What's up?" said Landers.

"Our boy must have some pull. They got a warrant to search the place. Feds will be here within the hour."

"Jesus," said Gibson. "What's the deal? Who is this guy?"

"Don't matter. Everyone stay in the cabin. Shut down the computer, the router, everything." Wolfe opened his phone and pulled the battery out. "And take the battery out of your phone. We're gonna have a little fly by." He moved back to the window and studied the sky.

"What?" said Landers.

"Feds are going to do a little fly by. Take pictures and thermo-image the place."

"Thermo-image? What the hell's that?" said Landers.

Gibson slapped the laptop shut and unplugged the server. "They measure the temperature inside a structure to determine how many people are inside. They're able to pick up body temperatures. Probably sweeping the place for electronics as well. It'll pick up anything emitting electromagnetic or wireless radiation, like a cell phone or computer."

"My phone's turned off. What're they going to do?" asked Landers.

"Pull the battery, like he said. Even if the phone is off, they can pick it up on a radiograph," said Gibson. "Hell, they can even pull off your phone number. This is like the recon we used to do in Baghdad. They can pick up about damn near anything. That's how we picked out terror cells before we blew the shit out of them."

"You want the guy's phone?" Landers asked, gesturing toward Nick's cell.

"No," said Wolfe. "Leave that one just as it is."

Wolfe leaned toward the window and kept an eye skyward. "After the fly by, a bunch of feds are going to come with a warrant. Search the place."

"You want this stuff out of here?" asked Gibson, gathering his electronics.

"Nah, just sit still." He leaned into the window, getting a better view over the towering pines. "There she is."

Gibson and Landers rushed to the living room window.

"Sons a bitches," Landers mumbled. "They can get all that from that far up?"

"They're looking for a body count," said Wolfe. "Problem is, they aren't going to find the body that they want."

The plane silently disappeared over the house and out of view. Gibson moved back to his equipment. Wolfe extended a hand. "Sit tight. They'll be back for another peek."

Two minutes later the plane reappeared, re-tracing its path across the sky. Wolfe patiently watched until it was obscured by the trees.

He turned to face them, handing his phone and battery to Gibson. "Get all that computer shit out of here. All the weapons, ammo everything. Take it all up to the mine." Then as an afterthought, he said, "On foot. Don't take the ATV."

Gibson gave him a pouty glance.

"On foot," Wolfe said sternly. "I don't want that ATV near the mine. Drove it too damn much as it is. Landers, get that ATV off the property." Gibson grudgingly started jamming wires into his backpack. "And take the judge some food. Might be a while before we get back to him."

Landers grabbed two handguns off the mantle and shoved them into his belt. With one hand he snatched a box of shells and reached for the shotgun. Wolfe smiled. "No, leave the shotgun. Property owner in this part of the country always has a shotgun. Wouldn't appear normal otherwise. Now get moving. If you see or hear a plane, get under cover. I don't think they'll be back, but keep an eye out, just in case. I'm going to check on our boy."

Wolfe moved toward the back bedroom. Over his shoulder he shouted, "Once you're done, get back here. We have some visitors to greet."

Chapter 36

The door slowly creaked open. A muscular arm pushed forward, followed by a large man with dark hair and mustache. He was dressed in military fatigues, though his shirt hung unbuttoned over a wife beater T-shirt.

"Mr. James. How are you feeling?"

This was definitely the man Sarah had described. Nick rubbed his neck. "Fine."

The man pushed the door open and cocked his head to the left. "C'mon out. I'll make you something to eat." With that he was gone.

Nick walked out the doorway. A bathroom was on the right and another bedroom on the left. He poked his head inside the bedroom. It held two cots and no other furniture. Clothing was scattered on the floor. Cardboard fruit boxes were lined along one wall with more clothing stacked in them—a real hillbilly divan. Most notably, there was no Supreme Court justice tied up anywhere.

The hallway opened to the left where a ratty couch was parked in front of a fireplace. The couch looked like it had been re-commissioned from a roadside dump. A shotgun leaned against the brick facing of the fireplace. Nick looked to his right, and the man was bent forward pulling items from the refrigerator. Nick's thoughts of jumping for the gun evaporated as the man turned.

"Sandwich okay? I've got some lunchmeat. Should still

be okay." Catching Nick's glance at the shotgun, the man added. "No. It's not loaded. C'mon over. Sit down."

Nick slowly moved toward the kitchen, quickly noticing his wallet and cell phone on the table.

"Oh, right," the man said. "Here's your stuff," motioning to Nick's wallet with a butter knife. "Mustard or mayo?"

Nick shrugged.

"Mustard it is, then," said the man. He slapped a sandwich together and slid the plate across the table to where Nick sat.

"Am I free to go?" Nick asked.

The man considered this, spun a chair around backwards, straddled it, and placed his forearms on top of the seat back. "We're all free men, Mr. James. Free to do whatever we want."

Though he wasn't sure whether he should trust the man's hospitality, Nick was starving. He took a big bite of the baloney sandwich.

"Sorry about the misunderstanding," the man said.

Nick swallowed hard and spoke. "Misunderstanding? I was assaulted and beaten."

"Yes, yes. Sorry about that. One of my guys got a little carried away. You see, we've had some equipment stolen recently, and with you sitting on our property line doing whatever you were doing, my guys got a little antsy."

Nick stared for several seconds. "Your guys always bring chloroform to a fight? Interesting neighborhood watch tactic."

The man laughed. "Well, you can never be too prepared. Sometimes it's necessary to quickly disable your enemy. Avoids unnecessary injuries to all involved, I've found."

"Where's my bike?"

"One of my guys is getting it for you," Wolfe said,

thumbing over his shoulder. "But you don't want to leave just yet."

"Why not?"

"Just trust me on that. If you want to leave when he gets back, you certainly can, but I think you'll want to stay." The man dipped his head forward and rested his chin on his forearms.

Trust you? Nick thought. Yeah, good luck with that. Nick took a few more bites. "Who are you?"

"Me?" said the man, smiling. "I'm Ben."

"Ben what?"

"You're pretty inquisitive for a trespasser. Name's Ben Cameron."

Nick nodded and smiled. Of course, the man was lying.

"Figure I got a right to know who's holding me captive."

"You're not being held captive. Just a misunderstanding. You took a hit on the head, and we were gracious enough to provide a spot for you to rest and recuperate. Have a little lunch. We'll get your motorcycle and soon you'll be on your way to wherever you're going." Ben pointed at Nick. "Coffee?" Nick shook his head no. "By the way, what are you doing way out here? Not exactly in your back yard for a guy from DC."

"Looking for someone."

"Yeah? Who's that?"

"Sheriff Brager. You know him?"

"Heard of him; never met. Course, never will now. Why you looking for a dead guy?"

Nick paused, watching the man move toward the coffee pot. "Actually looking for the guy who killed him."

"You're in the wrong place. Guy was killed in DC. You oughta look there." He raised a coffee mug toward Nick. Shaking his head, Nick declined.

"Guy who killed him is probably around here," Nick said.

"What makes you say that?"

"I don't know," said Nick, swiveling his head. "Just figure this is a good place to hide."

"You don't know much about hiding," the man said. Nick's face squinted. "Best place to hide is never in a place like this," he said, extending his arms. "Best place to hide is in a crowd. The bigger the crowd, the better. Place like this is where a guy's liable to get caught, where he can get surrounded or cornered."

There it was again, never get cornered.

"Interesting theory," said Nick.

"Oh, it's not a theory; it's a fact. When your life is on the line, you'll realize I'm right.

"Where'd you learn your theory, as it were."

"Kabul. Been there?"

Nick shook his head.

"See, these punk coward towel heads, they like to surround themselves with women and children. Want to be called warriors, but they fight like little girls. If they were out in the open, we'd pick them off like nothing." He made a gun with his thumb and finger, firing it around the room. "Being surrounded by innocents gave them protection."

"Why do I think that didn't matter to you?" Nick asked.

This brought a hearty laugh. The man turned away and scratched the side of his temple. "Had a job to do. Part of my work ethic, you might say. When I have a job to do, it gets done. Those dirt bags were well hidden, just not safe."

Steps shuffled across the wooden porch, and the door swung open. A muscular man in jeans and a green plaid cowboy shirt burst through the door.

"Hey, Wol—" The man froze when he saw James.

Buzz haircut and muscles, just as Sarah described.

"Come in, Kevin," Ben said. "You remember Mr. James here, don't you?"

153

"Uhh. Hi."

Nick nodded.

"Kevin, I believe you owe Mr. James an apology for your unwelcome behavior." He paused. "Now would be a good time," Ben said.

"Oh, uh, sorry," he said, then motioned over his shoulder.

Nick stared daggers through Kevin.

Brushing his hands, Ben rose from the table. "There now. All better. As I said, all a misunderstanding. Now if you'll excuse me, Mr. James, it appears I have some business to attend to." He and Kevin stepped onto the porch, leaving the door ajar. Nick could hear them whisper, but couldn't make out what was said.

Ben walked back in and leaned against the door frame, crossing his arms. "You have some friends arriving."

Before Nick could respond, he heard the sirens. He stood to see two West Virginia State Patrol cars skid into the clearing in front of the shack. A sheriff's vehicle and two black sedans pulled up behind them, blocking all access to the driveway.

Chapter 37

Javier Lozano slammed on the brakes, and the sedan skidded on the gravel into alignment with the sheriff's vehicle and state patrol cars. He and Kate exited the vehicle and approached the cabin. Officers and agents took up defensive positions behind car doors and over the hoods of the vehicles, guns drawn.

Kate had secured a search warrant from the district court judge in Winchester. Federal judges in small states like West Virginia had less activity with Justice attorneys from Washington. They were less jaded, and in close cases like this, where there was more speculation than evidence, it made all the difference.

Agent Crichi from the West Virginia office had given the warrant to Kate when they met for a logistics run-down five miles from the cabin. Thermal imaging of the cabin showed the presence of four people. Visual scan revealed two out buildings and an assortment of vehicles and farm equipment. The electronic sweep had picked up Nick James' phone, but nothing else. They sure as hell better come up with something on the search or this whole thing would be a bust, Javier thought.

A large man in military fatigues stepped from the cabin onto the porch. Nick James was behind him, and a third man followed Nick.

"Ben Cameron?" Javier shouted.

The man smirked and raised his hand to half mast, stepping down to the yard.

Javier glanced at Kate. Her eyes followed Nick as the men separated, coming off the steps of the porch. Then he saw a flash in her eyes. She switched her game face on.

"Mr. Cameron," Kate said, stepping forward and holding her creds in front of her. "I'm Kathryn Buchanan with the Department of Justice. This is Javier Lozano, Special Agent, Federal Bureau of Investigation. I have a warrant to search the property. A copy has been served on Amber Milrose, who owns the property and rented it to you." She flashed the warrant and held it out for Cameron.

As Cameron casually ran his eyes over the document, Kate looked at Nick. *You okay?* she mouthed. Nick nodded.

Cameron folded the paper while staring at Kate. He handed it to the man next to him. "Hold onto that, Kevin. It'll make good kindling tonight."

A fourth man appeared around the side of the cabin. He wore oversized eyeglasses and shaggy black hair. Damn it, Javier thought, that makes four.

Cameron folded his arms and puffed his chest as he inhaled. He gave Kate a long stare up and down. "Aren't you a sassy one, Miss Federal Agent? Hope you're planning on giving me an enhanced pat down, sweetheart." His two cronies gushed with laughter. "Well, well, well," Cameron continued. "They send me a freakin' taco bender and some college chic. Don't your agencies hire *men* anymore?"

Javier lurched forward. Kate stuck out her hand to stop him. Cameron raised an eyebrow as if to say *bring it*.

"Watch your mouth," Javier said.

Cameron smiled in return and raised his hands in false surrender. "Sorry, Paco. *No habla* wetback."

"We're here to search the property," Kate said, stepping between them. "Please move aside."

"Now tell me, Missy, what gives you the right to search my property?" Cameron asked.

Javier hoped that Nick was on the right track on the Caprelli kidnapping, but they didn't have enough to legally make that the basis of the search. All they had was Nick's APB and the location by his cell phone. It wasn't much. With Nick present and accounted for, the search technically should end, but since they were here, they would see if they could dig up anything else.

The bigger problem was Javier didn't have anything as far as the investigation went. He had to just jump in somewhere and hope pieces fit together. That's why he'd made the trip. It would have been easy to stay in Washington, but this was their best lead, and he wanted to be front and center to evaluate the situation.

"Had a report that Mr. James had been abducted," Kate said. "And we already had a search out for him. His cell phone led us to your property."

"Well, Mr. James is right here," Cameron said, locking eyes with Nick. "We had a misunderstanding." He then turned to face Javier. "We've had some equipment stolen the past few weeks, and my guys saw Mr. James loitering on the edge of our property line." He leaned forward and put his hands into his front pockets. "They got a little excited. But Mr. James had a little rest. He just finished having a sandwich, and he's all ready to leave, so what's the search all about?"

"Sir, we have a warrant to search your property—" Kate said.

"No, Princess, you have a warrant to find Mr. James. You found him. You don't have the right to search anything at this point."

"We are going to search your property," Javier said firmly.

"Is that so?" Cameron said. He slowly moved his right hand behind his back. Javier quickly drew his weapon, and officers behind him rattled their firearms as they drew a bead on Cameron's chest.

Cameron smiled at the attention. He extended his other palm toward Javier and slowly moved his right hand from behind him. He was holding a can of chewing tobacco. Extending it toward Javier, he asked, "Pinch?"

Javier's heart fell from his throat. He'd nearly unloaded on the guy thinking he had a weapon behind his back.

Kate turned to the agents behind her. "Search the house."

Over the next two hours agents combed the house, finding nothing but a shotgun. No electronics, no cell phones, no weapons and, most disappointingly, no Supreme Court Justice.

Cameron and his two cronies took a perch on a dilapidated picnic table to the left of the cabin. From there they watched in apparent amusement as the search unfolded.

The agents checked for crawl spaces beneath the floorboards, false walls, and any space where a body could be hidden. The thermal imaging was right, Javier thought. Four bodies registered, four bodies accounted for. A perimeter sweep resulted in nothing. The place was almost too clean to be believable. Living out here in the sticks with no cell phone, no radio, much less a TV? Unusual, but not illegal, Javier thought.

In a brief conversation, Nick downloaded all he knew about his time on the property. It wasn't much, Javier thought. Not nearly enough. Nick had only been conscious for an hour or so before they arrived. He had one brief conversation with Cameron, but that was it. Nick wanted to launch into his Posse Comitatus theories, but Javier didn't have time for that. He needed to find something. He needed this search to get him on track.

Finally, Javier rounded up the officers and called the search off like a surgeon calling a patient's time of death. They had nothing. He'd burned the better part of the day on this, and they got nothing. Calls back to Wesley at headquarters revealed that they had nothing productive on any front.

He walked toward the picnic table. "Mr. Cameron, appreciate your cooperation."

"You boys all done?"

Javier nodded.

"Told you it was a waste of time," Cameron said. "Figure you'd have something better to do than violate our rights."

"This was a lawful warrant. What rights do you mean?"

"A man's home is sovereign," Cameron said. "The sovereign cannot be violated. A government that violates the sovereign ceases to be a government. It becomes a criminal enterprise."

"So you think I'm a criminal?" Javier asked as Nick walked up beside him.

Cameron leaned forward, gaze fixed on Javier. "I do indeed, sir. You are complicit in illegal conduct, from the President right down to the lowliest receptionist. You impose rules, regulations, taxes, fines; you name it."

"So where does this all go? You guys going to overthrow the government?" Javier said with a grim smile.

"The government overthrows itself."

"How does that work?"

"Mr. Lozano—"

"Special Agent Lozano, to you." *At least he's dispensed with the ethnic slurs.*

Cameron paused, smiled, and cleared his throat. "Mr. Lozano, those who cease to recognize the sovereign shall cease to exist. We shall all stand before the congregation for judgment." He stepped down from the picnic table onto the ground. "Your government works to crush the sovereign, but you can't. You know why?"

"Oh please, please tell me."

"Because the sovereign is in here," Cameron said, tapping his chest. "It's in here. In each of us. The government is an imaginary power. It only has authority because people have chosen to give it authority. It's all imaginary. You, Mr. Lozano, are just a man. Your title with the government doesn't make you more of a man. You're just a man. But when you make the government your proxy, you try to become what you are not. And you are living a lie."

"Nice speech. Doesn't change anything."

"Those who use their power as proxy for the government will meet in the center of the star." A smile crossed Cameron's face. "The center of the star changes everything."

"The center of the star?" Javier asked. "What's that?"

"Be patient, Pablo. I have a feeling you're going to find out."

Chapter 38

They wound through the mountainous backroads toward Interstate 66. Although it was April, much of the trees were still sticks, and in the gathering darkness they cast an ominous pall over their drive back.

Kate was driving, Javier was in shotgun, and Nick was alone in back. Occasionally Nick would catch Kate's eye in the rear view mirror. Her tone had softened, in part because the warrant had been served, the moment was over. In part it may have to do with the workday nearing an end. Nick hoped that the look in her eyes had something to do with him. Game face was off.

Was there emotion in the look? Nick wondered. Or pity? He trusted that she still had feelings for him, but her job would come first. It would always come first. Maybe that was the problem. On some scale he was a fugitive, but his current captor understood him. Could she love him? he wondered.

"It was a bad search," Kate said.

"No shit," Javier mumbled.

"No, it was a bad search," she said. "Cameron was right."

"So what?" Javier said. "We were there, we searched."

"The warrant was for Nick. We found him. Everything beyond that was a bad search. If we had found something," she continued, "it would have been excluded at trial. Fruit of the poisonous tree."

"Big deal. Somebody's kidnapped a Supreme Court Justice. I'm not going to get caught up in your legal niceties. I have a job to do."

"They aren't legal niceties. It's the law. I should have stopped the search."

"Breaking a case of this magnitude requires bending some rules," Javier said. "Always does."

"It's wrong," she said. "You're no better than them when you think like that."

The phone in Javier's hand rang, and he slapped it to his head.

Javier had fired several calls into headquarters. His reaction explained where they were—nowhere. Earlier with his elbow on the door and his hand cupped around his forehead, he pondered. Nick knew what he was thinking. It was a number; forty-eight.

In any kidnapping situation, unless the person was found or contact made for ransom within forty-eight hours, the chance of recovering the person alive dropped precipitously. They were rapidly approaching that critical moment.

Javier shouted over the phone at someone named Wesley. They got nothing in the search. Leads were dying as the news cycle pounded away at the bureau. "Get the photos to analysis. I want everything on this Cameron guy. I want to know where he went to school, where he's worked. I want to know where he gets his freakin' hair cut." He switched ears with the phone. "Yeah, he's with us. We'll see." A long pause ensued. "We'll talk about it later. Get me everything on Cameron. Pronto." Javier punched a thumb into his phone, ending the call.

"How can there be no background on the guy?" Javier mumbled. "I know some states don't have sophisticated records or databases that mesh with ours, but how can there be nothing on this guy Cameron?"

"'Cause his name's not Cameron," Nick said. "But even if you had his real name, you likely won't find him in any database."

"So what's his real name?"

"I don't know, but Cameron is an alias."

Javier turned to face Nick, placing an elbow on the seat back. "How do you know?"

"Bill Gale was one of the leaders of the Posse Comitatus revival." Nick paused. "Did you get that Blue Book I left for you?"

"Yeah," said Javier. "From the trash can? I looked at it. Just a bunch of mumbo jumbo as far as I'm concerned. What do they think, they're some vigilante force? That pamphlet has this badge on the cover, like a bunch of self-deputized Wyatt Earps cleaning up the communities. Figured you could save me from actually reading the damn thing."

"Gale wrote it. Guy named Beach later published it. Anyway, Gale gave speeches and met with church groups, lots of angry people who were looking for someone to blame. One of his first attempts at broader communication was a newsletter. He had a pen name he used for the newsletter. The pen name was Colonel Ben Cameron."

Kate glanced over briefly. "We have his photo. We can use facial recognition. We have access to the 3-D bioinformatics software and match it with anyone in the State Department, Justice, Intel, or major crime databases. We'll find out who he is. If he's got a driver's license, been in the military; heck, if he was in his high school yearbook, we'll narrow it down."

"It's possible," said Nick. "But there's a chance you won't find him."

"Really?" Kate said incredulously. "You're going to tell me this guy's never had a driver's license?"

"Might match his picture, but won't be to his real name. These guys are definitely Posse Comitatus. If there's a connection with what we consider mainstream, they've cut it and there's a good chance, depending upon where these guys come from that they won't appear in any database we've got. They're totally off the grid."

"That's not possible," Kate said. "We'll get a hit on the facial recognition program."

"The lab's got the photos," Javier said. "We uploaded them shortly after we served the warrant. So we should hear something soon. Nick, what's this sovereign bullshit Camer, the guy keeps talking about?"

"That's the core of the Posse Comitatus belief. Think of it as two identities, a state identity and a sovereign identity."

"So it's a split personality?" Javier asked.

"No, it's a choice," Nick said, leaning forward. "We're born with a sovereign identity. That's the identity God gives us. The other identity is created by the state, which they see as unlawful. The sovereign identity is forfeited when the state identity is adopted."

"What do you mean, forfeited?" Kate asked.

"They believe that the state is unlawful. All power resides in the local community. The Posse Comitatus, the community, is the source of all rights, laws, interactions. When you obtain a driver's license, heck, a fishing license, or any permission from the state or federal government, you accept and adopt the state identity."

"That's such a load of crap," Javier said.

"You don't have to agree with it," said Nick, "but to deal with them, you have to understand how their minds work." He hunched forward in his seat. "Guys like Cameron, or whatever his name is, these guys may have never obtained a state identity—or a lawful one anyway. So, no social security number, no driver's license, no tax returns, nothing."

"Wasn't objection to taxation one of their big things?" Kate asked.

"Well, that and avoidance of foreclosure. If you obtained a state identity, you submitted to the state. You allowed yourself to become controlled by the state; you're no longer sovereign. If you are sovereign, then state and local taxes don't apply to you. In their mind, anyway. It's as if they were a foreign citizen. They didn't affirmatively agree to be a subject of the state." He paused for emphasis. "And unless they do, they're not citizens."

"Crazy," said Kate, shaking her head. "So how did they hope to avoid debts? If they give up their sovereignty, aren't they just screwed? Even under their logic?"

"It's the same dual identity issue," Nick said. "I admit it sounds crazy, and it is, but Gale and guys like him were able to rally a bunch of scared and desperate people. You have to understand, when you're at your wit's end and someone comes along with a solution to set it all right, you want to believe it. Kind of like a miracle drug for terminal cancer or a reprieve on death row. Anyway, if the state identity takes a loan and can't pay it back, the person can reject their state identity and recapture their sovereign."

"Recapture their sovereign?" Javier said sarcastically.

"I know, but here's the theory. If you signed under the state identity, it wasn't your sovereign that signed the loan documents. Now, mixed in with all this is a conspiracy theory among New York bankers, Jews, and communists."

"Quite a hit parade," said Kate.

"You'll see many similar kinds of arguments among those who favor a gold standard and only value commodities as assets to be owned." Nick said, catching Kate's eye in the rearview mirror again. "Anyway, this cabal of bad guys said even if you signed several pieces of paper, it didn't matter because none of it was backed by real money. It's just numbers and words on a page. The sovereign can reject what's been done under the state identity. Further, as a sovereign, the person can create his own paper currency and documents. In a nutshell, they don't want to be subjects of the state, they want to be seen as peers of the nation. Their own nation. Their own sovereignty."

"Jesus, what a bunch of freakin' loons," said Javier.

"So that redemption receipt I sent you, that's a form of currency. They're also called fractional reserve notes, comptroller warrants, anything to sound official. These guys who were in foreclosure in the eighties created their own documents to pay off or cancel the debts they had to banks. Well, that was the idea anyway."

"But none of it worked," Kate said. "It was all a delay tactic. They all got foreclosed."

"Agreed. But in the mind of the Posse, it was all wrong; a continuing violation of their collective and independent sovereign. I've been following these guys for three years. The farm crisis of the eighties gave them a desperate audience, people who needed the solution they offered. Look at what's happening today."

"So they're coming back?" asked Kate.

"They never went away. By some estimates there are as many as three hundred thousand members of militia groups like the Posse Comitatus in the country today. I was tracking them. That was my job. Well, when I had one anyway."

"What's their plan?" Kate asked.

"I don't know. There are hundreds of branches of local militia groups. If I were to guess, this is an attempt to solidify them behind one organization, one leader. Use something big, something brazen to draw them together, not unlike the growth of the Tea Party groups."

"Tea Party?" Javier scoffed.

"This has nothing to do with the Tea Party," Nick said. "Just an example of how groups can rally around ideas, things that hit the national media. Supporters rush to join in."

"All this for some damn membership drive?" Javier asked.

"If they can pull off whatever they're planning, the emotion goes viral. Angry people have a cause to join. With economic crisis and people out of work, in debt, losing homes, this is the perfect Petri dish for their theories to take root. The government becomes an easy target of the anger."

"Oh, come on," said Javier. "You mean to tell me all these people have no social security records, no military records. Hell, what about a driver's license? You gonna tell me these guys don't have a driver's license?"

"That's exactly what I mean, for many of the hard cores."

"These guys may be whack jobs, but they drive cars, they have jobs. They can't be totally off the grid. No driver's license," he said sarcastically, turning back to face the windshield.

"They believe the constitution gives them the right to travel; they don't need authority from the state. So, right, no driver's license, no fishing license, hunting license. Not real ones at least. Nothing that gives the state power over them."

"Power?" Kate asked. "Isn't it just about being a citizen?"

"Let me tell you about a guy," Nick said. "Gets arrested in northern Michigan. He refuses to face the front of the court because he won't recognize the judge's authority. He refuses to sign anything because the state is stealing his sovereign. He revokes his fishing license in open court. The only document he possessed."

"Sounds like a typical goof ball," Javier said. "Did he have aluminum foil over his ears to prevent the government from brainwashing him?"

"Laugh if you want," Nick said. "But three years later this guy and his pal Tim McVeigh blew up the Murrah Federal Building in Oklahoma City."

"Jesus," Kate whispered.

Chapter 39

Okay, try it again.
You can do it.
This time go slowly.
And concentrate.

I am Silvio Konstantin Caprelli. My wife's name is Stella Dorning Caprelli. I was born June tenth, nineteen forty seven. I was born in Brooklyn...I was born at Victory Memorial Hospital in Brooklyn, NY.

My father's name was Bruno Giancarlo Caprelli. My mother's name was Margaret...Caprelli. My mother's name was Margaret... middle name was...Caprelli. My mother's name was Margaret...

My brother's name is Francesco. My sister's name is Antonia. My mother's name was Margaret...what?

We lived on Marine Avenue. Ninety-six-forty-two Marine Avenue. I graduated from Xaverian High School.

My mother's name was Margaret...

He squinted hard in the darkness, straining.

My mother's name was...

My mother...

He put his hands over his face and began to cry.

Chapter 40

"So you think Cameron and these guys are Posse Comitatus?" Kate asked, locking eyes with Nick through the rear view mirror.

"I'd bet everything I have on it," Nick said. "They have all the tell-tale signs. It's a combination of distortions of religion, world history, and the Constitution. Overlay that with individual liberty on steroids and you've got the recipe for indignant mayhem. The receipt left in the bar. The waitress gave me a description that nails this guy to a tee, even the vehicle they were driving. These receipts come with different names, certified fractional checks, redemption receipts, the wrapping changes, but the intended prize remains the same; a made-up piece of paper to pay off debts that they view as pieces of paper made-up by someone else. Before the Oklahoma City bombing, Terry Nichols tried to pay off a loan to Chase Bank with a 17,000 dollar so-called fractional reserve check. I'll bet we find nothing on these guys. They leave no trail."

They drove in silence, the headlights piercing the night. Despite the late hour, heavy traffic poured away from DC. Their lanes into the city moved freely.

"Let's assume you're right," said Javier. "Where do they get the money to pull off something like this? Rent a place, plan a kidnapping of a federal judge? That takes money, and they can't be using those bogus receipts everywhere they go."

"No, the receipt was definitely on purpose," Nick said. "They wanted us to find that. They're taunting us with it."

"Well, they can't have jobs, income, anything like that," said Kate. "These guys have to be totally on the lam. Where's the money coming from?"

"I don't know. These guys have been known to engage in petty crime, but nothing on the scale of what they need here."

Kate snapped her fingers and faced Javier. "So if he left the receipt in the bar, let's pick him up," Kate said. "Theft of services. Bingo. Bring him in. See what we can get out of him."

"I don't think so," Nick said. "We know who to follow now. We need to watch these guys. Post surveillance on them twenty-four seven. If we bring him in, we don't get anything. Misdemeanor for running out on a beer tab?"

"We damn well better have something more than that," Javier said.

"Other thing is," Nick said. "We got a young gal as our only witness. If we're right and these guys whacked two federal officers and a sheriff, that girl is good as dead if we bring him in. We'd be asking the girl a lot to stand in the fire for something that happened at her minimum wage job. Hell of a lot easier for her just to forget what the guy looked like."

They rode without speaking. The car hummed and the headlights ate up Interstate 66. Nick checked his blackberry and pondered. He knew he was right, but should he say anything. After all, it was just a theory.

"Whatever they're up to," Nick said. "It's going down on Friday."

"Friday?" Kate shouted. "How do you know that?"

"Friday is April 19. In sovereign circles and the Posse, it's like some kind of national holiday."

"What's so special about it?" Javier asked.

Nick leaned forward, elbows on the headrests. "Guy named Jim Ellison was a leader of a posse group. On April 19th, 300 federal agents stormed his compound and arrested him. Feds couldn't get a conviction, but one of his men, Richard Wayne Snell, was charged with murder."

"Yeah, so what?"

"He was executed on April 19," Nick said. "The shooting at Foster's Glen was six years ago, on April 19. It's going down on Friday, whatever it is. April 19, 1993, the FBI stormed the Branch Davidian complex. Seventy-six people were killed. The next year, April 19, the Thompson Ultimatum was issued charging Congress with treason and calling on militia units to take up arms against the government."

"What's the Thompson—"

"April 19, the next year," Nick said. "McVeigh and Nichols blew up the Murrah Federal Building in Oklahoma City."

Javier speed dialed his phone. "Scottie, I need everything on the Posse Comitatus, sovereign groups, everything. Get a bunch of agents on it. I want to know everything there is to know about them. History, names, groups, convictions. Everything." He paused. "Yeah? Okay. Yeah. Put him on." Javier leaned back, staring at the ceiling. "What's up?" He turned and whispered "Wesley" to Kate. "Yeah. Yeah. What?" he screamed. "Are you freakin' kidding me? When? God." He rubbed his face pulling back on his hairline like he was trying to peel his skin off. "Who's on it? Get someone good. Get them over there right now. God damn it." He slammed the phone against the dashboard.

Kate stole her eyes from the road and locked onto Javier.

"Judge Browning over in Winchester."

"Right," Kate said. "Judge who issued the search warrant."

"Gunned down in his driveway twenty minutes ago."

Chapter 41

Nick didn't tell them about his personal experience with the Posse Comitatus.

His father worked their farm outside Minden, NE as his father had before him. Land prices and corn prices rose. It was a bubble, but like all bubbles, one folks thought they deserved. At long last, agriculture was getting the benefits bestowed on other industries. Who were they to question it?

The McNally farm came up for sale, and Dick Wilcox at the bank said he'd finance it. The price was high, but prices were all going up, so it would all work out. The spreadsheets said so.

For the first time they had a new car, a Cadillac. They bought new equipment. Commodity prices went up, and their corn held in the elevator rocketed in value. Loans were made, payments were easy. New clothes and well earned vacations for the parents; it was all secured by escalating land values.

Then the crash came.

It wasn't so much a crash as a crack, a crumble, then a land slide. Property values fell. Bankers got scared. Commodity prices tanked. Words like *equity* and *securitization* were quickly changed to "work out" and "foreclosure." Suddenly, the farm was upside-down in debt, like many neighbors. Loans were called. His dad said it was temporary. The prices will go back up. Heck, he laughed, it was the only direction they could go. The laugh quickly turned to desperation. The bank called. They couldn't be serious. Dad said we just needed time.

In the winter of 1984, Nick was six. The plentiful Christmases of his past were replaced with solemn gatherings and church dinners. It was community, not charity, dad said. They'd given money to the church for years. This time they needed help. It was a withdrawal, not a hand-out.

His parents argued at night. In the morning, dad's eyes were red with pink rings. Just didn't feel good. One night it sounded like dad was crying, but it couldn't be true. Dad never cried. It was just Nick's ears playing tricks on him.

The Cadillac was taken one morning, soon followed by much of the farm equipment. Wilcox, the banker, wouldn't take his dad's calls anymore. When they ran into him in town, he bowed to Nick's mom, looked nervous, and said he had to go. Dad grabbed his arm as he turned to go. Wilcox said, "I'm sorry, it's just my job."

Dad got angry and left for a few days. Turns out he went to Topeka to meet with a group of men who had a solution. Bill Gale was the leader. They were getting screwed, and it didn't have to happen. Gale was a minister and lawyer who had once run for governor of California. He knew secrets that the banks and local officials wouldn't share. Turns out he was neither a minister nor a lawyer, but he did somehow garner 3000 votes when he ran for governor.

His dad came back full of vigor. He was pitched for a fight this time. He met with neighbors frequently. The farmers in the deepest trouble listened in earnest, and quickly joined the battle.

The banks had it all wrong. They were the ones violating the law. They were the ones who should be losing their assets. They were the ones who should be in jail. The rants became more frequent. Hunting guns were pulled from closets and toted in public.

His father and a dozen men marched up the street to the bank. Wilcox heard the uproar and locked the doors. Men were shouting and pounding on the bank doors.

The sheriff arrived and tried to calm the crowd. He tried to befriend them, told them nothing good can come of this, we've been friends for years. We went to school together, he said. The kids go to school together. We go to church together. We need to just take it easy and talk it out.

No one knew who fired the shot and, if they did, they didn't say. Sheriff Perkins was taken to the local hospital, but he was dead before they picked him up off the street. The crowd dispersed. Nick's dad came home, but he was still angry. Gale was right. They could take back their property from the bankers. It had been taken unlawfully.

A state patrolman came to discuss the matter of the sheriff's shooting. Nick's dad wouldn't let him in the house. He claimed that the state patrolman was acting illegally, that he was a pawn for the state. The state didn't have the right. The constitution was on the James's side. It was the first time Nick had heard the word.

Two weeks later they had to leave. His mom had to convince his dad to put down his gun. It was over. They would move to Grand Island and live with mom's sister and husband until they could get jobs. They would get through this. The Lord would provide.

The banker's men carried out all the furniture, kitchen appliances and guns. They were sold to folks in the front yard.

When it was over, the family had three suitcases, some photographs, and a bible. His mom never raised her voice until the man in charge wanted to see what she put in the suitcases. Then she really let him have it. He must have figured it wasn't worth the trouble.

Nick's dad never moved to Grand Island. He never left the property. The banker's men had sold all of the guns, except one; the one in the barn where they used to park the Cadillac.

Chapter 42

April 18

It was hard being a fugitive in the digital age. Data never went away, computer databases never forgot. They were logical and emotionless, but their output, in the right setting, could change the emotion of the user. Scottie found him. Now they had a name. David Allen Wolfe, wanted for war crimes in Afghanistan. The rest was spotty with big gaps in time, but this was their man.

Scottie had also run a spider program on the web traffic coming off the justice video. It wouldn't be perfect because Kate had had some success in getting the video taken down. National security and threat of prosecution was still a trump card that worked, especially among businesses that cared about their reputations. Despite these efforts the video was still on international sites and an abundance of blog sites.

Somebody had sent the video code out to the masses. Links to the existing sites that still carried the video flew through the bits and bytes of the Internet. Kate couldn't shut them all down, but she'd gotten the big boys. The State Department had to help with the international sites, but time for diplomacy meant nothing would happen fast.

Javier and Wesley had a heated argument about Nick, Wesley wanting him arrested, Javier wanting to wait. If Nick was right about the Posse Comitatus, Javier needed him. He knew more about the group than anyone in the government, probably more than anyone who wasn't a member.

"We don't know that he's not a member," Wesley reminded him. To his credit, Wesley's paranoia was an asset in difficult investigations. Javier valued that, but right now he needed all the help he could get.

It was purely Javier's call, but the compromise was a tracking bracelet on his ankle and an officer assigned to him anytime Nick was away from the team. He was officially in custody. It didn't satisfy Wesley, but the compromise worked for Javier and that's all that mattered.

~

The officer assigned to Nick had light duty. Nick hadn't left the FBI building since their return from West Virginia. He pored through the reports and combed through data. He was quick to dismiss all the chaff. He acted with the certainty of a four star general. Mostly he spent time watching the video. He'd pause, rewind, and play it again over and over. With his elbows on the table and his chin resting on his fists, Nick watched the video again.

It opened with Caprelli on the bench, reading from two sheets of paper in his hands.

> *Hear ye, hear ye, hear ye. The Supreme Court of Common Law is now in session. Justice Silvio Caprelli, Chief Justice, serving at the pleasure of the people.*
>
> *Whereas, the Articles of Confederation having been adopted on November 15, 1777 and duly ratified on March 1, 1781, and*
>
> *Whereas, the Articles of Confederation created the United States of America, and*

Redemption Day

Whereas, Article Thirteen of said Articles of Confederation provides that the Articles are perpetual and inviolable, and

Whereas, The Constitution of the United States has not and cannot suspend, repeal, nor amend the Articles of Confederation, and

Whereas, the United States Supreme Court affirmed the perpetual and inviolable condition of the Articles of Confederation in Texas versus White in 1869, seventy-nine years after ratification of the US Constitution, and

Whereas, Article Ten of said Articles of Confederation establishes the Committee of States and provides said Committee of States with the authority to exercise all powers of Congress when said Congress is in recess, and

Whereas, the Congress of the United States officially stands in Easter recess on today's date.

Now, therefore, the Committee of States acting through duly appointed sovereigns from a majority of said States has convened.

The Committee of States has lawfully ordered as follows:

The Congress of the United States is hereby abolished.

The Executive Branch of the United States does not exist under the Articles of Confederation. Said positions are therefore void and without authority.

A Citizen's Grand Jury has been duly empanelled in accordance with the Common Law to try those who usurped the authority from the People. The Citizen's Grand Jury is the keeper of the law of the land, the only authorized judicial body.

The sovereigns shall be released from refuge and avengers of blood shall be denied their justice.

The sovereign is supreme.

The people will control their destiny and their country.

So sayeth this honorable court, the Supreme Court of Common Law.

Govern yourselves accordingly, Redemption Day approaches.

The screen faded to black. Nick replayed it.

No question, this was the work of the Posse Comitatus. Of that, he was certain. All the fingerprints of the Posse Comitatus were present. It was all familiar to him except for Caprelli's phrase "avengers of blood." That was a new one. What the heck were avengers of blood and how did that tie in?

Before digging in, though, Nick had pulled Winters aside in the hallway.

"Why didn't you tell me you were on the Task Force?"

"Nick, I couldn't."

"Why would you lie to me?"

"I didn't lie. I just didn't tell you."

"Kate told me," Nick said.

"She's a rock star in her job. I'm just a schlub trying to keep my pension. I'm sorry, Nick, but you didn't have a need to know and, at this point, I'm not doing anything to risk my career. I've got too much at stake, and they'd love to take me out for some bullshit reason. Deny me my benefits. That's what they do. Ya know. Bunch of heartless pricks." He leaned in and whispered, "I love you like a son. I'd do anything for you, but I'm not taking any chances with these bastards. I vouched for you with Lozano. Told him you know more about these guys than anyone. That jerk

Wesley was trying to put you in jail. I convinced Lozano to put you on the team."

~

Within thirty minutes of the hit on Wolfe, a team of FBI agents and West Virginia State Patrol circled the cabin. They didn't have enough to take in someone who ran out on a bar tab, but they did have enough to detain him for his actions in Afghanistan. It might not be enough to stop whatever was planned, but they needed to take a chess piece off the board.

The call came back too quickly.

"Got 'em?" Javier asked.

"Place is empty. They're gone."

"*What?*" Javier screamed. "We had them under surveillance. What do you mean, they're gone? Where could they go?"

"I'm sorry, sir. We had two officers at the edge of the highway. Didn't want them to know we were watching. No one came in, no one came out. They had to have gone on foot, back into the hills."

"For Christ's sake." Javier rubbed his forehead like he was trying to erase it. "Get a team together. I want a grid search of the property. Call me when you've got them." He slammed the phone. Turning to Wesley, he said, "Get the plane back up again. I want to thermo the area. They're out there somewhere."

"Those guys are survivalists," Nick said. "They can hide for weeks, hell longer, assuming they haven't just slipped away."

Wesley shot an evil stare at Nick. "Thermo will find them," he said definitively.

"Maybe," Nick said, returning the stare. "Maybe not."

"Well, at this point we don't even know if these are the right guys," Wesley said. "All we got is this guy's theory." He made air quotation marks for the word "theory."

Nick turned back to the video screen of the justice.

"It's not a theory," Winters piped up. "Nick's been studying this group for three years. If he says that's who it is, then that's who it is." Winters gestured toward Wesley. "What the heck, it's not like you've come up with anything." Nick's eyes locked with Winters along with a nod that said *thanks for the backup.*

~

Across the room Javier waved his hands. "Get that bird up there and let's get some agents on the ground." He knew Wesley was right. They didn't have much. But without Nick, they didn't have a damn thing. He'd learned that, to be successful in this job, he had to trust. Right now he had to trust Nick. He needed a break in the case—a big break.

"Scottie, who you got on your spider?" Javier asked. The spider program ran an algorithm that tracked Internet traffic from one site to another. The graphic on the screen showed several circles connected by lines. It represented traffic on the video—the more traffic, the larger the circle. The colors of the circles represented the intensity of the connection between two sites. The technology was brilliant; the law enforcement theory they were chasing was not.

Scottie and a team of twenty tech guys had been tracking the largest circles and ones with the greatest intensity of color. From that they took the domain name, tracked it back to the owner, got a file on the owner, tracked all websites of the owner, then ran a content analysis crawler on the sites in question.

They were trying to find the source; where did the video originate on the web? The traffic on the web for the video exploded so quickly and in so many locations, they couldn't find a single point.

"It was a distributed release," Scottie said as if to himself.

"What do you mean?"

"There isn't a single point. This wasn't sequential. Not a chance. This thing was uploaded at multiple sites at the same time."

"Can you get to the sites?" Nick asked.

"Many are bogus, orphan sites."

"What do you mean, orphan sites?" Javier asked.

"They're like fake ID's of the Internet. Guy can buy a website with a phony credit card. Hell, can even buy them with cash in some places. If the person registered as the owner is even the current owner. They're used to circulate and distribute information on the web. Even if you track them down, it doesn't tie to a real person or entity. They're just tools."

"Can't you track them to a server?"

"You're imagining that these are real websites. These are all shared server systems. They're orphans."

"Scottie, you got a site called Sovereign Free Press dot com or dot something?" Nick asked.

Scottie tapped the keyboard furiously and slapped enter three times.

"Yeah, they're getting traffic. Not one of the original sites; can't prove they pushed video code out of that site, but yeah, they're pumping traffic on the judge's video."

"Who are they?" Javier asked.

"It's a website that's sympathetic to the posse," Nick said. "Rants on anti-Americanism, anger, overthrow of the government."

"What? A throw-the-bums-out site?"

"No, more like, kill the bums and burn the buildings."

Turning to Scottie, Nick asked, "You got an address?" Scottie's fingers flew over the keys.

"Yep, shit, it's right here."

"What do you mean, right here?" Javier asked.

"Well, not here, but in Leesburg."

"Nick, let's go," Javier said.

"You want *him* to go along?" Wesley asked.

"Yeah, Nick speaks the language."

"I'll go with you," Wesley said.

"No, I don't want to appear with too much force. Two is plenty. It's not like we have people to spare," Javier said motioning around the room filled with computer keys clicking, analysts scouring reports, phones tracking down leads. The room hummed with frantic energy.

Wesley grabbed Javier's arm and leaned into his ear. "You don't know this guy," nodding in Nick's direction. "If he's part of them, you could be walking into a trap. We've already lost a state sheriff, a federal judge, and two federal officers. You don't know him."

Javier's face revealed that the argument wasn't working. Wesley dug in again, whispering. "He comes up with Sovereign Free Press? What's that? Just out of the fucking blue and you're going off with him alone to maybe meet up with more of these guys. I don't know, Javier. I think his theory is garbage, but let's assume it's true." He tugged on Javier's arm for effect. "If he's right, these whackos kill anyone who gets in their way. Yet this guy waltzes into their cabin and waltzes out untouched. Think, man."

"Not exactly untouched," Javier whispered.

"He's still fucking breathing," Wesley said with a hiss. "He could be one of them. You gotta admit, it makes sense. He could be one of them. Take some back up."

Javier pulled away. "Nick, let's go. Kate, get a warrant. I want to nab their computers."

"A warrant?" she asked. "For what? I've got to have a theory, a reason. Judges can be kind of funny that way."

"You're a lawyer, think of something," Javier said. "Call me."

"I'll see what I can do, but—"

Wesley smirked. "Why don't you just flash some leg? The judge will give you anything you want."

"Fuck off, Wesley," she shot back.

"Okay, okay," Javier said. "See what you can do, Kate. And for crying out loud, see if we can keep from killing each other. We're on the same team. Remember?"

"Some of us are," Wesley grumbled under his breath.

"Son of a bitch," Scotty screamed. "Son of a bitch."

"What?" The room shouted in unison. All attention was on the tech.

"Got a new video."

Chapter 43

Scottie projected the image onto the wall. Slack jawed, the group stood and watched. It was the same shot of Caprelli, robed and seated at a high court bench. Behind him a circular sign read "Supreme Court of Common Laws."

His eyes were ringed and dark. Someone had applied make up, but it couldn't hide the bags under his eyes nor could it provide emotion, of which there was none. He read from a sheet of paper in a steely and flat monotone. His eyes met the camera sheepishly at the beginning, then dropped to the page.

"Hear ye, hear ye, hear ye. The Supreme Court of Common Law is now in session. Justice Silvio Caprelli, Chief Justice, serving at the pleasure of the people."

"He looks like hell," Winters said.

"Sshhh," several shot back.

"It having come before this court and as a remedial measure to correct the historical record. Men of corruption in a criminal conspiracy at the highest branches of the so-called Government of the United States have infringed the rights of sovereign citizens, and this Court shall correct that illegal and illicit misappropriation." He shifted in his seat, but kept reading. "The Thirteen Amendment to the United States Constitution shall be returned to the people, including Section Three regarding titles of nobility. Said language was passed by The Congress and ratified by the member states.

Section 3 shall have the full effect of law as said amendment was passed and ratified."

"What the hell is he talking about?" Wesley whispered.

"Furthermore, the Fourteen Amendment, as passed, does not affect sovereign citizens unless they accept and duly adopt said citizenship. Any other interpretation is contrary to law and hereby void. Sovereign citizens who have been misled and coerced into giving up their sovereignty shall forthwith have it returned to them, provided they do not subsequently elect, in an affirmative manner, to give up said sovereignty. Honest and law abiding men are freed from their obligations under the pernicious Fourteenth Amendment. The Sixteenth Amendment, not having been ratified by the several states, is hereby abandoned and declared void. Taxation by the Federal Government is illegal and unauthorized. Past, current, and future debts owed under this Amendment are hereby forgiven and deemed resolved. Pursuit of collection shall be punishable as theft under Common Law. Concerted action for collection shall be punishable as conspiracy pursuant to the Common Law. So sayeth this honorable Court, the Supreme Court of Common Law. Govern yourself accordingly."

Caprelli's eyes sheepishly sought the camera after he finished reading. His gaze was apologetic, as though defeated and resigned. An unseen gavel rapped three times and the video faded to black.

Kate stammered "What in the—?"

"I want a work up of that video," Javier shouted. "Same as last time, only faster. Noise, lighting, content analysis, everything deconstructed. Get it now. Kate, keep that off the Internet."

"I'm picking it up on international sites and local blog sites," Scottie interjected. "The guys we shut down last time are playing nice right now."

Kate nodded and punched her cell phone.

"The Thirteenth Amendment? What the heck is that?" Wesley said.

Kate covered the mouthpiece on her cell with the other hand. "Freed the slaves. Outlawed slavery."

"What?" Wesley asked. "They're saying slavery is back?"

"No," said Nick. "It's one of the classic posse claims. They believe that the Thirteenth Amendment was passed and ratified, then changed by corrupt officials."

"Right," said Wesley, rolling his eyes. "Happens all the time."

"They believed that the third section of the Amendment was eliminated dealing with titles of nobility."

"You mean like Archdukes, Barons, and Knights?" Winters asked. "Last time I checked we don't have any of those in this country. What are they talking about?"

Nick nodded toward Kate. "They're talking about her."

"Huh?" came back in unison.

"You mean Princess?" Wesley said sarcastically. Javier shot him a look of disgust.

"No," said Nick. "Esquire. Juris Doctor. Her law degree. The Posse believed that the states abolished titles of nobility along with slavery. Since lawyers carry a title of nobility, all lawyers were eliminated."

"First let's kill all the lawyers," Winters said in a mocking voice.

"Right, Mr. Shakespeare," Nick said. "If lawyers were abolished, then the court of common law was all that remained. There was no need for lawyers or appointed judges because all disputes were to be handled by a court of common law, where any sovereign could appear and present his case. There was no need for our judicial system, no need for an intricate court system and certainly no need for specialists in the law. They think that section was stolen from the Thirteenth Amendment."

"Okay," Javier said, motioning to speed up. "What's the deal with the Fourteenth Amendment? That gone, too?"

"Their argument regarding the Fourteenth Amendment is more subtle."

"By subtle, you mean insane," Wesley said.

"Remember, the Fourteenth Amendment was passed in the wake of the end of the Civil War," said Nick.

"Created rights for all people, to include former slaves," Javier added.

"Well, partly right. It created rights for some people. Under their reasoning, only residents of the District of Columbia and certain federal lands were citizens of the United States prior to adoption. Before that, everyone else was a citizen of their state or, more appropriately, their local community. The Fourteenth Amendment, in addition to creating citizenship for former slaves, also created a dichotomy of options for all residents. That is, they could keep their sovereign citizenship or accept citizenship of the US. Only the government didn't tell people that and tricked them into becoming citizens of the United States."

"That's crazy," said Winters.

"I know, but you have to understand where they're coming from. The Fourteenth Amendment was open enrollment into the federal system. Not just for former slaves, but for everyone. If you accepted, then you lost your sovereign citizenship and became subject to the laws, procedures, and restrictions of the United States. Again, people were tricked into accepting through taxes, licenses, social security, whatever. If you signed up, you became a US citizen; if you didn't, you remained a sovereign."

The group looked at Nick for several seconds in

stunned silence. Eventually they shook their heads and went back to work.

"Scottie, track that video and update me," Javier said.

"Damn, and I just paid my taxes last week," mumbled Winters.

"Kate," Javier shouted. "Warrant? Wesley, prepare a statement and get time to patch me into Jannsen while we're driving. Nick, let's visit that guy at the Sovereign Free Press. Good lord, this is getting more bizarre by the minute."

Chapter 44

Merton Jenkins didn't appear concerned nor surprised by their arrival. His mousy brown hair was disheveled and stuck to his head like day-old spaghetti. Horn rimmed glasses that might have been fashionable in the fifties made his eyes appear larger than actual size.

Jenkins was the master of his universe, and it operated in the basement of a townhouse off Thundering Pines Lane in Leesburg, VA. This was world headquarters for Sovereign Free Press, the Sentinel of Free Men as it was branded online.

Javier flashed his creds and handed Jenkins a business card. He introduced Nick as a subject matter expert consulting with the FBI. This raised an eyebrow from Jenkins.

Nick had wondered just how his involvement was to be described; an SME. In the government world the tag SME normally meant that he was off the normal pay grid, that because of learning and expertise, the government was willing to pay near market rates for that intelligence. Nick, of course, wasn't being paid at all.

Jenkins ushered them past a stack of unwashed dishes and a side table littered with the morning *Washington Times*. An elderly woman in an off-white night gown puffed on a cigarette watching a game show on the television. She was oblivious to the newly arrived guests.

"Sorry for the mess," Jenkins said. "If I'd a known you boys were coming, woulda cleaned up a little." They went down a no-frill, framed-out staircase to the command center of Jenkins' media empire.

He plopped into an overstuffed leather chair and motioned to a ratty couch against the far wall.

"So you mentioned the Caprelli kidnapping. I been reporting on that. Hell of a deal. How can I help you boys?"

Javier leaned forward, elbows on his knees. "We've been monitoring Internet traffic, particularly the Caprelli video."

"Which one?"

"Both, actually.

"Hell of a deal, ain't it?"

"Anyway, we're finding that your site, Sovereign Free Press, is responsible for a majority of traffic related to the video," Javier said.

"I have a deep and loyal audience. You're making it sound like I've done something wrong," Jenkins said, shifting uncomfortably in his seat.

"Not only is the traffic heavy, there's evidence that the video is being distributed from your site," Javier said.

"Look, boys, I have a popular site, and this Caprelli thing is turning out to be big for my readership."

"Lucky you."

Nick glanced around the basement. Several computer monitors covered one long desk with wires strung helter skelter down the sides. Two printers sat on the floor, probably in the same spot since they came out of the box. Stacks of paper littered the floor. Two standing file cabinets, drawers gaping open, displaying pages jammed in at odd angles. Housekeeping was not this guy's strength.

"Hey, I can't help it if the particular news of the day increases my readership. Go to any damn newspaper in this country. Bad news sells in this business."

"And what business is that?" Javier asked.

"I'm in the news business, Mr. Special Agent. You boys come out here to talk about trends in news readership? Or you have something else on your mind, cause I got a business to run."

"Why don't we start with where'd you get the code for the Caprelli video?" Javier demanded.

"What do you mean?"

"Well, if you just made the video available on your site, that would only take a link to the source code," Javier said. "Pretty simple. You, it appears, have been sending out the actual source code which allows the video to be posted up on numerous sites and servers. Where'd you get the source code?"

Nick knew that Javier had overplayed his hand. The information Scottie had provided couldn't prove the source code had been sent from the site. Jenkins may be unaware, but it was an aggressive bluff. Kate hadn't been able to secure a warrant, so Javier was just wading in as deep as he could get.

Jenkins leaned back and studied his visitors. "Funny thing, that US Constitution. Them boys that wrote it was pretty smart. See, they knew that government couldn't be trusted, and they knew that if government could get control of newsgroups, they could control the country. So them boys put the First Amendment into the Constitution. Fellas ever heard of it?"

"I don't need a history lesson," Javier said. "Where'd you get the code? We've got a Supreme Court Justice that's been kidnapped. We don't have time to play games. You can either tell us or I'll get a warrant and take in all this equipment and find it for ourselves." Javier waved his arms as if gathering up all the equipment. "Course, might take us a few months."

"See, it's always interesting to me," Jenkins said with a wry smile. "When an individual citizen wants to claim his rights, he's playing games. But when the government claims its rights, it's urgent. Drop everything to help the almighty government. Sorry, boys, I ain't playing that game."

"I'll get a warrant."

"I'll get my attorney," he said, sitting forward, fists clenched. "I'm a journalist. That's what I do. I have sources, same as any self-respecting reporter in this country. Gotta tell you boys, these courts have done this ring-around-the-rosey about a journalist and his sources. Y'all outta do some reading."

"We're not talking about a source," Javier said. "We're talking about a thing, electronic video code that would be evidence in the abduction of a Supreme Court Justice."

"Oh, I get it. You want a thing, not a source." With finger to his lips he pondered this. "Kinda like them Pentagon Papers and Wikileaks files. Y'all want the thing. Sorry, boys. Seems like you been wasting your time. I can't help you."

"You mean you won't help us," Javier said.

Jenkins leaned back and casually put an ankle over a knee. "I got a couple hundred years of legal precedent on my side that says I have a right to protect my sources. You come in and threaten me, then ask me for a favor? Not sure where you learned that little trick, but she don't work with me."

"You better hope your records are all in order, taxes, registrations, licenses," Javier said, pointing toward the filing cabinets. "We're liable to go over them with a fine toothed comb. Bet we find something. You travel much? Might end up on the watch list if you're not careful."

"Take your threats out of here or I'm calling my lawyer."

Javier stood preparing to leave. Nick stayed seated. He

motioned to Javier to hold on. "You a bible-fearing man, Mr. Jenkins?" Nick asked.

Jenkins looked at him for the first time since the conversation started. He smirked, but didn't respond.

"Tell me what avengers of blood means," Nick asked.

"Y'all oughta read the bible. Find out for yourselves."

Undeterred, Nick continued his questioning. "What's Redemption Day?"

Jenkins smiled, but no response.

"Where you going to be tomorrow, Mr. Jenkins?" Nick asked. "Got any plans?"

Jenkins' smile broadened into a grin. He looked down and shook his head.

"Okay, how long have you known Brother Wolfe?" Nick asked.

Jenkins squirmed in his chair and the leather squeaked. "Don't know who you're talking about."

"Did you help Brother Wolfe when he was on the lam from his stint in Afghanistan?"

The leather chair squeaked again, Jenkins scratched his jaw and stared at Nick.

"You see," Nick said, "if you helped Brother Wolfe hide; you know, kept him safe, then the First Amendment isn't going to help you. You'll stand for aiding and abetting. And if we find out you know the whereabouts of Justice Caprelli, then you're aiding and abetting the kidnapping of a federal officer. Last time I checked, that gets you fifteen to life. But you're a reporter; you could investigate that."

"I think it's time for you boys to leave," Jenkins said.

"Oh, we're leaving," Nick said, now standing. "Probably coming back soon, but before we go, I do have a few more questions. Do you know Earl Wayne Baker?"

Jenkins gave Nick a menacing stare.

"I'm done talking."

"Were you with him up at Foster's Glen? You know, where Baker killed the state patrolman?"

"Baker didn't kill no one. Man was railroaded," Jenkins said defiantly. "Witnesses I talked to said the agent was shot by his own partners. Then they shot that Jackson boy in cold blood. Shot him in the back. That's what I know about Foster's Glen."

"Rumor has it that several men escaped from the camp into the woods," Nick said. "Sheriff's department never found them. Bet there's a pretty good chance you were one of them, weren't you, Jenkins?" Nick paused for a moment. "See, if we tie you to that shooting." He turned to Javier shrugging. "Hell, or even reasonable suspicion that you were involved in that shooting, we can take all this equipment and take our sweet time reviewing it while you sit in lock up. Heck, I bet we find some of those certified fractional checks here somewhere. You pay your bills with those things? Just like Wolfe?"

Jenkins pointed to the stairwell. "Leave."

"You're the mouthpiece for a criminal enterprise," Nick said. "You can hide for a while behind the First Amendment, but once we can prove you were active in the conduct, you got nothing to hide behind. We're going to talk with Mr. Baker. See, he's on death row. Man on death row's got no reason to keep secrets."

Jenkins kept pointing to the stairway.

"We'll be in touch," Javier said.

The two trudged up the steps, through the hanging cigarette smoke and out of the townhouse.

~

A telephone line engaged from the basement of the townhouse. The call was answered on the third ring.

"Brother Wolfe? I had a few visitors this morning." He listened, flipping Javier's business card. "Yep, him and a guy named James. They don't got shit, but I got a bad feeling about that James guy. He seems to know more than a guy oughta. Wanted to know about you after Afghanistan, Foster's Glen, and asked about Redemption Day. I think they're going to see Earl."

Chapter 45

Nick and Javier entered the passageway. The door behind them hissed and clunked as the deadbolt sealed. Four feet ahead a similar door held them captive. They were in the lock down in Sussex State Prison.

A heavyset guard checked signals on his walkie talkie. Seconds later the door ahead of them hissed and clunked. An electronic beep rang out. The door opened, and they walked into the prison.

"Sergeant Walker," the guard said, extending a hand.

"Javier Lozano, and this is Nick James," he said, grasping the hand.

"I know."

"Here to see—"

"Earl Baker. Gotcha."

Of course he knew, Nick thought. They'd been through the security checkpoint, provided ID's and produced the DOJ form needed to meet directly with a death row inmate. Everybody knew why they were here.

Sergeant Walker spun on his heels and moved down the hallway. He escorted them through another electronic pressure locked door and farther into hell.

White painted concrete blocks and polished laminate flooring framed their vision, occasionally interspersed with windowless metal doorways. At the end of the doorway, Sergeant Walker barked into his walkie talkie and jammed a large iron key into the door handle. He pushed the door in and stepped aside to allow them to enter.

The room was ten by ten, though it felt smaller with four walls of concrete block and no windows. There was a metal table and three chairs, all bolted to the floor. Nick and Javier entered.

"Five minutes, unless we have a problem," Walker said, then he pulled the door shut, locking them in with a definitive clang.

Javier sat in one of the chairs and turned to Nick. "First time in the big house?"

Nick nodded.

"Yeah, all the death row guys are here in Sussex. Just remember, we're the good guys," said Javier. "We get to go home. These guys don't."

Nick stumbled to one of the chairs and collapsed in it. He drew a deep breath and sat upright.

"This guy isn't going to give us anything," Javier said. "He's going to the hereafter; he doesn't care what happens. Guy's had no contact with anyone—maybe his attorney, but that's no help. Visitor log shows nothing for six months. Mail log is zip. Hell, he hasn't even been on the Internet—if he could operate a computer anyway. This will be a bust." Javier threw an ankle on his knee and leaned back.

Nick blinked and considered the remark. He had run through the same scenario. It wasn't that Baker didn't know; he might not. The problem was he wasn't going to give them anything if he did, at least not knowingly. Baker was the link to Caprelli, the only link that made sense. He was convinced they weren't going to get the answer from Baker, but maybe they could uncover a clue.

This was a poker game. Baker wasn't going to show his cards. Nick had to find a tell. He had to use Baker's strength to reveal the weakness. From his research he knew

Baker's strength was arrogance. He had to find the tell in the arrogance.

The door clanged and opened. Walker and two other guards surrounded a small balding man in an orange jumpsuit. Baker's eyes darted around the room, finally centering on Nick. A chill went through Nick, and he jumped up facing the man. Baker smiled. His wrists and ankles were secured with a chain running between the two. There was enough slack in the ankle shackles to allow him to shuffle into the room. Baker kept his eyes on Nick and slid into the room, turning sideways around the table and into the open chair.

He raised the locked wrists upward toward Walker. "Hey, how 'bout some courtesy with the cuffs?"

"You're here to talk, not do sign language," said Walker.

Baker laughed at him.

Javier stepped over and whispered something to Walker. The sergeant nodded and pulled the door shut.

"Howdy, boys." Baker was enjoying this. He was the center of attention.

Javier sat back down. "I'm Special Agent Lozano. This is Nick James with my office."

"What's your office?" said Baker staring at Nick.

"FBI," said Javier.

"That's a joke," Baker said, with a disgusted huff. "You don't know the first thing about investigations, but here you are purporting to represent it. That's a good one. The whole Federal Bureau of Investigation is a myth. It's an unlawful creation of a corrupt government. A reincarnation of the Cushing Doctrine." He smiled smugly.

Javier shot a glance at Nick.

"What's your deal?" Baker said, nodding at Nick. "He do all the talking. You the dummy in this ventriloquist act?"

"We—we're investigating the kidnapping of Justice Caprelli," Nick said.

"Ain't that a hoot. Well, let me make it easy for you guys. I didn't do it." He laughed hard. "And I think I got a pretty good alibi. You see, I don't get out much." He gestured around the room with his locked wrists. "And where would I keep a kidnapped justice? They check my cell every two hours."

"You know who's holding him," Nick said.

"I know what I read in the papers."

"That wasn't the question."

"You didn't ask a question. You made a declarative statement. I'd expect you to know the English language," he said nodding to Nick. "I wasn't too sure about your spic friend here."

Javier shot upright lunging toward Baker, then caught himself and sat back slowly.

"Figured you were new to this country. Just snuck in to steal a little healthcare and some American's job."

Javier sat back down. "You're a funny guy for a cop killer."

"Perhaps you haven't heard. I wasn't even there. Jokers arrest me a week later in Missouri. I didn't kill anyone. The man did die. And he deserved to. But I didn't do it. As it turns out, I wish I had."

Nick felt the conversation spinning out of control. He gestured for Javier to take it easy, then turned to Baker.

"We're here to make sure your friends don't die."

"Well aren't you charitable? Who's going to die?"

"Your friends who took Caprelli."

"Oh, is this the point where I tell you who has him? Then you go rescue him, is that it? I'm kind of getting lost here." Baker sneered and continued. "Kidnapping a federal officer comes under the Lindbergh Law. They face your government's death penalty if Caprelli is dead or life imprisonment if he's alive. Not much incentive to keep him alive, if you ask me, but I didn't make the stupid law. What's your point?"

Baker was right, but Nick couldn't let him turn the conversation.

"It's not about living or dying for those guys," Nick said. "It's about the death of the cause. Your actions need to serve your revolution, not destroy it."

Baker considered him for a long minute, then smiled.

"Finally got someone who understands the situation. So, tell me, smart guy, why do you think I'd know who has Caprelli?"

"Because he denied your death row appeal," Nick said.

"Any of them would have. What? He just made the unlucky draw?"

"And because the Posse wants to use the authority of his office," Nick said, then paused. Baker's smile collapsed into a sickening grin. Nick ignored him and continued. "To re-write the Constitution."

"Not re-write it," Baker said. "But get it right. To conform to the real law. To follow the common law. This government blatantly stole the 13th Amendment as passed by the states and has so distorted the 14th Amendment, it is unrecognizable."

Baker took a deep breath and eased back in his chair. "Our aim is to throw out the thieving bastards who are distorting the law. I am being held illegally, by an illegal government. I am a prisoner of war. I do not recognize this government. It does not follow its own law."

"You were tried by a jury and convicted of murder," said Javier. "What do you mean?"

"I am a sovereign citizen. The person who was tried was not the sovereign. They tried my straw man. I can only be tried by a court of common law. I have not been charged with a crime by a court of common law."

"I'm tired of all this common law crap," said Javier.

"Common law is biblical law. It is the law of sovereign men."

"This is all bullshit," Javier shouted. "We have laws, you violated them, you're guilty." He gave a dismissive wave toward the shackled inmate.

"Your government follows the common law, when it is convenient to its selfish purposes."

"Common law makes up much of our law," Nick said. "That and the statutes passed by the legislature and our constitution."

"Thanks for the civics lesson," said Baker, scowling. "Are you familiar with the history of assisted suicide?"

"What?" Javier asked.

"Assisted suicide. Are you familiar with its history?"

"You mean like Kevorkian?" Javier asked.

"Yeah, like Kevorkian. In 1990 the illegal State of Michigan could not find a way to stop Kevorkian when he helped sovereign citizens enforce their self determination. Their so-called statutes did not define what he did as a crime."

Baker's chains rattled as he sat upright with his folded hands on the table. "The Michigan constitution did not give the state the right to detain Kevorkian for his conduct. They could pass a law, but even they were not so unlawful as to create an ex post facto law to criminalize the good doctor's prior conduct. A new statute would only prohibit future conduct. So what did the shyster government in Michigan resort to? Huh?" He asked, leaning forward, eyes wide. "What did they do? Their laws were no good. Their corrupt system had failed them. So the State of Michigan applied the very laws that you and others say don't exist. The State charged Kevorkian with common law murder. So don't tell me common law doesn't exist."

"Kevorkian was acquitted that time," said Nick.

"As it should be. The government, as usual, was trying to distort the law to achieve its illegal purpose. The people would not allow it. But see, your illegal government takes the people out of the process. It is run by shysters, criminals, and the god-less. They twist the law to their aims and take away the rights of the people, imprisoning them in their system."

"What sovereign is holding Caprelli? And where?" said Nick.

"Why should I help you?" he said. "You're part of the criminal enterprise. I will not help you impose your extortion on my brothers."

"Men will die, like the fire fight in Foster's Glen. That doesn't need to happen."

"That didn't need to happen when good citizens took their freedom from the British, but it did," Baker said defiantly. "Blood is shed for freedom. Always has been. And you two punks ain't about to change that."

"You may not care about Justice Caprelli or the officers who'll get him back, but you have to care for your brothers who'll die and be injured. This doesn't solve anything. Nothing will change when it's done, just a lot of death."

"Plenty will change," Baker said, leaning forward and glaring at Nick. "Many will learn that they don't have to give in to this lawless government. The people will wake up. They're starting to already. They will understand. The world will learn about Posse Comitatus. They will learn to take back their rights. They will learn to respect the sovereign citizen. And you," he said, pointing with a jangling cuff on his wrist, "you will teach them."

"You're drawing your last breaths," Nick said. "You must want to go to your maker with a clean conscience. That you've done the right thing. That you've stopped unnecessary deaths."

"Do not argue about God in front of me. My God believes in the sovereign. My God believes in retribution for the murder of his son. My God does not shy from battle. He leads his tribes to victory. Redemption Day shall come. God is on our side. I have to die, others have to die, but Redemption Day is coming. When the people wake up and know what has happened, the government will be thrown out, the leaders will be killed, the shysters will be imprisoned. The people will control, as it is meant to be."

Baker stood slowly and shouted, "Walker!" He turned to Nick and spoke in a low tone. "You guys are boring me. Imagine that. I'm in lock down twenty-three and a half hours a day. You boys are so boring, I'm going back to my cell."

The door swung open. Walker and two other officers stood in the hallway. Javier stood and moved against the wall to allow Baker to shuffle by.

Baker half turned in the doorway. "The avengers of blood shall be turned out. It starts in the center of the star, and there's nothing you boys can do to stop it."

He laughed and slid into the hallway. "Long live the Posse Comitatus. The time is upon us. Redemption Day is coming. Long live the Posse Comitatus."

Chapter 46

Water lapped the side of the boat. The two men stood facing one another, not speaking. This was a negotiation.

The next person to speak would be the loser.

Beyond them, the Chesapeake opened and fishing boats rocked as they pushed away from the marina. Two other boats floated as they waited for departing crafts to clear so they could make it into their slips. Nearby, an obese man with lightning fast hands effortlessly filleted a rock fish, tossed the meat onto the counter, and grabbed another. A teenage boy watched in awe.

"Fair offer," Willie Jackson said finally, trying to get his mark to open up.

"Nope."

So much for getting him to open up. The man didn't move away from Jackson, so it was still on.

"Look," said Jackson. "I'm talking cash. No checks, no bank loans. Ten minutes you walk away from here and pay all your bills, then buy everyone a round over at The Tethered Fin."

"Got more in it than that."

"What you got in it don't matter. That ain't my problem. I'm telling you eighteen cash American. Hell, you're the one who ran the ad."

"Ad says twenty-five thousand."

"I know what the ad said." Jackson stopped himself.

He stared at the man, then looked around the marina. He waited. The man said nothing, but he wasn't moving away. He was still on the hook.

"She's a twenty-eight foot Packman with a drop down front hull, only eight years old and got twin Evinrude 130's."

"I know what kind of boat it is. I also know what money's worth," Willie said, standing defiantly.

"Gotta have twenty-five. Can't let her go for less than that."

Jackson waited patiently, then extended his hand. The fish reached for it, thinking he'd won.

"Nice meeting you," Jackson said and turned to walk away.

He slowly took two steps and smiled when he felt the man shifting his weight on the dock.

"Nineteen-five, but that's it."

Chapter 47

Slade Richenbacher downshifted the Diamond Rio and signaled his exit off Interstate 95. He'd finally reached the Rogers Clark exit, which not only had a truck stop with good food; it had a massive asphalt parking lot.

Although Richenbacher could back an eighteen wheeler through a slalom course with his eyes blindfolded, it was smart to park his rig with plenty of space to avoid being boxed in by some soccer mom in a kid mobile.

He left the engine running, locked it, and lumbered off the rig onto the parking lot. His first step took him sideways. A casual observer might think that first move demonstrated that he was intoxicated, but it was caused by six hours behind the wheel. He'd left Atlanta before sunrise and, if he'd timed things right, he could get through the DC beltway before rush hour hit. Two hours beyond that he could drop his rig for the local boys. His cargo was a tanker of unleaded.

Southern Maryland was the last stop on the gas delivery system originating at the Gulf of Mexico. Slade made this run six times per month, so he knew the traffic patterns, the cheapest diesel fuel, and the best truck stop food every inch of the way.

Richenbacher was an indie, the last of a dying breed. He was never good with bosses, and the thought of reporting into someone made his skin crawl. If he wanted work, he got work. If he wanted to go fishing, he went fishing. His petroleum distribution gig was good. He had steady work, they paid on time. It wasn't the highest paying turn, but it was consistent. If he wanted to be unavailable, he could. Southwick Petrol always put him back in the steady rotation.

The Diamond Rio had one payment to go and was only nine years old. He could get several hundred thousand miles out of her yet, and being paid off, he could take a little more time on the water pursuing the elusive bone fish.

His grip contained a daub kit and clean shirt. He would get a quick shower in, grab a hoagie sandwich, a liter of Coke, three packs of cigs, and be rolling north toward DC in twenty minutes.

Living a life on the road was what he chose. It was a living, and he was damn good at it. Being alone on the road constantly, he felt anonymous everywhere he traveled, even though he recognized the help at the stops he frequented.

Anonymous was good.

Slade Richenbacher got his shower, his hoagie, Coke and cigs, but he never made it to DC.

The stranger knew a thing or two about big rigs; that's how the conversation started. Just two truckers swapping stories about the beasts they drove. Seconds later Slade was staring at the wrong end of a snub-nosed .45. A set of plastic cuffs made Slade's hands of no help and they exited the truck stop.

He'd heard of random highway jackings and always figured that the cargo was what was wanted. He might get abandoned on a lonely road and have to file a claim for a stolen rig, but he wouldn't be harmed. What was the point?

As they continued driving Slade Richenbacher realized he was heading down a bad road and there was no turning back.

Steve O'Brien

Richenbacher's last breath was two miles off the interstate, on his knees facing away from the truck toward the creek bed. He wasn't a religious man, but he quickly bargained with his maker a split second before three bullets ripped through the back of his skull. His body tumbled forward into the creek. He flipped onto his back with dead eyes staring back at the man holding the gun.

~

Frank Jackson sneered and spat onto the ground. He quickly surveyed the roadway, casually skirted the Diamond Rio's bumper, and climbed back into the driver's seat.

Five minutes after the gunshots, the Diamond Rio shifted smoothly and accelerated up the onramp of Interstate 95, headed toward DC.

Chapter 48

Late afternoon had arrived before Nick and Javier returned to the city. Crossing over the 14th Street Bridge into DC, they received simultaneous emails from the Sovereign Free Press announcing "Redemption Day is coming."

"What the hell is this Redemption Day stuff all about?" Javier said.

"Not sure. They appear to be using it as some kind of rallying cry or there's some kind of message attached to it that only they understand."

"And what? Jenkins is just taunting us with it?" Javier asked, looking over his left shoulder shifting lanes.

"I guess. Here's what I can't understand," Nick said. "You gave Jenkins your business card. Right? It had your email address on it. But how did he get my email address?"

Javier shrugged. "You ever have it on business cards or anything?"

"Nope. This is my private email account. I can't access my old Center Tech email account. That's the only one that would have been recorded somewhere."

"Well you're a popular guy." After a long pause, Javier added, "What's this Cushing Doctrine crap?"

"Another of their distortions. Caleb Cushing was the Secretary of State prior to the Civil War. He instructed that all able bodied men above the age of fifteen could be enlisted by a US Marshall to put down uprisings. Essentially makeshift armies of men."

"What's wrong with that?" Javier asked.

"Well, at the time it was passed, the primary use of these groups was to pursue and capture slaves who had escaped in the South. Later, after the Civil War, the doctrine was used to protect newly freed slaves, and a part of the country wasn't too happy about the US government's role in what they deemed a local dispute."

"So Baker thinks were some makeshift army out to get them?"

"Something like that," Nick said. "Once the Cushing Doctrine was inverted to protect slaves, Southern Congressmen pushed to repeal it. They passed the Posse Comitatus Act."

"You're kidding. There's an act called the Posse Comitatus Act?"

"Yep, it was pushed through Congress with heavy support from Southern states, and it said that no federal army or navy could be used within the country unless specifically authorized by Congress."

"So who was in charge?"

"The local community. The local Posse Comitatus. It was a device to allow Southern states to enforce different rights for new citizens. That is, former slaves. It set the civil rights movement back about eighty years."

"What about the National Guard?"

"Well, it wasn't until Little Rock in 1955 before a President ever authorized federal intervention in state issues. The Posse Comitatus saw that as illegal then, and they think it's illegal now."

They drove in silence for several minutes, then Nick turned in his seat. "I think I know someone who might be able to help us with the avengers of blood stuff."

"Who's that?" Javier asked.

"Father Flaherty at Georgetown. Theology professor over there."

Javier pulled the car up to the entrance to the FBI underground garage. A slab of metal slowly lowered to allow the car to enter. "I can't spend anymore time out in the field today, and you'll need a chaperone. Take Wesley."

"I'm not exactly feeling the love from Wesley. He's pretty sure I'm full of shit on all this."

"Well, see if Kate is available and let me know what you find out."

~

Thirty minutes later Nick and Kate were seated in straight back wooden armchairs in front of a massive maple desk covered with stacks of papers, magazines, and newspapers. Sunlight cut through the third floor window; shadows of tree branches danced on the floor.

Father Flaherty settled himself into his leather desk chair. At nearly seventy he wasn't teaching on a regular basis, but the university still allowed him to inhabit an office. He was like a priest on vacation, not wearing the standard Catholic collarino, but rather attired like a professor on any nameless college campus.

His disposition was composed of the gravitas of a serious man of letters. Age had thinned his once copious Irish mop to a small hedge ringing the sides and back of his scalp. Somehow his eyebrows had maintained their growth curve and appeared even bushier behind the wire rimmed glasses. He slowly leaned forward on his elbows.

"How can I help you, Nick?"

"I need your help solving a riddle that I think involves the Bible."

"Hit me with it," Flaherty said in a gravelly voice, rubbing his hands together.

"Well, I don't have all the information, but do you know what avengers of blood means?"

"Hhhmmm." His eyes rolled up the ceiling as he pondered. "There are several books of the bible that discuss avengers of blood. What else do you know?"

"Something about refuge," Kate offered.

"Well, refuge in the Lord is a pretty common reference throughout the Bible, but I think you're talking about cities of refuge, Book of Joshua, also Deuteronomy. Actually the second half of Joshua, one of the least understood books of the bible—well, in fairness, either least understood or most boring. But here goes." He cleared his throat and leaned back in his chair. "Avengers of blood refers to family members, both blood as in kinship and blood as in death. In that time, if someone killed a member of your family, the biblical law allowed you to avenge that death."

"Eye for an eye?" Nick said.

"Yeah, something like that. So it was common for a family to send out one of their strongest sons to find the person who killed the family member. When they found them, they were entitled to kill them." He clapped his hands together as if washing his hands.

"The book of Joshua created sanctuary cities or cities of refuge," the priest continued. "If the person didn't mean to kill the person—manslaughter in today's world—the person could flee to a city of refuge. There were six of them in the area controlled by the Israelites. Anyway, the person would meet with the city elders and describe what happened. If the elders believed the death wasn't intentional, they took him in and gave him refuge. If the avenger of blood arrived at the city, the elders wouldn't turn the killer over—he was protected."

A pendulum clock on the wall clicked of seconds like a marching soldier.

"That's it?" Nick said. "So the guy was protected as long as he stayed in that town?"

"Yep."

Nick shared a glance at Kate. This was no help. Her eyes held the same reaction.

"There's got to be more to it than that," Kate said.

"I'm afraid not," the priest said, then as if catching himself in thought, he raised a finger. "Well, the killer could eventually go free."

"Go free?" Nick asked. "How? Wouldn't the avenger of blood be waiting for him?"

"Not clear whether the avenger lost his rights or if the change in circumstance allowed the killer to go free," Flaherty said.

"How does he go free?" Kate asked. "What's the change in circumstance?"

"All killers had to stay in their respective city of refuge until the one time when they were freed."

"What allowed them to go free?"

"One event." Flaherty leaned forward, placing his hands on the desk. "The holiest man of all in these cities was the chief magistrate. When the chief judge died, the killers were free to go home to their families and the avengers of blood weren't permitted to touch them."

Chapter 49

Dahlgren fountain glistened in the fading light. An icon of Georgetown campus, it was framed on all but the west side by academic buildings. It served as a meet up location for students or a place just to hang.

Kate and Nick descended the stairs and exited the Ryan building into the Dahlgren quad.

"So he's going to kill Caprelli?" Kate asked.

"Yeah, I think we've known that all along."

Except for the ride over in the taxi, this was the first time Nick and Kate had been alone together. He found himself stealing glances in the fading sunset. *Did she still have feelings for me? Did she ever?*

Working a kidnapping case was hardly the place to rekindle a relationship, but despite the urgency and uncertainty, he felt at ease. It was the first time in several days that he had truly relaxed. He had a compatriot, a true advocate and friend. *Did he have more than that?*

They strode toward the fountain. She gave no clues. Her mind was all business as far as Nick could tell. But she'd been like that at times when they were together. He couldn't say yes, but knew it didn't mean no either. He'd take that.

"But what's the avengers of blood deal?" she asked. "They go free?"

"I think so."

"So who are the avengers of blood?"

Nick paused, glaring up at the fading sunlight. "We are, I guess," he said. "When Caprelli dies, they'll claim they're freed. Kind of like the Year of Jubilee, where all obligations are balanced. Redemption Day could signal their freedom from the past. A starting over point. The Posse tried some Jubilee notions in the past, largely to avoid foreclosures and argue for debt forgiveness. This seems bigger than that."

"Do you think Caprelli's already dead? I mean we don't know how old the videos are. Maybe they've already killed him."

"And are running out tapes like Al Qaeda? Maybe, but I don't think so. These guys are into show. They want a spectacle," Nick said as they approached the fountain. "They've learned about publicity after Ruby Ridge and the Tea Party success. They're pushing a movement. In the early days this had to be done face to face or through the mail with poorly constructed newsletters. Like everyone else, now they're linked by the Internet. They recruit, train, indoctrinate, and rally for their cause the same as a political party or dot com start up. They're planning something big, something newsworthy."

"What exactly is their cause?" she asked.

"Mostly it's anti-government, anti-bank, pro liberty movement. They portray themselves as victims or targets of oppressors who support minorities and statism. The Posse Comitatus concept is ages old. It's based upon the notion that locals within the community should be in charge of enforcing local laws. You can see how this played out in the Civil Rights days. Home rule versus integration."

Nick and Kate had their backs to the fountain as they talked. The sun was quickly dropping from the sky behind them. Shadows were stretching to fill the quad.

The two men Nick noticed earlier while crossing Healy Lawn were in the corner of the quad. Something wasn't right about them. The shorter of the two was bald and talking on a cell phone. He looked their way; the other, taller man with long blond hair, wearing a gray hooded sweatshirt, sat on the bench appearing bored. Nick locked eyes with the bald man; he didn't look away.

"Let's get out of here," he said, grabbing Kate's arm and moving around the far side of the fountain.

"What?"

"Gotta bad feeling. Let's move."

Nick looked back, and between the spray and shooting water of the fountain, he could see the two men start to move their way, casual, but direct.

"When we get to the tunnel under New North, we're going to run."

"What are you talking about?" Kate asked.

Nick accelerated his pace, reaching back for her hand. Fast enough to create space, not fast enough to be obvious, he thought. "There's two guys back there. I saw them when we arrived. They don't fit." He glanced over his shoulder again. "And right now, they're following us."

New North was a red brick building housing classrooms and professor's offices. A broad archway had been carved by the architect that allowed students to walk under the building to connect the quad with the rest of the campus.

Kate started to turn her head.

"Keep moving," Nick said.

Just as they entered the tunnel, Nick looked back. The taller one had his hand in the pocket of his hooded sweatshirt. Gun, Nick thought. They were certainly following them and nearly breaking into a light jog.

As soon as they crossed out of sight, Nick yelled "*Run!*"

They ran through the archway and took an immediate right, cutting through a hedge moving parallel to the New North building. He knew their pursuers were behind them and likely running. He'd worried that Kate might not be able to keep up with him, but for the former all-conference lacrosse star, running at high speed wasn't a problem. As they cleared the building, Nick motioned to the right and they scampered across the grounds to a side door of the Healy Building.

Please be unlocked, please.

Nick grabbed the door and flung it open. With adrenaline rushing through him, he nearly ripped the door from the hinges. Kate rushed in as he looked back. The men were about forty yards behind them crossing the lawn. He slammed the door and quickly scanned for a weapon. In the corner he spotted a wrought iron pole. It was used to open the transom window, a relic in an air conditioned world. Nick shoved it through the door handle and across the limestone jamb. "Up," Nick said, spinning around.

He'd taken two steps when the men yanked on the door. The pole held, but he noticed it had slipped slightly with the rattling from the door. A few more tugs and the pole might just slide to the floor. Hopefully they would buy some time and possibly frustrate these guys. They'd get impatient and try a different door.

Nick scampered up the marble steps behind Kate. At the landing they burst into the hallway. To the right the nave of the building opened to offices. Straight ahead was another stairway leading to the front of the Healy Building. Nick motioned to the left at two enormous wooden doors that marked the entrance to Gaston Hall. They quickly slipped inside.

The hall was dark and empty. Several rows of auditorium seats stood before them, a stage to the left. Gothic architecture and ornate carvings filled the walls. The ending rays of sunlight filtered through the stained glass and curved windows. Dark wood paneling absorbed the light as did the inlaid ceilings.

Nick grabbed Kate's wrist and tugged her to the right. A stairway led to the upper seating area in the auditorium. "Hide up here. I'll be back for you. I'm going to lose these guys," he whispered.

Kate shook her head, gathering her breath. He urged her up the steps. "They'll think we split up," he said. "I can lose them, then I'll be back." She reluctantly started up the steps. "Turn your phone to vibrate," he said.

"I'll call Javier," she said.

"Okay, but keep quiet and out of sight," Nick said as he moved back toward the entrance. "Don't leave. I'll be back."

Chapter 50

Nick descended the stairs two steps at a time and burst into the landing on the main level. An elderly man and a young woman walked away from him down the hallway. The rest of the building was silent.

He turned and walked out the entrance of the building onto the lawn. His pursuers were nowhere in sight. They were here somewhere, he knew, as he walked toward the circle adjoining Healy lawn. He made himself as visible as possible, walking into an open area of the lawn. Beyond the lawn was Welcome Gate, and cars puttered along 37th street.

He spotted the bald man talking into his cell phone while his partner stood talking to someone inside a beat-up white van. Nick quickly moved across the lawn to an exit onto the street forty yards to the south. Fortunately, the van was aimed in the other direction. When he reached the sidewalk, he stopped and waited for them to spot him. In an instant the men on foot were after him.

Nick raced across 37th street toward Prospect Avenue. He looked right and considered running down a steep, narrow stairway that connected Prospect to Canal Road. Locals called them the exorcist steps because a classic scene in the 1970's thriller was filmed there. He'd be a sitting duck on the steps though. He continued down Prospect Avenue.

At 34th Street he took a left. Once out of their line of sight he scurried over a temporary construction fence and squeezed between two plywood boards into the building site. "New Townhomes in Georgetown," the sign read. Having just been framed, the site provided needed cover. Nick ran up an improvised staircase and crouched near the front of the structure overlooking Prospect Avenue.

The bald man pointed up 35th Street and waved toward what must have been the taller man. Baldy looked up at the structure, causing Nick to duck down completely out of sight. The taller man jogged back into Nick's view, and the two talked briefly. The white van rolled up to the intersection, and both men climbed in. He watched the van pull away and eased back against a wall and exhaled.

He would give them a few minutes, then head back to get Kate. Nick pulled his phone and dialed Kate. No answer. He clicked off without leaving a message. Maybe she was on the phone with Javier. He sat and waited, catching his breath.

Eventually, Nick stood and stretched his legs. Just as he prepared to move toward the stairway, he spotted the van. They were back. It crept slowly in front of the construction site and stopped. Baldy and Blondie got out of the cargo door and pointed toward the window where Nick was hiding. Baldy went left, the other right.

Nick scanned the floor for a weapon or escape route. Nothing. Just scraps of cut plywood and a roll of tarp plastic were available.

Once these guys got into the structure, they'd have him cornered. The back of his second floor room was open to an alleyway. It was a drop of about fifteen feet to the ground, but would do him no good as he was still inside the construction site. A brick wall about eight feet high marked the edge of the property, but it was a long distance from the building. Could he jump that far?

He rolled the tarp plastic to the landing in front of the stairway. Nails creaked as plywood was pulled away below him. A cracking sound came from the other side of the structure as one of them tore his way into the building. Footfalls could be heard coming nearer on the floor below.

Nick pushed the roll of plastic into the stairway sideways and it jammed. He stomped on it several times to push it farther into the opening, effectively blocking the stairway. It wouldn't hold long, but could buy him some time.

He retreated to the front of the building and ducked down. Soon he heard steps on the stairway below him. From the stairwell opening he could see Baldy, a handgun leading him up the steps. He was scanning the area above him. They locked eyes for a moment. Baldy smiled and motioned to Blondie behind him. The roll of plastic started to move. Nick couldn't wait any longer.

Nick ran as fast as he could and launched himself out of the back of the building. His legs bicycle kicked as he flew toward the brick dividing wall. He couldn't clear it. He was falling too fast. Nick pulled up his legs and hit the concrete cap on the top of the wall. His momentum carried him on, and he flipped forward off the wall and into the alleyway. He tumbled forward and landed on his back.

Unable to breathe, he slowly turned onto his knees and pulled himself upright. He didn't have much time. Before they could get over or around the wall, he had to be gone. Nick limped toward 34th Street, crossed it, and kept in the alley to the next block. From there he was able to move at a slight jog and turned down 33rd Street toward the Potomac.

He raced through moving traffic on M Street and took the footbridge across the C&O Canal to Water Street. He forced open a side door to an abandoned warehouse and collapsed onto the floor, his breath coming in heaving gasps.

Nick knew Georgetown well. One thing he was sure of was that following by vehicle would take time. Stoplights and limited access roads across the canal would buy him needed time. Just to be safe he removed the battery from his cell phone. His pants were torn below the knee and blood oozed down his shin onto the tracking device on his ankle. Couldn't be, he thought.

Several minutes passed. He worried about Kate. He would give this some time, then put his battery back in and call her. Right now he needed to rest and stay hidden. Traffic on Water Street was light all the time. Most travelers on the road were headed to the boat house or to parking spaces to access the hiker biker trail. This time of day, there would be no traffic.

When headlights bounced off the water-damaged walls, he thought, no way. He leaned forward to look just as the white van rolled to a stop outside the warehouse.

Nick found a back door and ran west along the canal. His socks stuck to his leg from the drying blood. He clomped along at the highest speed he could attain. He dove into a stairwell where Whitehurst Freeway dumped into M Street and was soon above the canal crossing back into Georgetown proper. This time he took the exorcist steps and lugged his way to the top. His limp had become more pronounced as he tried to catch his breath. He had to get to a safe place, call Javier, then go back for Kate.

He slipped the battery back into his phone and dialed a number.

"Turn off...the bracelet," he said, wheezing.

"Nick? Where are you?" Javier asked.

"Turn...off...they're...tracking me..."

"Who? Where are you?"

"Trying. Stay alive." He gasped for breath. "Guys. White van. Chasing us. Kate."

"Where's Kate?"

"Hiding. Georgetown. Turn off. Bracelet."

"They're not going to take you if they know you are wearing a tracking device."

"These guys...won't have...problem...cutting off my foot."

"Nick, we're coming."

He ended the call and immediately punched Kate's number. He struggled to get his breathing under control. As he crossed Dumbarton he heard a car engine accelerate. The white van was headed directly at him.

Nick disengaged the call, broke into a choppy gait and moved to the alley. He had to get off the alleyway or they'd just run him down. Halfway through the alley he scampered onto a carriage house just as the headlights lit up the alley. He jumped from the carriage house into the brick-enclosed back yard. From the main house a yapping dog gave him away.

Kiki.

Rather than frightening off the bad guys, this guard dog was leading them to him. The van's engine went silent.

Nick limped and drug his leg onto the porch. "Kiki, it's me," he whispered. He tried the back door. Locked. "Kiki. Shhh."

He turned to see Baldy drop into the back yard, followed by Blondie. Baldy was smirking; the taller guy just looked annoyed.

"Thought you could get away, huh?" said Baldy. "Can't hide from us." His gun was drawn as the two slowly approached the back porch. Baldy's smirk deepened into a yellow-toothed grin. Nick scanned the area, but he was trapped on the porch. If they wanted him dead, he only had seconds left.

A shotgun blast ripped through the night sky. The pursuers looked up. Mrs. Mac pointed the weapon from an upstairs window.

"Get off my property. Leave the boy alone," she yelled.

Baldy squinted to see who was holding the gun, then chuckled and continued forward. The distinctive cha-chuck of the pump action discharging the spent cartridge and reloading a fresh one came milliseconds before the next blast. It tore a hole in the ground at Baldy's feet and sprayed his lower legs with buckshot. He jumped back, holding his hands out.

"My pappy gave me this here gun, and he damn well taught me how to use it. Now get off my property." Mrs. Mac pumped in a new shell. "You got three seconds."

The men looked at each other and began backing away. They unlatched the fence and slipped out of sight.

Nick looked up at Mrs. Mac adorned in a flowing nightgown with a cigarette bouncing on her lips. She tossed him a lanyard with a key attached. "Let yourself in. I'll keep a watch for these guys."

No sooner had he shut the door and picked up Kiki, the sirens and lights lit up the sky in front of the house.

He watched Javier jump from an unmarked cruiser and jog toward the door. A real tribute to the accuracy of the tracking devices, Nick thought.

He quickly punched Kate's cell number again. It rang twice, then clicked. "Kate," he shouted.

"Hello, Mr. James." It was Wolfe's voice. "I'll see you in the center of the star."

The line went dead.

Chapter 51

Red neon flooded the slight opening in the faded grey, moth eaten drapes. Four seconds on, two seconds off. The word "ancy" was the only part visible. Kate blinked several times. To her right was a tattered green armchair just past the magic fingers coin slot. The bed was soft like asphalt, and the brown imitation crushed velvet bed cover transmitted unknown bacteria on a continuous basis, but that was the least of her worries.

She'd been chloroformed repeatedly from the time the two men had pinned her to the floor of the Gaston Hall balcony. They weren't the same guys who had chased them, but clearly played for the same team. Just when the fuzz was wearing off the edges, she was sent back to lala land with another blast of the juice.

Her arms were pinned behind her, hogtied to the roping around her ankles, as she lay on her right side. She tugged and wriggled, but soon found it a waste of time. After bouncing and shifting her weight, she was able to flip to the other side. From here she could see a cloudy mirror above a crusted linoleum counter and sink. The entry to the bathroom was to the left, and an open closet with scattered hangers was on the other side.

A key slid into the door, and it chunked open, dragging on the orange shag carpet. Wolfe's silhouette filled the doorway. He was talking to someone outside the door, more directing an order than making conversation. "No one in or out," was the part Kate heard.

Wolfe closed the door behind him, keeping his eyes on Kate. A smirk covered his face with a sinister twist of his mouth on the left side. He stepped to the window and tugged the drapes completely shut. With one quick move he lifted the green chair and spun it facing Kate. He leaned in slowly and ripped the duct tape off her mouth.

She shook her head, wincing. "You're a dead man."

"Now, now, is that any way for a lady to behave?"

"Kidnapping a federal officer. You're toast."

"I've never had much use for your laws, missy lawyer. Seems you don't fully comprehend the situation in which you find yourself. And your rationale is fundamentally faulty. Most of your laws are." He leaned forward, leering at her. "See, here's what's backwards. If I let you go, I could die. If I kill you, I could die. Here's the little pickle you've pointed out. If I kill you and no one knows about it, who's going to kill me? But if I let you go, you're gonna tell on me, and that's actually worse. You see, deary, your logic means it's better for me to kill you than let you go. Course, most of the garbage you folks consider laws are similarly flawed. So this isn't surprising. What is surprising is you thought I might be dumb enough to go along with you."

She stared silently. He waited. "So isn't this the part where your boyfriend comes busting through the door to save you?"

"Who are you talking about?"

"Mr. James."

She ground her teeth, but didn't speak.

"I can tell he's your little man friend. I could just see it in your eyes when you were together. Well, and truth be told, I had some intel on both of you." He tapped his fingers on the side of the bed. "He sure was trying to reach you by phone, but you were a little predisposed at the time. So I talked to him for you." Wolfe shrugged, with his hands up as if to say *what's a guy to do?* "Did he tell you he was coming back for you? Is that what he said when he left you in the auditorium? How sweet."

"You're a pig."

"Oh, that's just hurtful. You've already gone to name calling. And you haven't even bothered to get to know me."

"I know plenty about you. I know you're wanted for war crimes in Afghanistan. I know you kidnapped Justice Caprelli. I know you killed two Secret Service officers. I know you ordered the killing of Judge Browning in Winchester. I think I know enough to support my opinion."

"And when you argue for the death penalty for someone who violates your laws," he said with *violates* in his most sarcastic voice. "You claim it's for the good of the country. When you levy big fines against companies and their workers lose their jobs as a result, you're doing it for the good of the country. When you prosecute citizens for failure to pay the exorbitant taxes, yet allow untaxed workers to slide across the border, you're doing it for the good of your country. When your President declares war to protect the price of oil, you round up the poor and uneducated, give them a gun, and tell them to hunt the enemy, that's all for the good of the country."

"Save it," she said.

Undeterred, he continued. "Many of those boys get their arms and legs blown off, if they aren't lucky enough to actually be killed in combat. I've seen it first-hand, sweetheart. All the while, they're fighting a bunch of kids in bare feet and hand-me-down clothes that people in this country tossed away. The kids from both sides have no idea why they're trying to kill each other. When your country does that, it's supposed to be honorable, for the good of the country. Excuse me if I think the good of the country is a bunch of self serving bullshit. The criminals running this country distort history and make rules to serve their interests. And good soldiers like you make them work." Wolfe leaned forward, elbows on his knees. "Well, those criminals won't be in control much longer. The people are taking over."

"Oh, is that who you're doing this for?" she said. "The people?"

"The power is always with the people. People in the local community. Not some jerks in suits with Ivy League degrees that distort facts."

"The Posse Comitatus? Is that your idea of power?"

"Posse Comitatus isn't a group. It's an ideal. It's about self-determination, responsibility. Local control, not some bloated federal infrastructure."

"You sound just like the Taliban. If we could just go back in time, everything will be wonderful. You can't go back."

He smiled as if lecturing a child. "We don't go back. We have an awakening. This country is on the verge of an awakening. Redemption Day is coming."

"You're nuts," she said. "You can't win this. I don't know what your deal is, but you can't win this."

He laughed. "I've already won. Every piece is a victory."

"You won't get away with this."

"See, that's the problem you have," he said, smirking. "You think 'getting away with something' is the goal." He leaned back, stretching, as though he was contemplating his next thought. "I learned a little something from those godless terrorists I killed. The mission is the goal. How could someone fly a plane into a building? Sure it caused destruction, but the pilot and his pals were killed. Who would do such a thing? Made no sense to Americans before 9-11."

"Sure, compare yourself to 9-11 terrorists," she said. "You're a lunatic."

"Each part is a step toward completion of the mission. I have my role. And now you'll have your role. This is bigger than me. I'm just the blasting cap. I start the sequence. I start the chain reaction."

"I'm not a part of your game," she said, looking away from him.

"Yes, my dear, you are. Not willingly, mind you, but you'll be playing a crucial role. Your name will go down in history. It's a history that you won't like, but history nonetheless. You see, you have to stand trial."

"What are you talking about?"

"You have to stand trial before the court of common law, the good judge Caprelli presiding. And I'm afraid to say, the chances you'll be found guilty are high. Very high indeed." He stood, pulled his shirt out of his pants, and began unbuckling his belt.

She bounced and scooted to the far side of the bed. "Get out of here."

"But before we get to that, my little firecracker," he said. "You and I have a little business."

Chapter 52

The doorbell chimed through the cavernous house, reverberating even from the front porch landing where it had been engaged. Darkness shrouded the street aptly named Centrillion, Haden thought. This is where the affluent hid from society, behind gated entrances with auspicious street names. This was "in your face" wealth of the new variety.

Haden heard footsteps approaching the door and stepped back slightly. He gingerly touched the outside of his jacket to make sure the envelope was in the breast pocket. The envelope contained his back-up solution. Contingencies were necessary in this game. Haden played to win. Inside the envelope was his potential salvation and Elliot Galbert's worst nightmare. Having it with him boosted his courage. There was power in this business-sized envelope, more effective than Kryptonite.

The gap in the door frame was filled with Galbert's face as the door swung open.

"Come on in, Maxwell," Galbert said dismissively as he turned his back and walked away.

"Nice place," said Haden. "What? No butler to open the door for you?"

Galbert harrumphed as he continued down the hallway past the curved double staircase. He was dressed in jeans, a wrinkled dress shirt, and Ugg slippers. "Wife's gone to her damn Pilates class, and the kids are off at school. Sometimes I feel like I live here all alone."

Haden followed him into a spacious, wood paneled study. A fire crackled in the fireplace, framed by two overstuffed leather chairs. Galbert motioned to them. After Haden settled into the near one, Galbert raised a glass from behind his massive desk. "Want a drink?"

"No, I'm good."

"I'm not very happy right now." Galbert said in a flat tone.

"You should be elated. Your phone is going to ring in the next two days, and the funding for the DOMTER contract is going to be back. Probably double the original fee. You're going to make a bundle, my friend."

"All the bullshit you've pulled, I'll be lucky if I don't go to jail," Galbert said. "I didn't sign up for this, and I sure didn't sign up for the amount of money you've extorted."

"That's such a hurtful word. I'm accomplishing what we agreed. You wanted the contract back, I'm getting it for you. Given what you have to gain, the three hundred thousand is a drop in the bucket."

"Was supposed to be seventy five."

Haden slid backward into the chair and tapped the armrests lightly as if judging the quality of the leather. "Things got complicated, my friend. You know how that goes. The early money would be wasted if we didn't get the prize, now, wouldn't it?"

"Yeah, well, I thought you'd go through channels, talk to people. Not take hostages and kill a bunch of innocent people." Galbert took a slug of his scotch, ice cubes clinking. "That's crazy."

"We do what we have to do, my friend. Sometimes the traditional way doesn't work or isn't expedient enough for our needs. You paid for an outcome; you'll get the outcome you wanted. That's the deal."

"I'm not a party to any of that."

"You're up to your eyeballs," Haden said glaring into Galbert's face.

Galbert picked up a bulky manila envelope from the desk and tossed it to Haden. "That's it. No more. This isn't worth it. This is insane. I'm officially out."

"You're not out. You'll never be out," Haden said.

"Anyone comes to me, I'll tell them about everything. You, this Posse Comitatus crap, everything. Take your money, and I never want to see or hear from you again."

Haden cocked his head and gave Galbert a sad face. "I'm sorry to hear you say that after all I've done for you." Haden's voice raised and he gestured menacingly at Galbert. "I've watched you take millions out of the government over the years. You've got this freaking mansion, nice cars, vacations. I've watched you do it all. Then when some little guy like me gets a taste, you want to screw me." Haden scooted forward in his chair, sitting erect. "Well, it doesn't work that way. I did what I said I would do and you're going to turn me in? Not happening, my friend. You think the government is going to give a damn about me? You're the tuna. You're the one they'll want to indict. I'll get immunity. You'll do the perp walk. You need me. Understand? That's how it works."

Galbert reached down into a desk drawer and pulled a glock. Haden dropped the manila envelope and quickly threw his hands up. "It's over when I say it's over," said Galbert. "Do you understand?"

"Hey, no need for all this," Haden said, hands extended while slowly rising from the chair. "We're in this together. We need each other."

"I don't trust you. Never have. It was a mistake from the start, and now there's only one way to end it. You're the only thing that can link me to all this. I'm going to cut the link." Galbert motioned to the French doors leading to the concrete porch and swimming pool. "Outside."

"What are you gonna do? Shoot me in the back yard? Don't want to dirty up your fancy library?" Haden moved slowly toward the desk.

Galbert gripped the gun with both hands. "I said outside."

"Whoa, whoa, whoa. I've got something I need you to see," Haden said. "This will help you understand. Explains everything." He reached inside his jacket pocket holding the other palm toward Galbert, reassuring him. Haden slowly pulled a letter-size envelope from his inside pocket and extended it across the desk. Galbert hesitated. Haden shook the letter, encouraging Galbert to take it.

Without taking his eyes off Haden, he reached out and grabbed the envelope. Haden quickly ripped the envelope away from him. Galbert yelped and pulled back his hand. Two streaks of blood striped Galbert's middle and ring fingers. He held them up to his lips with a curious eye. He shook the gun motioning toward the deck.

"What the hell—"

"Tell me, Elliott, you ever been to the Pacific Coast of Colombia?" Haden said calmly. "And not British Columbia for skiing and shopping, but the real deal—the jungles of Western Colombia. Figure a rich guy like you would have traveled there once or twice. You know, one of those showy vacations that demonstrate to your friends how desperately you care about the welfare of the planet."

Galbert shook his head and blinked several times.

"They've got these toads," said Haden. "Well, actually they are frogs." Then as if talking to himself, he said "never was sure the difference between toads and frogs. Anyway, they're called Poison Dart Frogs."

Galbert's head began to nod, and the gun drifted down as if it was too heavy for him to hold.

"See, these frogs excrete this toxin through their skin.

The natives would dip their arrows in the toxin and use it for hunting. They'd use blow guns. Hence, the poison dart. Fascinating stuff, don't you agree?"

Galbert stumbled toward the desk and tried to hold himself upright. He teetered for a moment, then collapsed to the floor.

"The toxin is two thousand times more powerful than a cobra bite. And fast acting. It causes instant paralysis. Early Europeans never knew what hit them."

Galbert tried to speak, but only wheezing came through, nothing resembling words.

"Imagine those Spanish conquistadors feeling invincible with their fancy gunpowder rifles. Then they get taken out by a nearly naked guy with a blow gun." Haden snorted and chuckled. "Well, guess you can, can't you. But don't worry. You're not going to die from the Poison Dart Frog."

Galbert lay on the floor, his eyes wide open, but unable to move. Haden stepped around the desk. "You just couldn't wait, could you? I had everything fixed and you got scared." Galbert's eyes stared straight ahead, and he lay on the floor. "I know you can hear me. That's one of the more frightening aspects of the toxin. Aside from being quick, it disables the muscular system, but doesn't impact the brain stem, so even though you can't move, you observe everything. Just can't do anything about it, my friend."

Haden moved behind the desk and stood over Galbert's body while he pulled on latex gloves. "Great thing about the poison dart frog toxin is that it stays potent for up to two years, provided the toxin comes from a frog in the wild. See, domesticated frogs lose their toxicity. The frogs are on the extinction list. Illegal to bring into the States. But those diplomatic pouches come in handy. One of the benefits of government work. One of the few."

He reached down and picked up the gun where Galbert had dropped it. He positioned the glock in Galbert's hand and held it to the man's temple. It was like moving a person in his sleep. The muscles provided no resistance. Galbert's eyes stared straight up. Haden could sense the fear in them.

This guy doesn't deserve all the money he's made. It's not about being smart or even being connected. Many people had that, including him. These guys start something like Center Tech, and demand pushes their stock into the stratosphere. The money becomes a scorecard rather than a means to survival. Now it was Haden's time to take his share.

"Goodbye, Mr. Galbert. It was a pleasure doing business with you." He jammed Galbert's index finger against the trigger. The gunshot shattered the soothing crackle of the fireplace. Haden blasted a hole through the man's head, spraying blood and brain matter on the fine Egyptian rug and stained walnut bookcases.

Haden stepped away, grabbed the two envelopes, and exited through the front door. With his split, plus what he'd skimmed off the prior installments, he'd be able to buy that cottage just outside Port Saint Lucie and spend his days fishing. His desires were simple. He would live the good life, thanks to the government and the boys in the Posse.

His was the only car operating on Centrillion Drive as he steered onto Georgetown Pike and headed home.

Haden dug his cell phone from his pocket and dialed. The line engaged. "Yeah, all done. Shit, that stuff is scary good. Went just like you said." He looked over at the envelope and stash of cash. "Where are you?" He listened for several seconds. "Yes, I've got the cash. See you in thirty. You bring the scotch, my friend."

Chapter 53

Locals called it Water Street. It was one of the ways Georgetown residents rejected being part of greater DC. To DC natives or geo-tracking navigation devices, it was K Street, an extension of the power boulevard that cut through downtown DC and provided homes for the prestigious lobbying shops that shaped the country's laws.

Water Street dead ended just below the Francis Scott Key Bridge that joined Georgetown and Rosslyn, VA. Haden parked just shy of the bridge and continued on foot. The stench of human waste and puddles of God knows what caused him to pick up the pace and step lightly.

Beyond the archway suspending Key Bridge, the Georgetown Boathouse sat in darkened silence. It was a private club of canoeing enthusiasts and rowing fanatics. At this hour no light was emitted, and there was no evidence of human habitation. The chain link fence was shut, but an unclasped padlock dangled from the chain. He slid the fence open and stepped through, pulling it back closed. A long wooden dock ran along the edge of the Potomac and provided easy access for members from the warehouse storage building where pleasure boats and racing sculls hung on racks like sleeping bats in a cave.

"Hey," Haden whispered as he stepped onto the dock.

"Back here."

Haden stepped around the rack of upside down canoes and followed the voice.

The man sat on a faded folding chair. The yellow stripes had long since given up their pride and turned dusty white. A matching chair was across from him. He raised a plastic glass of scotch, a bottle of Johnny Walker Blue at his feet.

"What took you so long?" the man asked.

Looks like he's already downed several glasses, Haden thought. "No problem, my friend. All is well." He sat, placed the manila envelope on the floor, and leaned forward pouring a glass. "Tell you what, that frog juice is some wicked shit." He shrugged and leaned like a man falling sideways. His friend laughed. "No kidding," Haden said, pausing. "It was like ten seconds and the guy was done."

"Good to hear," the man said. "Most of those international trips I make, I only bring back some form of bionic flu bug. Glad to know that at least one trip was successful."

His friend held his glass forward in toast. "Here's to us." He tipped his head back and downed his glass. Haden laughed and followed suit. The man leaned forward and picked up the envelope.

Haden coughed and wheezed.

"The Blue stuff is the best, isn't it?" he said.

Haden nodded, coughing again, his fist over his mouth.

The man set his glass on the ground.

Haden looked up, his eyes terror-stricken. He couldn't breathe. He couldn't draw any air in. The empty glass fell from his hand. He slumped forward and fell onto the concrete.

~

"Shit is some good stuff, I tell ya."

Haden made gasping sounds. No movement. He lay curled on the ground.

"One thing to be hit by a poison dart. Another thing entirely to drink the stuff, my friend," he said mockingly.

He grabbed Haden's ankles and began to drag him to the front of the boathouse. The paralyzed man's eyes were wide and unblinking. If he had control of any facial muscles, terror would be written all over his face.

"You do good work. I'm impressed." He slid the body to the edge of the dock and scanned his surroundings. Sensing the coast was clear, he stepped near Haden's torso and leaned over to look into his eyes. "I know you're in there." He chuckled. "You've been valuable. But now your usefulness has run out. Swim with the fishes, my friend."

He hooked his foot under Haden's shoulder and rolled him off the dock. The body submerged like timber rolling into the river. It splashed brackish Potomac water onto the wooden flooring. His head bobbed up, eyes pleading, but with the aid of gravity his face slipped under, causing an eruption of bubbles as the water replaced the oxygen in his lungs.

He looked out over the waters toward Virginia. The river moved in quiet splendor, carrying the winter run off from the Appalachian Mountains down to the Chesapeake Bay. Just as quietly, Haden's body would drift, mouth open and eyes of disbelief.

He walked back into the boat house and kicked over the glasses, as well as the Johnny Walker bottle. Donning a handkerchief, he picked up the base of the bottle and spilled the remainder on the floor. "So sad," he muttered. "Such a waste of good scotch." He walked out, dropping the bottle and the handkerchief into the Potomac.

Chapter 54

April 19

Kate was still drowsy as the door creaked opened. Wolfe and another man entered. She could hear a car engine running outside the motel door. Sleep evaded her, but fatigue and fear had ground her down. Darkness illuminated by muted lights poured through the doorway. It had to be the middle of the night.

Wolfe untied the rope while the other man scoped the room, looking apparently for anything they might leave behind. Her hands remained bound behind her and mouth gagged, she glared at the two men as though ready to jump them if given chance. At least the roping around her legs hadn't been deemed necessary.

"Let's go," said Wolfe, and he lifted her into a standing position with one hand. She was pushed forward out of the door where a van sat idling. It had been backed up to the motel, and the rear doors were open. She could see what appeared to be two figures in the cargo area of the van, but couldn't make them out.

Wolfe led her with a firm grip around her bicep. She balked. If she got into the van, she was sure she'd never be seen again. Wolfe urged her forward, but she skittered sideways away from the vehicle. She scanned to the right. Two lone cars were parked in front of rooms, but not a soul was up at this time. Even the lights of the motel office at the entrance were out. Her scream was muffled by the duct tape. She tensed and tried to break free.

His hand around her arm was like a vise grip. As she tried to move away, he threw her toward the van. Her knee slammed into the bumper. She fell hard, face-first onto something solid on the floor of the van. Dazed, she slid down. Anything to avoid the van. In a flash she was airborne. Wolfe had her by the arm and one hand gripped the back of her belt. He tossed her into the van like a sack of fertilizer.

"Dumb bitch," he mumbled.

The doors slammed shut behind her.

Chapter 55

Willie Jackson pushed away from the dock and jumped behind the steering wheel. Smoke filled with oily residue separated from the water where the Evinrudes idled impatiently. He pushed the throttle forward enough to engage the props and the boat's nose veered in response.

This back bay cove off the Potomac was glasslike in the early morning mist. Bell Haven, on the waterfront, was seven miles from his destination. He had plenty of time. He didn't want to appear rushed.

He notched the throttle forward. The engines gurgled, and water slapped the bow of the boat as it accelerated slightly. A *no wake* rule was in effect once inside the Memorial Bridge. Willie was well away from that point, but he was mindful of the time and didn't want to draw any attention to himself.

The white bow and hull gleamed as the sun ate away the fog off the surface of the river. A green tarp covered the rear half of the vessel and a similar covering enclosed the special U-shaped hull ahead of the windshield. The driver's compartment and a small space across the aisle were the only open spaces on the craft.

Willie looked at his watch and grinned. Easy does it, he thought. I'm gonna be right on time.

~

Kate's stomach was twisted and nauseous. For an hour and a half they wandered through the blackness. She was tossed and turned as the van lumbered on. From her position in the back of the van, she could see little, an occasional sign, a light post, mostly darkened tree limbs. It was a barren rural area, but beyond that she knew nothing.

Wolfe was riding shotgun. The one Wolfe had called Kevin was driving, and a bespectacled wimp rode in back with them. She couldn't make out their occasional conversation. Some laughter and sharp remarks, but she could hear nothing of substance.

It had to be a painter's van. Small wooden ladders and drop cloths framed the front of the van where the wimp sat. The smell of gasoline or varnish of some kind added to her nausea.

She'd reached out behind her as far as her shoulders and bound wrists would allow, searching for anything she could use as a weapon, an old screwdriver, a sharp nail, anything. There was nothing. Kate scrubbed her binding against the frame of the van, hoping to cut the rope, but several minutes of activity resulted in nothing.

Judge Caprelli, tied and gagged like her, sat slumped against the other wall of the van. She could see he was defeated. He had the eyes of an old hound beaten with a garden hose. He could barely hold her glance.

A man of his intellect, who had authored hundreds of opinions that shaped the legal world as they knew it, sat helpless, accepting his fate, whatever that might be. Though they'd never met, she'd studied his opinions in law school. Everyone had. His leanings were farther right than Kate's, but she had to respect the man. Law school seemed ages past and that esteemed justice was a different man than the one across from her now.

With the frequent bumps and jostling, she tried to

maneuver into a position where she could see where they were going. It did little good. The wimp, the one they called Gibson, would give her his fiercest stare as if to say, don't make me use this gun.

What kind of punk needs a gun to watch two bound prisoners?

His glare was counterfeit. Behind it she could sense his real emotion. It was fear. This gig was bigger than he could handle. She'd seen that look in opposing counsel's eyes just before the jury came back with a guilty verdict. He was outmatched. He was in over his head.

The sun lit the sky ahead of them. They were traveling east. In itself that didn't do her much good. She didn't know where they had started; she didn't know where they were going.

Somehow the sun gave her hope. She blinked hard. She would not cry. She wouldn't give them the satisfaction. They controlled the game. They made all the rules. Despite all that, she wouldn't let them win. Even if winning was merely breaking her spirit, they would not win.

~

The Diamond Rio eased forward, then stopped. Cars shifted ahead, and the rig shimmied forward only to stop again. Moving an eighteen wheeler across the 14th Street Bridge was never an easy task. In the late morning rush hour it was even more unpredictable. Frank Jackson danced on the clutch and brake maneuvering like an elephant among flitting gazelles. He downshifted and hit the gas, causing the engine to roar out its approval.

An airliner's engines screamed above him. Halfway across the 14th Street Bridge was in the landing and takeoff pattern of Reagan National Airport. In fact, this was the bridge the Air Florida Flight 90 crashed into after takeoff, its wings caked in ice.

Frank looked out to the right, and a half dozen boats were bobbing along. He didn't focus on them as he wanted to get into position on the bridge. He knew his brother Willie was out there, but wasn't sure if that was one of the boats he'd spotted.

Focus, he told himself. Willie has his mission, I have mine. Need to make sure mine goes perfectly. If mine goes perfectly, Wolfe's will go perfectly, and that was what they'd spent the past months planning. He was in the home stretch now.

He checked his watch. Five minutes behind where he needed to be. He put on his signal to shift to the left lane. It was a promise rather than a request. Frank would let a car or two clear, but when he wanted that lane, he would take it.

He tugged the wheel to the left and let loose with a blast on the horn. A silver Prius was hanging off his front bumper, apparently afraid to achieve the speed limit. More than two car lengths were open ahead of it, but the hybrid held position. The blast from the horn caused the driver to swerve. After another long blast, the driver got the hint and shot forward. Frank filled the far left lane. From here he would flow onto 14th Street and toward downtown DC.

The Jefferson Memorial glistened off to the left. Crowds had already jammed along the reflecting pool, merging among the late stage cherry blossoms.

Ahead, the Holocaust Museum approached on his left, and the white frame of the Willard Hotel beckoned in the distance. His rig wasn't made for this kind of morning commute traffic, and cars zipped in and out of lanes ahead of him. He pulled to a stop at the light on Independence Avenue.

Another block and he'd make the first of two left turns. He'd run this mission four weekday mornings in the past two weeks, so he knew where he had to be at the appropriate time. A glance at his watch told him he was two minutes behind schedule. He'd made up ground. Running the route for practice in a pickup truck was a totally different experience, but he'd logged enough time in big rigs to accurately estimate the difference.

Making up the final two minutes would be a piece of cake. He might take off a car's front grill or a few bumpers, but that was the price. From here on out, he wasn't stopping for anything. An illegal turn wasn't out of the cards either. From this point forward, no one could stop his mission—not cops, park police, and certainly not a bunch of damn commuters and pedestrians.

No, he was in control both of time and mission, exactly the way Wolfe laid it out.

~

The road had straightened, and Kate felt them pick up speed. She knew they were out of the back roads and onto a heavily traveled highway. Road sounds from other vehicles surrounded her. This gave her encouragement. Perhaps she could cause an accident, throw herself against the driver and cause a collision. She might die in the process, fly through the windshield and be crushed. If defeating them meant she had to risk her life like those on Flight 93 on September 11th, that was the price she would gladly pay.

From her vantage point, she could see the portions of the green highway signs as they flashed overhead. Not enough information to read them, but they were traffic signs. They were on a major roadway.

Kate slowly tucked her legs under her little by little to avoid detection by Gibson. A quick glance at Caprelli caught his eyes lighting up. Was it surprise or encouragement? She paused and waited. In one move, she'd be able to get to her feet and spring toward the driver.

She had to wait for Gibson to turn forward more fully. She closed her eyes to slits. Maybe he'll think I'm nodding off, let his guard down a little. The three of them were talking; mostly Wolfe was talking and the other two were agreeing. Gibson shifted from his seat on one of the folded stepladders.

Ever so slowly, Kate tucked her legs. She waited, trying to keep her breathing steady. Be patient. Be patient.

Now!

She leapt toward the front of the van. Her feet slid on the metal flooring, and she fell against the ladder hitting the back of Wolfe's seat. Gibson yelled. She pulled her feet up and used her shoulder to elevate her upper body to spring again. She would shoot between the two seats and into the driver.

As she rose and jumped again, she was met with an elbow to the face. She crumpled at Gibson's feet. Wolfe turned, still holding his elbow out. Pain seared her nose and eye socket where he'd smashed her face. Kevin shot a glance back at the commotion, then swerved back to focus on the road ahead of him.

"Jesus, Gibson, watch 'em, will you? The fuck are you doing back there?" Wolfe yelled.

Gibson grabbed Kate by her hair and tugged her backward. He jammed the gun in her face and pushed her into the back half of the van.

"Watch it, bitch," Gibson said, shoving her. She fell backward onto the floor of the van. Blood ran from her nose, and her eyes were blurred and watery. "Don't fuck with me. I'll take you out right here."

"Just keep a watch, will ya?" said Wolfe. "No more drama. Girl and an old man; figured you could handle that."

248

After nearly an hour their pace slowed. They were entering a congested area. She could see the tops of taller buildings, apartment buildings, but from this angle nothing was familiar. The van veered left, then right, eventually slowing to a crawl. As the vehicle eased into a right turn, she spotted a sculpture of a man riding a bull.

They were crossing the Memorial Bridge into DC. Ahead would be the Lincoln Memorial.

Kevin gestured toward the left, and Wolfe leaned over to get a look. Then Kevin motioned to the other side of the bridge. They sure as hell weren't sightseeing, she knew.

The van was crawling toward downtown DC.

Chapter 56

Hunched over a computer terminal with bleary eyes, Nick tried to make some sense of everything. Two hours of restless tossing on a conference room bench down the hall had done little for his mental firepower. The computer was flanked on either side by manila folders of research and data.

How could I let Kate out of my sight? How stupid. The one person he cared about, the one person who meant something to him, and he abandoned her. He replayed the events over and over. *Why did I do that? How could I do that?*

Nick could envision dozens of alternative strategies, all of them ones he didn't take. His past was like a funnel drawing him down one exit. He couldn't stop the spin. He couldn't slow the force of the flow. The ending was always tragedy, always with Kate captured and him responsible. His idiocy had put Kate in grave danger. He had to get her back safely. That was the only option.

Nick knew working through the night wasn't the answer, but at least it prevented him from playing the recording of his failure over and over again.

Javier looked no better than Nick felt.

The urgency had become frantic. Nearly all of their fellow agents worked through the night. If Nick was right, and he was willing to bet everything that he was, today was the day. At two am the FBI had alerted the DC Police,

Maryland, and Virginia State Patrol, Secret Service, Park Service, and national security offices that something was imminent. They just didn't know what or where.

Wolfe could be anywhere, but their information led them to believe he was still in the Mid-Atlantic region. It was agreed that nothing would be said publicly. Though debated vigorously with Jannsen and Schaeffer, the decision was not to unnecessarily alarm the public. Hell, they couldn't even describe what to look for or what may be suspicious.

Nick rose wearily and shuffled the seventeen steps to the coffee pot to refill his paper cup. He passed Javier, who was staring at computer print outs of various threat assessments they had made.

"You get another *Redemption Day is Coming* note from Jenkins?" Nick asked.

"Yep. Guy's a broken record."

What was their plan? Nick was confident that they would kill Caprelli. That much fit the plan, but how and where? And even if they knew, how in the world could they do to stop it? Of course, that assumed that Caprelli was still alive.

It was possible that they would kill him on video, then send the tape out as they had done with Caprelli's prior videos.

Nick collapsed back into his chair and tapped the keyboard. "Center of the Star." *It made no sense.*

Nick, along with forty FBI analysts, had searched every entry on all the search engines. They'd tried decoding the phrase and overlaying it on other phrases. They'd attempted to create a web address from it. Nothing.

"We got another video," Scottie shouted, causing thirty or so heads to snap in his direction. Nick jumped upright in his seat and spun around.

"Caprelli again," Scottie said, pulling his headphones down to hang around his neck.

"Where'd it come from?" Nick asked.

Scottie clicked several keys. "Sovereign Free Press had it first."

"Son of a bitch," Javier said. "We should have brought that dirtbag in yesterday."

"For what?" Nick asked. "We had nothing on him."

"Because I don't like the creep. That's good enough for me. What's on the video?"

"Looks like the same old common law bullshit as the other two," Scottie said. "But they released a verdict today."

"What verdict?" Nick shouted.

"Kate was found guilty."

"Of what?"

"Treason and obstruction of justice."

"Jesus," Javier mumbled. "What the hell does that mean?"

"Posse Comitatus jail?" Wesley asked, a bit too casually, drawing angry stares.

"Was Kate on the video?" Nick asked.

"No, just Caprelli. Head shot like the others," Scottie said. "Read the verdict."

Nick leaned forward. "Did Caprelli say anything about a sentence?"

"Just the same old center of the star crap," Scottie said. "It's getting old."

Nick closed his eyes and leaned back against the headrest. This was all his fault. He should have never left Kate alone.

Javier and Wesley rushed to Scottie's computer, and the video was cued up.

Nick rubbed his eyes. He turned in his chair to look at the video. As an afterthought he reached for his coffee cup. As he stood, the coffee cup fell from his grip, hit the side of his keyboard and splashed coffee on the files next to his machine.

"Shit."

He quickly scooped up the files and brushed them to get the coffee off. Several documents fell from one folder and slid across the floor, underneath the desk.

Nick knelt to pick them up, careful to avoid the coffee that dripped from the desk's edge. He picked up a handful of documents and froze.

He stared at the document and blinked several times. Then he shouted.

"I know what it means. I know what Center of the Star is."

Chapter 57

The Diamond Rio crept past the Jefferson Memorial as it merged onto Interstate 395 southbound toward Virginia. Cars dodged around the lumbering sled like fleas around day old-mayonnaise. Frank Jackson shifted and floored the rig. He needed speed.

The good news was the road ahead was clear. No vehicle directly ahead of him prevented his acceleration. Cars passed him and kept on moving. They'll make it home safe tonight, he thought. Those behind him, not so lucky. He keyed the mic on his CB. "On the ramp. Tango out."

The black box squawked back. "Copy that, Tango. Godspeed, Brother."

He merged from the right lane onto the highway. A steady stream of cars poured past him on the left as they streamed off 14th Street. Ahead, more cars merged in from the left as Interstate 395 turned to cross the 14th Street Bridge. In a few hours much of the traffic on 395 southbound would come from the House and Senate office buildings just a short mile away. At this time of day traffic was relatively light.

Frank jammed another gear and slammed the accelerator down. Smoke poured from the exhaust pipe like a bear roaring as it approached its prey. He stole a glance in the left rear view. It didn't matter what was there; he was going to make his move whether traffic objected or not.

The .45 that had killed Richenbacher was tucked into the back of his jeans. The other weapon lay on the console behind the gear shift. He tugged on the lever and powered up another gear. Now he was rolling. He took the other weapon and slid it under his t-shirt, tucking it in front to secure it. An additional cartridge was on the console, and he slid that into his front jeans pocket, just to be sure.

He was approaching the necessary speed, but he still ratcheted it up. A quick glimpse of the dashboard clock said 11:29—game time.

~

The van circled the block in heavy congestion. It seemed to Kate that they just kept going around in circles. What were they looking for? They were downtown, in the business area. What were they doing?

After what seemed like half a dozen times around the block, Wolfe motioned to the right. The van stopped and reversed. They were parallel parking. Wolfe turned and stared at his two prisoners. Gibson was getting antsy. He stretched his legs out and shook his arms as if relieving the tension. Kevin kept a watch in the side view mirrors. They sat motionless. He and Wolfe spoke, but she couldn't make out the conversation.

Wolfe checked his watch and turned back toward Kate. "Won't be long now, sweetheart."

~

Willie Jackson puttered west on the Potomac. Moving slowly aroused less suspicion. He was eager to open up the engines and get to the destination. He had to be calm. Timing was everything. He wondered where Frank was as he slipped under the Fourteenth Street Bridge.

The steady drone and clip clop of tires hitting seams in the bridge served to drown out every other sense. The three spans of bridge that comprised the Fourteenth Street corridor across the Potomac were preceded by a metro line bridge that crossed the river from the Pentagon toward L'Enfant Plaza.

The Washington Memorial stood firm on the National Mall to his right. The hump back bridge on GW Parkway and the LBJ Memorial were to his left. Tourists flooded the area to his right. The area to his left was vacant, as if the monuments on the Virginia side didn't count.

People stood and took photographs of those damn pink trees, he noted. Pictures with family, pictures with monuments in the background, close ups of cherry blossom buds; they did it all in moronic tribute to nature. It was as if the opening of these buds somehow ushered forth the spring season.

I've got something that will open the season, he thought. And it's right here in the boat. I'm going to open something more than some paper thin pink flower. I'm going to open a can of whoop ass on this town. That's for damn sure.

Ahead, the glistening white form of Memorial Bridge lay. A constant stream of cars poured back and forth from the Lincoln Memorial to Arlington Cemetery.

Willie looked up and watched the silver bottom of an airliner pass directly overhead as it approached National Airport for landing. The sound trailed the plane by a second, then came roaring toward him like a wave. His mind drifted back to his days on the USS Harry Truman in the Suez Canal. They were just begging those damn Iranians to make a false move. Times were simple then. The roar meant power; the carrier's presence meant the ability to back it up.

He gazed toward the south and thought of the souls laid

to rest on the hill at Arlington. *They were warriors. They were like me. They gave their lives for freedom.* Willie would do the same, although he didn't plan to give his life at this time. He would strike a cause for freedom. At some point he may face that life or death situation. If they could accomplish this goal, he was ready for that moment. The men and women in Arlington were heroes.

Willie would be a hero, too. It was just a matter of moments away.

~

Mitch drove carefully, ensuring that he didn't exceed the speed limit, but not too slowly to draw attention. For someone used to driving fast, it was taxing. Kirby Mients sat in the passenger seat and stared out the window. This was like the moment before walking onto the field for the Super Bowl. Each person knew his assignment, each had come to grips with the consequences, and each visualized the task ahead of them.

"Can you drive a little faster?" Kirby said, staring at his watch.

Mitch looked over, then back at the road. This was the mountain man's equivalent of *fuck you.*

"My part's the only one where I can't control the timing. I gotta be in position, 'cause I don't know how it's going down. Understand?"

Mitch looked over again, then back.

"Don't be a prick. Just pick it up a little. Jesus, Mitch, my grandma just flew by us on a bicycle."

Looking straight ahead, Mitch finally spoke. "Got plenty of time." He shifted lanes and prepared to exit off Jefferson Davis Highway near what was called Crystal City. "We practiced the past three days."

Crystal City was a series of high rise office buildings and apartments perched between Interstate 395 and National Airport. Because of the height restriction on buildings in DC, the structures looked like Manhattan from the distance. But it wasn't the buildings that were of interest to Kirby. It was the metro system. Crystal City station was two stops from the Pentagon and three stops from the first metro entry point in the District of Columbia.

Kirby leaned forward. "Look, your part is easy. A piece of cake. Mine's gotta have timing."

Mitch ignored him and turned left through the underpass of the highway. Kirby gave up, crossing his arms and leaning back, staring out the side at the shoe shops, restaurants, and offices along Crystal Drive. He crossed his ankle over his knee. Below him was a backpack.

Mitch drove another block, then pulled to the side of the road. Kirby huffed, opened the door, and jumped out, swinging the backpack over his shoulder.

"Godspeed, Brother," Mitch said.

Kirby slammed the door.

~

Mitch drove west on K Street. This was home to the most expensive lobbyists in the country. At Connecticut Avenue, vehicles veered to the right. To the left, the road led to the OEOB, the old executive office building, a gray ornate structure that sat next to its more famous and shiny white neighbor. He checked his watch.

He did have the easiest part of the plan. Well, Tommy did, but Mitch only had to drop off Kirby. Other than that, his was a piece of cake.

At Twenty-first Street, K Street dropped into a tunnel below Washington Circle. Beyond that, the road

Redemption Day

dropped and separated as the extension of K Street ran under Whitehurst Freeway. Mitch was five blocks from his destination.

Whitehurst Freeway was constructed in the mid-sixties as a temporary structure. It was built on twelve by twelve steel beams that by appearance were clearly insufficient for a permanently supported roadway. It was a rhinoceros on ballerina's legs.

The rhinoceros dies today, he thought. Commuters had gotten too accustomed to the convenience of skirting Georgetown and getting onto the Key Bridge into Virginia or onto Canal Road which took drivers to Maryland. Whitehurst Freeway was a standing tribute to the fact that DC served Virginia and Maryland and that it would never be the other way around.

Like so often happened with the US government, a one-time initiative quickly became institutionalized. The Whitehurst was a symbol of Washington, Mitch thought. Well intentioned, underfunded, and temporary, that through special interest need had become permanent and immovable. Until today.

Mitch pulled through four way stop signs to the point where traffic dropped off. K Street reached a dead end under Key Bridge. Beyond that, it became a hiker biker trail which followed the C&O canal. Tommy had already parked on the north side of the street. Mitch parked across from him on the south side.

They were in position and had plenty of time.

Chapter 58

Frank glanced in the side view mirror, then swung all his strength into turning the wheel hard left. The rig jerked and groaned as the front wheels skidded. Cars around the Rio slammed on the brakes and swerved to avoid the sliding tanker.

Frank held on as the truck tipped to the right and the left side separated from the earth. The fuel in the tanker sloshed precisely as physics required and shifted the weight up and against the direction of the turn. The truck creaked and teetered, then crashed onto its side, sliding along the pavement.

The Diamond Rio lay like a downed dinosaur, steam pouring out of the grinding, coughing diesel engine. The scent of burnt rubber and diesel fuel filled Frank's nostrils. The rig blocked three of the four lanes of the bridge. Frank quickly pulled himself up. With one foot on the console and the other wedged into the steering wheel, he pushed the driver's door open and scampered on top of the toppled rig.

Behind him, the traffic was already snarled. Several cars had collided as they veered to avoid the truck. Drivers were in a stunned haze as they stood on their brakes and surveyed the scene.

Frank knelt and reached down for the grab iron, then lowered himself and dropped to the ground. He backed away onto the quickly emptying bridge behind him. He nodded approvingly, noting how he'd almost perfectly blocked the middle lanes of the bridge.

Coming back to their senses, drivers started to move around both sides of the downed eighteen-wheeler. Frank moved to his right as a black SUV started to inch around the front of the rig.

He raised his gun and fired twice into the windshield. The driver jerked as if hit by a bolt of electricity and slumped to the side. Two plumes of red mist puffed in the vehicle, splashing the driver's window. The SUV lurched to the left and slammed into the concrete dividing wall.

Frank smiled. The angle with which the SUV hit the dividing wall almost perfectly blocked following traffic. He skipped toward his left as a Honda sped past behind the downed tanker. A pickup truck also slid through. Frank stepped into the line of traffic and held out his open palm. A man in a Toyota sedan hit the brakes and stopped just short of Frank. The driver had a white dress shirt and black tie.

Fucking bureaucrat, Frank thought. He lifted the gun and fired two shots through the windshield, then fired two into the engine block of the Toyota. Steam spewed out of the engine. The bureaucrat slumped forward over the steering wheel.

With the outbound bridge effectively sealed, Frank ran a few yards away from the truck. The pavement from that point to Virginia was wide open, no vehicles were left. Above the noise of the diesel coughing and sputtering, Frank could hear the horns honking, and impatient travelers hoped to move the blockage by imposing their frustration on the surroundings. Childish, Frank thought.

Frank slipped another clip into the .45. He raised the gun and fired three times into the tanker portion of the truck. Fuel started to shoot from the silver tanker, and the ground was soon colored by the leaking petroleum. Frank backed up several strides and pulled the other weapon from behind his back.

Frank loaded it and aimed. A pop was followed by a hissing sound. He had a large and ever growing target, so his chances of success were fairly good. The projectile fired forward, spinning like a high school rocket experiment. Even in the daylight the trailing fire from the load burned Frank's eyes.

The flare spun, landed on the concrete, and shot into the side of the downed tanker. It lodged under the rounded edge of the tanker and continued to spew fire. It was the perfect weapon. A split second later the fire ignited the spilled fuel. There was a flash as the air above the pooled petroleum caught fire, then a split second later, the tanker exploded, sending a mushroom cloud of flames shooting into the sky. Frank's mouth hung open as we looked skyward at the erupting smoke and flames. He tossed the flare gun over the side and began running toward the Virginia side of the 14th Street Bridge.

~

Time crept slowly. Kate's heart pounded, and her breathing was shallow. No one had spoken for several minutes. Gibson had his elbows on the headrests, but frequently turned to see if Kate had moved. From behind the wheel Kevin gestured in front of them as if playing tour guide. They spoke in hushed tones. Wolfe checked his watch again.

Then they all tensed at once. Kevin's mouth was agape, and he stared at Wolfe. Wolfe just stared straight ahead. Seconds passed, then Kate noticed it. Through the windshield she spotted the mushroom cloud as it rose far in the distance.

They'd blown up something. Was it the White House? The Pentagon? It was hard to tell how far away it was, but from their direction, it could be either target or a federal building. Hell, it could be Reagan Airport for that matter.

Wolfe snapped open his cell phone. As he spoke, he gave a thumbs up to the other two, then slapped the phone closed and checked his watch again.

He slowly turned and with one hand lifted one of the stepladders and moved it away from the back of his seat. Beneath it was a drop cloth covering something. He smiled at Kate as he peeled away the drop cloth to reveal a coil of rope with a pair of nooses in the center.

~

Kirby walked past the cookie shops and shoe repair closets that lined the underground shopping area of Crystal City. This subterranean area divided the Metro station from the automobile traffic and office buildings above. Thousands of commuters trekked these halls as they hustled to get to work in the morning or get home in time to have a life at night.

He glanced at his watch and picked up the pace. He tugged his backpack tighter to his shoulder and double timed it toward the metro. With his fare card in hand, he swiped it through the electronic turnstile and jumped onto the escalator down toward the westbound trains. A sign read that the next westbound metro train would arrive in four minutes. He was okay on time as long as there were no delays on the system.

A young couple was embraced and kissing fifteen feet up the station platform. Kirby stared at them. Their lives are going to change and they don't even know it, thought Kirby. Depending upon where they were going, their lives might end in a few minutes. He stared at them. They were oblivious of him. They were just oblivious.

Moments later the metro train pulled into the station. Kyle scanned the cars as they went by. He wanted a train car that was light on passengers, preferably where he could get one of the bench seats in the middle of the train. He quick stepped back toward the front of the train. He got onto the car just steps behind the two lovebirds.

He excused himself between the people milling around the doorways. They held onto railings and overhead straps, but didn't move away from the doors, as if getting easy access on and off the train was preferred to actually sitting down and riding. Kirby slipped into one of the middle bench seats. He slid his backpack onto the floor and pushed it under the seat in front of him. Then he gazed out the window.

The next stop was the Pentagon City metro station, then they would travel to the Pentagon station. In the reflection of the window he could see the boy and girl. They were giving their lips a break. The male lovebird gripped the support railing and held her hands in the other. Their eyes were locked.

Kirby scanned the other folks in the rail car. No one was giving the slightest attention to the two lovers. In fact, no one was giving attention to anyone on the car. Each was absorbed in a book, newspaper, smart phone, or simply gazing at the floor or the advertisements along the rail car walls. Kirby smirked. These losers won't even see it coming, so self-absorbed that they don't have the slightest idea what was going on in this country. Idiots were so self-indulgent that they didn't realize that the country and their freedom were being stolen right in front of their eyes. Bunch of sheep.

Kirby watched the lights in the tunnel flash by, then

light flooded the train. The train slowed, then burst into the Pentagon City metro station. About half a dozen people got on, a similar number got off. The lovers decided to sit and took a bench across from Kyle. Probably going to hump her right here on the metro seat, he thought. The doors slid shut, and the train jerked back into motion.

His heart sped up, and he took a deep breath. The time was now. He checked his watch. He would be a little early, but close enough. Sweat beaded on his temples, and he swiped them off. His chest tightened, and he tried to expand it with multiple breaths.

Again the rhythm of the flashing lights was interrupted when they decelerated and entered the Pentagon metro station. Aside from being below the headquarters of the most powerful military power ever to walk the earth, the Pentagon metro station was also one of the largest commuter congregations on the system.

Commuter buses by the dozens moved through the expansive parking lot, dropping passengers who escalated down to the underground metro station. Hundreds of others walked from the nearby apartment buildings perched across Interstate 395. A child care center reserved for Pentagon employees was a few hundred yards away from where the buses dropped their human cargo.

Kirby pulled himself up, just as the metro engineer called out "yellow line train, next stop L'Enfant Plaza."

As designed, the yellow line of the metro tunneled toward the Potomac, then rose above ground and over the river into DC. The elevated rail line ran parallel with the 14th Street Bridge. Kirby slipped between standing commuters just as the doors were shutting.

The couple sitting across from him gave each other an odd glance. Kirby moved quickly toward the door. The man yelled, "Hey, buddy, you left your backpack."

The backpack contained a product with a fancy name—pentaerythritol tetranitrate.

In the explosives community it was called PETN. In the service they just called it "boom." A small amount was all that was needed for a nice explosion. PETN was easy to disguise, easy to carry, and simple to detonate. For a closed area explosion like this, PETN would be more than enough.

Kirby pressed the sequence on his cell phone and ran for the escalator to get out of the Pentagon. He wasn't running because of fear; he ran to avoid the blowback. If everything went according to plan, the explosive would go off before the train exited the tunnel and was above ground.

Chapter 59

Knocking down bridges was like knocking out a heavy weight champ. The admonition of champion boxer Smokin' Joe Frazier's was elementary, if you kill the body, the head will die. Some fights had to be won that way. Therefore, they attacked the body. Mitch and Tommy had the easiest of the tasks.

Whitehurst Highway was like the legendary bumble bee. No one had told the bumble bee that it was physically impossible for it to fly. For the Whitehurst, it wasn't impossible that it was a bridge, but beyond plausible that it remained standing for so many years, spans of concrete supported by toothpick-like H beams.

With their vehicles in the appropriate spaces, Tommy and Kevin got out and walked west about forty yards to the next set of H-beams. Keeping an eye on the street and sidewalk, they tracked one on either side of K Street. The street below Whitehurst started to narrow as it neared the entrance where it ran into the hiker/biker trail just below the Chesapeake and Ohio canal.

Mitch watched the street for vehicles, namely police, while Tommy unhooked two backpacks and strapped one around the base of the two nearest H-beams. Once it was in place, he stepped into the street and kept a look out while Mitch did the same for the beams on his side of the street. As with everything, they had practiced, then practiced more.

Wolfe was a stickler for perfection. Even after several perfect runs of this simple task, Wolfe would have them do it again. In his scenarios cops mysteriously appeared; how would they react? A goodie-two shoes citizen might intervene; what would they do then?

As they had practiced so often, nothing happened. No cops, no citizen protectors, nothing. There wasn't even any traffic to speak of. They moved eastward back toward their vehicles. Rather than getting back inside, they continued past them. Ten feet beyond the vehicles, Tommy removed his cell phone and hit a number. Mitch crossed the street back to the north. "All in position," Tommy said into the cell, then he slapped it shut.

Mitch removed a cell from his pocket. He didn't place a call, but he sent a message with it nonetheless. The wireless signal pulsed outward and triggered the countdown on the four bombs they had just placed. Mitch nodded at Tommy, and they continued eastward. They tried to maintain a leisurely pace, but they couldn't help themselves. When they turned left up Wisconsin Avenue, they slowed to a normal walk. Leaning forward and trudging up the hill, they glanced at one another. A sheepish grin spread across Tommy's face.

Half a block farther up, they heard the explosion. They stopped and turned back to look. Over the Ritz Carlton smokestack a mushroom cloud was forming. It wasn't their bombs; too far east. This was on the Roosevelt Bridge. They looked at one another, then heard three pops in sequence, this time below them and to the right. Tommy turned and moved up the street. Mitch paused for a minute.

It wasn't much of an explosion. Almost like loud firecrackers. Something better happen Mitch thought, or Wolfe's going to kick some ass when he finds out.

Seconds later a creaking sound came from the direction of K Street. It started off slowly, then progressively got louder.

A seismic crack came next. Mitch's mouth dropped open as a section of Whitehurst collapsed onto K Street.

Like dominoes, sections of the bridge kept falling with concrete dust sending up puffs of surrender. A black sedan tumbled into the intersection of Wisconsin and K below him. "Shit, that came from the bridge," Mitch muttered.

Mitch turned, and Tommy was nearly to M Street. He hoofed up the hill after him. "Jesus, we did it. We really freaking did it."

~

Willie had the toughest job of all, unless killing people came easily. The Roosevelt Bridge was built in the nineteen sixties. Willie had studied it. The bridge was a project in honor of its namesake to get the country back to work. Six lanes across, the bridge connected the west side of DC with Rosslyn, VA. Millions of commuters pounded over this bridge to get to the western reaches of DC from Virginia commuter communities.

Roosevelt Bridge was built to last. Six feet of solid concrete filled the joined pillar. It had been driven deep into the muck below the Potomac. Five feet above the water line, each of the concrete bulkheads divided into four narrow pillars that actually held up the roadway.

Willie puttered toward the bridge like an unarmed serf approaching Windsor Castle. In his twenty-eight foot powerboat, he was no match for the steel and concrete monstrosity that was Roosevelt Bridge.

But the serf came with ammunition. The boat carried a cocktail of fifty four bags of ammonium nitrate fertilizer, seventy-five gallons of liquid nitro methane and a crate of Torex. It was half of what McVeigh used on the Murrah Building. It might not knock down the Roosevelt Bridge, but, according to Kirby, it would certainly disable it.

Willie dove into the brackish waters of the Potomac. His boat was securely tied to the base of the bridge span. After pulling himself from the muck onto Roosevelt Island, he removed his cell phone from a zip lock bag, punched a code, and watched his handiwork.

Chapter 60

In a split second phone lines lit up and activity hit a frenzied pace. Winters and Wesley were typing furiously. Scottie was cursing at his computer to run faster. Phones were slammed, dialed, and slammed again.

"I need a map," Nick yelled.

"Damn city's coming apart," Wesley shouted.

Javier pointed at Scottie. "Get a map up on the wall."

Quickly the wall was illuminated, and Scottie pounded the keys. "Of what?"

"DC," Nick shouted.

"Somebody rolled a tanker truck on the 14th Street Bridge and it exploded," Wesley said.

"Perfect timing for a damned accident," Winters said.

"No accident," shouted Wesley. "We got shots fired. The whole outbound bridge is shut off, backing up into the city. What the hell's going on?"

"Jesus," Scottie screamed. "The Roosevelt Bridge is closed. Some kind of explosion."

"Metro's down," Maggie said. "Explosion just outside the Pentagon Station. Underground."

"What the hell's going on?" screamed Javier.

"Whitehurst is down," Scottie said.

"What do you mean, down?" Wesley asked.

"I mean down on the fucking ground. Damn thing got blown up."

"What in God's name—What are they doing? Cutting off the city?" Javier asked.

"More like locking us in the city," Nick said.

A map of the DC metro area filled the wall. Nick jumped around an empty chair getting to the map. "Zoom in."

"What are we looking for?" Javier said.

"The star."

Wesley and Winters moved closer, and the four of them stared. It suddenly seemed quiet, just hearts pounding. Winters gestured toward the map. "Here's a star. Ground zero." He pointed to the north end of the Ellipse, just below the White House.

Nick shook his head.

"What about the capital?" Wesley said. "All the streets form a spoke around it."

"Same with the White House," Javier added.

"No," Nick said as he stepped closer.

"Here," shouted Winters. "The Washington Monument, the center of the National Mall. How could you get more center than that?"

"Not enough traffic," Nick mumbled.

"What are we looking for?" asked Javier.

"Busy intersection," said Nick. "We need a high traffic area."

"Why?" asked Wesley. "What difference does it make?"

"It's the posse code. Part of the blue book." He handed Javier the Posse Blue Book and leaned in closer. "Scottie, zoom in on the downtown area."

"It's the code," Nick said. "The center of the star was right on the cover of the Blue Book all the time."

Javier held up the book studying it. "More of a pamphlet than a book. Where's it say center of the star?"

"The star is a badge. A sheriff's badge," Nick said,

272

keeping his eyes glued to the map. "Look at what's in the center of the badge."

"Looks like a book, a sword, and a noose."

"The book is the Bible. The sword represents individual self-determination, and the noose is for cleansing."

"Cleansing?"

"Eliminating violators of the code. Killing."

The map resized on the wall and came into focus. "Bill Gale, one of the founders of the posse movement," Nick said. "He commanded it?"

"Commanded what?" Javier said.

"Government officials who disobeyed the Constitution. He ordered that they be removed by the posse to a populated intersection of the town and at high noon to be hung there by the neck until dead, to be an example for those who subverted the law."

"They're going to hang the justice on a city street?"

"And Kate, too, if we can't stop them."

"That's crazy," Winters mumbled.

Nick traced his finger on the map, then tapped. "There." He pointed to the downtown area. "There's the star," he said, outlining it with his finger. "DuPont Circle, Logan Circle, Mount Vernon Square, Washington Circle, and the White House. The center is…"

"Sixteenth and K Street," shouted Wesley.

Nick spun and raced toward the door.

"How can you be sure?" Javier asked.

"I can't, but it's almost noon. It's our best shot." He was out of the room.

"Get DC Police to that intersection," Javier shouted as he followed Nick.

"The city's gridlocked," Scottie said. "Nothing's moving out there."

"Call for back up," Javier shouted over his shoulder. "I

need officers, with fire power."

"Let's go," said Wesley.

~

Wolfe turned to the geek and said, "Get 'em ready." Geek handed his gun to Wolfe, then stood crouching in the van. In one hand he had two burlap sacks. He quickly fitted the first over Caprelli's head. Poor man, he's totally given up, Kate thought.

Geek turned toward her, and she flung her legs out, catching him behind the knee. Geek fell backward, propping himself on the far wall of the van.

He crouched and turned toward her. He leaned in with his knee and pinned her between the side and floor of the van. She struggled for breath as he compressed her chest with the full force of his weight.

She threw her head side to side and forward to avoid the burlap sack. In the end, it was no use.

She was shrouded in darkness. Breathing became more labored as he shifted his position, but kept pressure on her, smashing her into the corner of the van. Next, the sack tightened around her neck. It was snug, but not impacting her breathing as much as the knee across her midsection.

Then with one further compression, he was off her. He'd bounced one last time to get upright. She inhaled deeply, filling her chest. The bag smelled like dirt and mothballs, but her lungs welcomed the air from any source.

From the shuffling, she knew that a noose was going around Caprelli's neck as well. The van rocked slightly, and Wolfe's voice called out, "Let's go." The driver and passenger doors opened and shut. All too predictably, the back doors of the van swung open.

Kate could hear the clambering of the stepladders

being shuffled out of the van. Caprelli went with little resistance. She knew to fight every opportunity. Whatever they wanted her to do was exactly the last thing she was going to do. There had to be several dozen people outside; someone would do something. They wouldn't just let two people hang in downtown DC.

The noose tightened around her neck and pulled her toward the back of the van. She resisted, even though her airway was cut off.

"She won't get out," she heard the geek say.

Wolfe's voice was annoyed, "The hell she won't."

~

Nick barreled out of the FBI building and sprinted up E Street toward 14th. Anger fueled him, anger at himself. How could he have not seen it? How could he have let Kate down? Wesley trailed him by half a block. The streets were jammed with traffic and horns honked in a futile attempt to move through unmovable spaces. With the 14th Street Bridge down, along with Whitehurst Freeway and the Roosevelt Bridge, gridlock was imminent throughout downtown DC. There were just too many vehicles and not enough exits. It was like a burning theater with several of the exits chained shut.

With the Metro explosion, there was nowhere for people to go. Like rats in a cage, if the cage was big enough, they would just leave one another alone. Make the space smaller and add more rats and soon they would be attacking one another over food, territory, or simply fear for survival.

Unarmed and with no plan, Nick ran headlong into a situation he couldn't comprehend.

~

The noose constricted suddenly. She lay choking, but not cooperating. Kate was suddenly dragged out of the van, and she fell to the pavement like a box of rocks. The rope pulled her upward. To breathe, she had to loosen the pull on the rope. Soon she was upright and being pulled toward the sidewalk.

She missed the step onto the sidewalk and fell, banging her head against a parking meter. The blow dazed her, but didn't erase the nightmare unfolding. Kate tried to scream, but the tape on her mouth and the pressure from the noose prevented sound from exiting the burlap sack.

The rope yanked her upward and away from the van. She could hear horns honking and people yelling, but couldn't make out the sounds.

Then Wolfe's voice boomed through. "Just a demonstration, folks. Nothing to worry about. Just a protest demonstration."

Kate felt herself being tugged along the sidewalk. People in DC were jaded enough and had witnessed enough demonstrations in this city that Wolfe's assurance would be enough to convince people to look the other way and keep moving. The walk paused for a moment and the noose loosened. She inhaled as deeply as she could, trying to get her lungs as much air as possible. She knew the respite wouldn't last.

~

Nick blew through 15th Street barely slowing. He skipped through the standing traffic, horns blowing and frustrated drivers making threatening gestures at their competitors for the next six inches of street to open up.

Wesley caught Nick as they turned down Pennsylvania Avenue. It was the part of Pennsylvania that had been closed to traffic for over twenty years. The little stretch that was the most famous address in the country, 1600 Pennsylvania, was on their left.

"Nick." Wesley heaved. "Hold up, man."

Nick looked over, but continued on, angling toward Lafayette Park.

"Seriously, hold up." He reached out and got a grip on Nick's bicep, slowing him to a steady walk. "We need backup. We can't go barging in."

Nick turned and ran on. He didn't trust Wesley. In fact, Wesley might be in on all this. Someone sure as hell was. Trying to slow him down just would give them more time to execute their plan. He had no idea what he was running toward, but he needed to get to 16th and K as fast as humanly possible.

That, and pray that Kate and Caprelli actually were at 16th and K.

~

After several seconds Kate was yanked hard from above. What was she supposed to do? Levitate? She got on her tip toes, but couldn't loosen the rope nor lessen the tension. She was pushed from behind. She kicked something and heard it slide across the pavement. It sounded like wood against pavement.

She was pushed from behind again. It was the stepladder. She stepped up one rung, balancing precariously with her hands bound. The pressure continued. Soon she was up three steps, but the pressure didn't stop. She reached her foot up and out, but couldn't find another step. She was at the top of the stepladder.

The rope kept tightening. She was on her tip toes, but couldn't get any air in her lungs.

She could feel the veins in her neck pulsing, and her face turned cold and painful. She couldn't balance here much longer as she was becoming light-headed. In a matter of seconds, she knew she would pass out and fall from the stepladder.

Wolfe's voice boomed through the din of traffic and horns honking. "Silvio Caprelli and Kathryn Buchanan, having been found in breach of your duties as federal officers, having violated the Constitution of the United States, and having been found guilty by a jury of the common law court of the United States, you are both to be punished by hanging until dead. The sentence carried out by the Posse Comitatus. Long live the Posse Comitatus."

The geek and Kevin's voices resounded, "Long live the Posse Comitatus."

The stepladder wobbled under Kate. She tried to keep it balanced. Suddenly her feet were scrambling in the air, searching for anything. Her head snapped face up, all air was cut off, and she started spinning.

Lights flashed in her mind, despite the darkness of the sack. Blue, red, and white lights exploded behind her tightly closed eyelids. She thought she heard voices. Shrieking and pounding sounds filled her ears. Was that Nick, yelling, "Kate?"

Then she could feel nothing at all.

Chapter 61

Washington, DC was a cacophony of honking horns and angry voices. All of downtown was gridlocked. Cars snuck into the intersection hoping that the path ahead would open, but it never did. Crosstown traffic was locked down in a tangle of stationary vehicles.

With the bridges down, there was no way to get toward Virginia, and those cars hoping to go north toward Maryland were crimped in the same blockage. Too many vehicles, too few open roads. Rage and resignation were the only emotions visible.

Pedestrians crossed, seeking a path to an open metro station or a nonexistent bus. The metro trains were all shut down, and stations were filled with disillusioned passengers. The buses were swarmed by smaller vehicles and not moving at all.

Nick sprinted up Wisconsin toward K Street. From the distance he witnessed what he feared most. Two bodies extended by ropes from a light post. Passersby gazed in wonderment and moved on, jaded by the thousands of protests staged annually in the city.

It was a city where nothing was real and, if it looked real, it was certainly not.

Nick shot sideways between two vehicles and jumped over the hood of another car where no space allowed him to slither through.

"Kate!" he screamed.

Two bodies hanging; it was obvious who each was.

For another the choice to save a sitting Supreme Court Justice or a young able-bodied woman might be a conflict. For Nick, there was no decision to make. He jumped onto the sidewalk, grabbed Kate around the knees, and lifted her. "Kate, I'm here. I'm here."

She slumped backwards. He was able to take the pressure off the noose, but she started sliding sideways, and he couldn't control her. He wasn't able to get all the pressure off her, but he held her up as high as he could. "Help! Get some help over here!"

Wesley was behind him, grabbing the justice with one arm and pulling his revolver. He gestured toward the rope. "Get that untied."

As he said it, a slug shattered the window of a green sedan parked behind them. They both turned. Wesley was trying to leverage the justice up higher and searched the crowd for the gunman. The sidewalk was jammed with pedestrians, some looking slack jawed at the group, others moving with heads down trying to find an avenue home.

Wesley aimed left and right searching for the gunman. He locked on a target and fired, just as a slug shattered his forehead, spraying blood and brain matter onto the green car's trunk and back windshield. He tumbled backward onto the sidewalk. His gun clattered off the curb into the street. Shrill screams rang out, and pedestrians ran in a scrambled mass. Several people dove onto the ground behind any form of cover.

"Help," Nick shouted. He was winded by the run and struggled to get his voice. "Get that untied." Another bullet slammed into the vehicle behind him. They were sitting ducks for these gunmen.

To his right he saw Javier fire three times. The crowd

scattered and one body fell. The geek with the glasses went down. He could see Wolfe and another man duck into an office building. Two uniformed police officers rushed forward. One grabbed the justice; the other tried to lift Kate, but Nick shook him off. Javier and another man furiously worked on the rope that was anchored to a fire hydrant.

It only took seconds, but it seemed like hours. The rope slackened, and Kate fell onto Nick's shoulders. He quickly placed her on the ground and tore the noose off. He ripped the sack off her head and peeled away the duct tape over her mouth.

Her face had a bluish tint. Blood smears covered her chin and cheek. Red marks formed a necklace around her throat. He gently slapped her cheek. "Kate, Kate."

Javier was down on one knee next to him, keeping an eye toward the building where Wolfe escaped.

They shared a quick glance. Nick opened her mouth and cleared it. He shifted to get down and give her mouth to mouth. As he pinned her nose shut, her eyes fluttered and she coughed. "Kate, it's Nick. I'm here."

Her eyes opened slightly, but moved as though awakening, no sign of recognition. Her chest heaved in shuddering gasps. He tapped her face with an open palm and she coughed more. "Get a doctor over here!" Javier shouted.

One of the officers knelt next to Nick. Kate's eyes focused and she mouthed, *Nick.*

"Yes, I'm here."

She glanced around and tried to lift her head. After a wince she laid back down.

Javier had checked on Wesley and shook his head solemnly. "I'm going after Wolfe," he said.

"I can't leave her," said Nick.

Javier nodded and stood, surveying the area and waving for approaching police officers.

Kate's eyes locked on Nick. "Go," her lips said. Barely a sound was emitted. Then in a raspy voice a louder "Go" came out. The officer patted him on the back.

"EMT is on the way," said the officer. He looked around. "They're on foot. Will be here as soon as they can."

Nick looked back to Kate. Javier turned toward them. "Go," she said, then a fit of coughing consumed her.

Nick jumped up. The other officer was talking to Caprelli, but he couldn't tell if there was a response. He rushed to Wesley's gun, turned with Javier, and they ran to the building.

Chapter 62

Javier braced himself against a concrete pillar, Nick just behind him. Four feet separated the pillar from the revolving door. Floor to ceiling glass gave them a view of the interior. Javier peered around the pillar. "Let's go."

The entry space was vacant. A marble partition served as a check-in desk. Two elevator banks framed the narrow space behind the partition. An exit door lay straight ahead at the far end. Javier pulled the glass door open adjacent to the revolving door and kept low. He held his gun in both hands. After two steps he waved Nick to the right. If someone was behind the partition, they needed to be separated to create a crossfire.

Javier held his hand palm-out to stop Nick's advance, then he moved slowly toward the marble partition. He lifted his head quickly and dropped back down low. He lowered his gun and motioned to Nick. He rushed around to the open side of the structure.

A security guard's feet stuck out. As Nick neared, he saw blood splatter on the desk. The headshot had ripped most of his forehead open, and grey matter ran onto the floor. Javier checked for a pulse, but it was a foregone conclusion.

He stood and waved two more officers into the building. "How many floors?" Nick asked.

"Don't know. Probably eight," said Javier.

The four of them stood looking at the lights on the elevator.

"Okay, we're going to go top to bottom. Nick, you stay here. You," Javier said, motioning to one of the police officers, "call for back up and go around to the alley. Keep the back exit covered. You," he said to the other officer, "come with me."

He punched the elevator call button. The other officer spun through the revolving door and raced down the sidewalk out of sight. The ring of the elevator brought them to heightened awareness, and they drew weapons from the side as the door split open.

They entered the elevator, and Nick was left alone.

He backed to the front of the marble and steadied his weapon on the structure. From here, he could hit anyone coming off the elevators. All was quiet; too quiet. He turned and saw that medics had arrived and were swarming around Kate and the Justice. He waited.

None of the elevators moved. It would take several minutes for Javier to clear the floors. It wasn't a huge building, but every office and cubicle would have to be cleared—too much time.

Nick stared at the red illuminated exit sign. They could have gone straightaway out the back of the building, and they'd be wasting their time shaking down this building.

He slowly stepped toward the exit. A twelve inch square window provided the only view through the door. Nick cautiously straightened and looked through the window just as the elevator to his right chimed. He slipped to the floor and aimed toward the opening.

His hand shook as the door slid open. No one got off. Someone could be hiding out of his vision, so he froze, locked on the opening.

Nothing moved.

He rose to one knee and crept quietly toward the opening. Positioned low, he led with his gun in both hands.

Nick extended his left foot over and quickly slid sideways on his right knee. An empty elevator stared back at him.

Nick took two deep breaths and stood. He wiped his forehead and scanned the area. Footsteps pounded behind the exit door. Nick jumped back against the wall, flattening himself so that he couldn't be seen from the exit window.

The footsteps kept going. It couldn't be Javier, but it could be just a building occupant. The last thing he needed to do was blow away an innocent secretary.

He twisted the knob and slowly cracked the door open. He saw a blue jean clad leg and work boot circle out of vision down the stairwell. Nick slipped through the door.

Footsteps made a shushing sound as they descended. The stairwell dropped ten steps to a landing, then jackknifed another ten steps to the basement floor. A metal door emptied into the alley. An alarm was attached to it, so they hadn't opted for that.

Nick stepped as quietly as possible down the stairs. At the landing he poked his head around. No one was at the bottom of the stairs. The room extended to his right.

He listened.

The HVAC drowned out anything discernable. He crouched and took two more steps down. No sound. Two more steps, then it was the point of no return. His legs would be visible.

He got low and tried to get a glimpse of the room. Boxes were stacked along the right wall. Two gray metal doors lay ahead; one open, one closed. Nick reached the concrete floor and backed to his left behind the stair railing.

There were shuffling sounds behind the open door. Nick gripped his gun and took aim on the doorway.

"Wolfe," he shouted.

Just as the sound left his lips a gunshot cracked to his side. He spun and saw an arm extend from behind one of the stacks of boxes. A second shot clanged off the railing.

Nick fired at the edge of the boxes, then twice more through the corner of the boxes, chest high. Landers's body tumbled to the floor; his gun skittered across the concrete floor.

Wolfe stood in the open doorway, his hands empty. Nick slipped to one knee and aimed for the chest.

"Mr. James," he said calmly. "I guess it comes down to this." He started to step forward, moving toward Landers's gun in the middle of the floor.

"Stop right there. You can't get out of here. Officers are coming."

"I know about you, Mr. James. I know about your father." His lip curled up on the left side, and he snorted a blast of air through his nostrils. Despite Nick's armed advantage, Wolfe treated him like an errant teenager.

"I mean it, don't move." The gun shook despite being held in both of his hands. He had experience with firearms, but aiming at paper bull's eyes couldn't prepare one for holding a weapon on a human target.

Where was Javier? What the hell are they doing?

"He was part of the Posse," Wolfe said. He shifted his weight, taking him closer to the gun on the floor. "You knew that. But your father was weak. I think you're like him. I think you're weak." He took another step.

"Stop."

"I didn't know your father, but I've known many men like him. See, your father wanted to believe in the Posse. There's a difference between wanting to believe and actually believing." He chuckled as if to himself. "Your father didn't believe. That's why he put a gun in his mouth. It's what cowards do."

Where the hell was back up? They had to have heard the shots. Nick stood, the gun trained on Wolfe's chest. He tried to take a deep breath.

Stay calm. Help's on the way. Just a little longer.

Wolfe kept his eyes locked on Nick and slipped forward a half step. He was only four feet from the gun.

"Step back."

Shoot him. In the leg. Just wound him.

"You can't stop Redemption Day. You can't stop the Posse."

"I don't have to stop the Posse," Nick said. "I only have to stop you. That's all that matters."

"Going to play the hero, is that it? You weren't meant for that role." Wolfe lips curled at the edges. "That Buchanan gal. She your girlfriend?"

Don't let him provoke you. Don't give him that advantage.

"You're a dead man," Nick said.

This brought laughter from Wolfe, a whole-hearted belly laugh that was more play acting than real. "Funny. That's what she said."

Nick stood motionless, his jaw clenched tightly, his teeth grinding. "She was right."

Kill him. No one will know.

Wolfe took another half step. "I understand she was your girlfriend." His lips flared, and he continued chuckling. "She was mine, too. She's a sweet one, for a Fed."

"I mean it. You move a muscle and I'll blow you away." Nick flexed his fingers, never removing his right index from the trigger. His pressure on the gun had whitened his fingers, and he loosened them to get circulation back. He squeezed and released. His heart hammered in his chest. His breathing had become so shallow, his body cried out for a deep breath. The thought of Wolfe touching Kate sickened him. He squeezed the gun as if he would crush it.

Shoot him, just shoot him now.

Wolfe huffed. His eyes moved from Landers's gun to Nick. "No, you won't. You know why?" Wolfe laughed. "You know why? Cause you're a coward, just like your old man. A punk coward."

Pull the trigger.

Wolfe began falling. The move disoriented Nick. But it wasn't a fall; it was a drop and roll. In one motion Wolfe swept up the gun and was on one knee, lifting the gun into a dead aim on Nick.

Dad? Dad? What do I...

Two shots exploded before his brain connected with his trigger finger. Fear and anger swept over all other thoughts and emotions. In that moment there was no reaction; there was only action. There was no thinking. There was no analysis; just two pieces of lead flying in one direction.

The first bullet ripped through Wolfe's chest, the second splattered his neck just below the jaw line. Wolfe's body violently flipped backward, arms flailing until they slapped in unison against the grey concrete.

Nick kept pulling the trigger. The chamber was empty. The gun just clicked in his hands.

Chapter 63

The hallway was familiar. Nick's heels clicked on the marble floor and echoed in a predictable fashion. Four days had passed since the shooting. The city was in shambles. Repairs to the bridges would take months.

The Metro took part of the yellow line out of service, but was still able to operate detouring from that route. Six people died in the explosion and twenty-seven more were gravely injured. Fear had caused ridership to drop. Many were still in a state of shock and couldn't make it to work. Businesses remained shuttered, too hard for workers to get into the city. The wound was still too fresh.

He turned the hallway. Most offices were empty. He paused as he passed his old doorway. The office was vacant, but the trappings of the new occupant covered the desk and walls; pictures of family, smiling wife, happiness frozen in time, all the things Nick didn't have. He lingered a moment, then entered the adjoining office.

"Hi, Dave."

"Nick. How you doing? Good to see you," said Winters, lighting up like a rescued puppy. He rose and shook Nick's hand.

Nick sat across from the desk and crossed an ankle over his knee.

"What have you heard on Caprelli?" Winters asked.

"Still in the hospital."

"Hell of a deal."

"Word is he's going to retire."

"Can't blame the guy," said Winters. "And Kate? How's she?"

"Pretty bruised up, and voice is pretty raspy, but docs say she's going to recover; well, physically anyway."

"Jesus, that must have been traumatic," Winters said, shaking his head.

"She's going to need some time off. She's had round the clock protection. Not sure who else might be associated with Wolfe looking to extract some revenge."

"Can't be too careful," Winters said, nodding.

"Nope, not when Wolfe's insider is still running loose."

"What do you mean?" Winters looked more surprised than he sounded.

"Wolfe clearly had a mole on the task force. It took a while, but I figured out who it was."

"Oh yeah, who?"

Nick had practiced this interaction in his head over the past days. He nodded toward his friend. "You."

"Me?" Winters said, laughing. "That's crazy."

"No, it's not crazy." Nick sat forward in his chair. "The thing I couldn't figure out was where the money came from."

Winters leaned back and considered Nick with cautious eyes. His fingers were steepled in front of his mouth.

"Then it made sense," Nick said. "Someone had worked a deal with Elliott Galbert."

"Didn't Wesley work for Center Tech at one time?" Winters said quickly.

"Yeah, that made good sense," said Nick, nodding slightly. "A check of Galbert's bank records showed big withdrawals from several banks, plus several visits to his safe deposit box. Guy was smart enough to keep the cash movements small enough to stay under the Patriot Act levels, but because he had several accounts, he amassed a good amount of cash in a short period of time. Of course, we can't find the cash, so figure that's how the posse was funded."

Nick stood and walked behind the chair, leaning his arms on the wooden back. "Course the money trail went cold. We're sure that Wolfe got a good share, but the insider surely skimmed. That's the Washington way."

"What did you find in Wesley's bank records?" Winters asked, a quizzical look on his face.

"Nothing unusual. But it wasn't Wesley."

"I think you're wrong," Winters said, his eyes narrowing. "I wondered about Wesley from the get go. He never trusted you. I backed you all along. He had problems with Kate. Hell, he had problems with everyone. That's your man, Nick. Not me."

Nick looked up at the ceiling as if contemplating his next line. "Someone provided the phone number to my Blackberry and my personal email account."

"Nick your info was already in the records. Anyone could access that." Then Winters' voice took an edgy, defensive tone. "I didn't, but even if I did, so what? You were under an APB. I have a responsibility to assist with law enforcement. That's my story, and it's rock solid."

"Someone broke in to steal my gun. When I left to have drinks with the gang, you knew I'd be occupied for a while. You knew I had just bought that Smith and Wesson. You or someone went to my house and broke in to locate it. Problem was, the door was left ajar. That wasn't smart. You knew where I lived, Dave."

"That's crazy. Why would I do that? Anybody in the government could get your address. That's no state secret."

"So you could have Brager killed and pin it on me."

"Nick. I think you need to calm down." Winters leaned forward on his desk and gave his best imitation of a compassionate friend. "I don't know if you're stressed out. I could sure understand if you were, but you're making no sense at all. If there was a mole, it was Wesley."

"Nope. Here's how it went down. First, I lost my job at Center Tech because of the DOMTER cancellation—"

"Many people did, Nick. It wasn't just you."

"Yeah, but I knew more about the Posse. That's why Sheriff Brager reached out to me, if he even did."

"What do you mean?"

"Well, he certainly was directed to me. I had no recollection of the guy, and it's odd that he would meet with someone who no longer worked in the agency versus someone in Homeland. Odd, don't you think?"

Winters just shrugged.

"What bothered me was that someone was using information from my bracelet to track my whereabouts when Kate was kidnapped. They weren't interested in kidnapping me, though. They planned to kill me. That's why it didn't matter that I was wearing a tracking bracelet. They just had to catch me."

"Everything points to Wesley," Winters said defiantly.

"You know what was strange, Dave? I was there when Wesley was shot. There was no recognition in his eye, not a glimmer. Also, if he was in on it, they would make sure and kill me, not Wesley."

"I heard Wesley fired one round, but missed. Might have missed on purpose and was shot by accident."

"Well, I can understand him missing," Nick said. "Wolfe and the other guys were hiding among a crowd. Plus, he was struggling to hold the judge up to release the pressure from the noose. Kinda difficult to get a clean shot."

"Nick," he said, making a tsk tsk sound. "I think you need some help. You're coming apart from the stress."

"You were unhelpful in the investigation. Maybe you

just suck at your job, but that's suspicious," Nick said. "You knew what was coming down and when."

The two stared across the desk. A clock on the wall clicked out the seconds. Only heartbeats and blood pulsing made any movement.

"You were cashing out. Take that federal pension, a nice bonus from the Posse, and scoot out of town. Problem is, you haven't deposited the cash anywhere yet, so there's a good chance it's at your place. That's why a team is planning to execute a search warrant as we speak. Wolfe and his pals were killed, so we can't ask them. Galbert was killed. Pretty convenient for whoever was in on it."

"Galbert committed suicide," Winters said, defiantly.

"Did he? Sure looked like a suicide. His widow is no dummy though. Gals who marry to that level can afford good advice. See, suicide might interfere with big insurance payments, so she ordered an autopsy. Funny thing; why would you do an autopsy on a guy with a bullet hole in his head, but they did. Found a strange trace in his blood work."

Nick glanced at a piece of paper he'd pulled from his shirt pocket. "Batrachotoxin, an alkaloid poison. Medical guys had to do some research, apparently don't come across this stuff every day. Turns out it comes from frogs. See, Galbert had some cuts on his fingers—not unusual by themselves, but they figured out that's how the toxin got into Galbert's system. Pretty fast-acting, I understand. Anyway, you'll be happy to know the widow's gonna get all that insurance money because it was a homicide, not a suicide."

"So what?"

"You know the mistake the killer made?"

Winters shrugged.

"He forgot what business Galbert was in."

"What do you mean?"

"Galbert was a tech guy. Hell, the name's right in his business. How could the killer be so stupid?"

"Yeah? And?" Winters said.

"Well turns out the house was wired for video, including his study," Nick said. "His wife coughed up that news after the autopsy came back. Her lawyer was pretty smart. See, if it was a suicide, they didn't want visual evidence. They risked blowing the insurance claim. Lawyer knew it was better for him and the grieving widow not to know what was on the tapes, so they kept them sequestered. When the autopsy showed poisoning, they had what they needed, so she released them to the authorities. You'll be interested in the video."

Winters tried to laugh it off. "What? You've come to tell me I'm on the video killing Galbert?"

"Not exactly."

"So what exactly is your point?"

"Guy named Haden Maxwell was on the video. Know him?"

"Yeah, he works downstairs. Why don't you go interview him?"

"You know I can't." He let the statement hang in the air. "DC Police found a floater off Hains Point yesterday afternoon. Turns out it was Mr. Maxwell."

Winters shrugged.

"You have to admit it's kind of suspicious. So they ran a tox screen on the guy. Guess what?" He shook the piece of paper in the air. "Batrachotoxin. What are the chances?"

"And this affects me, how?"

"Well, you'd better hope you ditched all that toxin or else the search team is going to tie this together."

"You've got nothing. This is all bullshit," Winters said, waving him off.

"Oh, yeah, found Maxwell's car." Nick paused. "Underneath Key Bridge. Guy must have been in a hurry. He forgot to take his cell phone."

A look of shock shot through Winters like he'd been tagged with a cattle prod.

"Guy calls you just before he dies of poison or drowning or whatever. Had quite a few phone conversations with you."

"We work together. Everyone knows that. So I talked to the guy. Doesn't prove I killed him or knew anything. This is all bullshit. Nothing you've got implicates me."

"Well, maybe not directly, but a bunch of people are in ten by ten cells based on circumstantial evidence. Maybe you've heard."

"This is a bunch of crap. I don't have to listen to this." Winters started to stand.

Ignoring him, Nick continued. "You know what sealed the deal?"

Winters sat back down. "No, please tell me what sealed the deal," he said sarcastically.

"Wolfe knew about my dad."

"So what?"

"Nobody knew that." Nick paused, then continued. "You're the only person I ever told about that. About what really happened."

"Anyone could have done research, looked through old newspapers, microfiche, checked records."

"If they did, they wouldn't learn what Wolfe knew. See in the obits in small towns, they don't use the word *suicide*, so all anyone would know was that he died and was buried."

"What about law enforcement records?"

"Well, if someone knew to look, and again, little reason for someone to do that, but if they did get those, it said nothing about the Posse, just reported a distraught farmer with a fatal, self-inflicted gunshot wound while his property was being auctioned off. I've seen the records, Dave. Nothing about Bill Gale and the Posse. So how did Wolfe learn that?" Nick paused, letting it sink in. "He learned it from you, Dave. There's no other explanation."

"You're insane."

"It's over, Dave. I just want to know why."

Winters rubbed his face with both hands. The clock ticked like a terminal disease, consistent and inevitable. "Fucking town. I watch scumbags like Galbert get rich taking money from the government. I'm just a damn pawn in the system. Sure job's secure, but I'll never get rich, never have what those guys have. Damn three percent raise. Big deal. I'm just months out from retirement. Everyone steals in this town."

"You're supposed to protect people. That's the job. You ended up killing them."

"You'll never prove it. Never."

Javier Lozano walked through the door flanked by two uniformed officers. "Dave Winters, you're under arrest for the murder of Haden Maxwell and conspiracy to murder Elliott Galbert. I'm sure some snappy prosecutor will think up a bunch more, but that's the opener for now."

One officer stepped forward and cuffed Winters.

"You have the right to an attorney. If you cannot afford an attorney—"

Nick stepped out of the room and walked down the hall. At his former door he rested his forehead against the cool metal doorframe. He could hear the Miranda warning in the background.

It had been a little over a week since he last stood here. His job, his office, his career, had all been shattered, like the family pictures on his former desk. Everything was a signal that he didn't belong here anymore. The problem was, he didn't know where he belonged.

Nick and his former mentor locked eyes as he was escorted down the hallway. No words were necessary. The officers marched their man down the marble walkway. After several seconds Nick turned and looked at them.

"Oh, Dave, one other thing."

Winters turned back. "Yeah?"

"You sucked at your job."

Winters stopped in his tracks, looking back down the hall. One of the officers tugged him back around, and they continued walking.

Javier slapped Nick on the shoulder. "Thanks, man."

Nick nodded, swallowing hard.

"Stick around. I'll buy you a beer tonight. Hell, I'll buy you dinner."

"Nah, can't," Nick said, walking away.

"Why not? Where are you going?"

"I've got a meeting."

Chapter 64

Nick slung his backpack over his shoulder and elbowed the car door shut. With a beep and flash of the headlights, the car said goodbye. He walked through the parking garage as lightning ripped through the sky. Sheets of rain cascaded on the pavement in a series of bursts. Rain was good. Something had to clear away the grime from the city. If only something could wash away the recent memories. Nick's only shelter was the open air walkway from the parking garage to Sibley Memorial Hospital.

Out of habit he cranked through his Blackberry while waiting for the elevator—nothing, not even junk mail. He slogged forward, lighting up the button labeled four.

The intercom called out doctor's names and indecipherable codes. The female voice droned over the loudspeaker. She could have been reading sports scores or astrology predictions for all he cared. Nick rode the elevator lost in thought, just plain lost.

When the elevator doors parted, Nick spotted Kate sitting at the end of the hallway, head down and arms wrapped around her shoulders. She was like a small child waiting to be scolded.

The terror of the past week had shredded the confidence and self-assurance that was her persona. Her hair was perfectly styled and pinned back, such a contrast to the moments on K Street several days before.

She was out of her hospital gown and dressed in street clothes. This was progress. A turquoise turtleneck covered the marks around her neck. No one would notice. But her injuries weren't apparent by any visual means.

She smiled, but her eyes seemed emotionally disconnected from her lips. A reddish tone, noticeable perhaps only to Nick, shone around her eyes.

Euphemistically, Kate was being "monitored." It was a neutral grey word for medical holds on otherwise healthy patients. It was a head fake on insurance companies that allowed traumatized patients to receive therapy without being admitted for a mental ailment. After today's session her doctor would make a recommendation on discharge.

He hugged her tightly and kissed her temple. "Told you I wouldn't be late."

She shivered and nuzzled her chin over his shoulder.

"Don't leave me," she said.

Nick didn't know if she meant right now, today, or forever. It didn't matter. The only thing that mattered was this moment.

He wrapped his arm over her shoulders, and they moved back toward the elevators. "We've got a little time. Do you want some coffee?"

Her head bobbed slightly, her hand over her mouth.

His Blackberry chimed. He pulled it out with his right hand and opened the message for a few seconds.

"What is it?" She asked.

"Nothing."

They walked along in silence. She tucked the side of her face deeper into him.

As they passed a trash container, Nick reached out and dropped the Blackberry into it. Kate was oblivious to the maneuver and didn't notice it rustle papers, magazines, and coffee cups before it clanged hitting bottom.

They continued down the hallway slowly. One step at a time, one second, one minute, one hour, one day; the healing would come. Time and space was all they needed.

He shifted his backpack and smiled down at Kate. Her eyes said *I'm trying.* That was all he needed to see.

The flame was still there; weak and dim, but still glimmering. It needed tender kindling and a soft breeze, but it would come back. The fire would return, of that he was sure.

At the bottom of the garbage can, the light on the Blackberry dimmed. It would reside there until the battery ran out and would be forever buried in refuse and discarded possessions of an immediate gratification society.

The final message on the Blackberry read, "Redemption Day is Coming."

Author's Note

All of the historical statements and events attributed to the Posse Comitatus in the book are true, with two exceptions. The Foster's Glen shooting is fictional; however, it is modeled after many actual incidents between law enforcement personnel and the Posse Comitatus and Sovereign member groups. Second, although there are biblical references throughout much of the Posse's beliefs, the incorporation of the cities of refuge concept from the Book of Joshua is my own creation.

If you would like to learn more about the history of the Posse Comitatus and Sovereign Groups, Daniel Levitas' *The Terrorist Next Door, The Militia Movement and the Radical Right,* is a must read. Levitas' research is deep, and the writing is compelling.

As a young attorney in Nebraska, I had interactions with Posse members. Thankfully, my interactions did not involve violence, but were tragic nonetheless. Many farmers lost everything in the farm crisis of the 1980's. Desperate to hold onto their farms, reputation, pride, and dignity, several turned to the Posse Comitatus, which led them to believe they could avoid foreclosure by using the Posse's distortion of the law.

It was a hoax, but like a dying patient hoping for a miracle drug, some bought into the righteous indignation that certain members of the Posse sold. And sell it they did. The more enterprising members of the group hawked legal documents and seminars as if they were weight loss programs on late night TV.

Desperate people do desperate things, and the Posse preyed on that.

The Posse engendered an indignation that fueled violence. Statistics show that membership in militia groups is rapidly rising and, although I am not an alarmist by nature, the country must guard itself against terrorist attacks from within with the same vigilance as those originating outside the country.

Acknowledgement

I am deeply grateful to every reader. Your choice to spend a portion of your life holding the words I crafted is my greatest honor.

Thanks to Larry Brooks for penetrating insight on story structure, to Michael Garrett for extreme patience and tolerance in editing and to Geoff Brewer for challenging me to find deeper layers of meaning in storylines . . . and in life.

Also my appreciation to Mrs. Svoboda, my seventh grade teacher, who one day, out of the blue, said "you're a pretty good writer." You changed a life that day and I never had a chance to say thank you.

Thank you posthumously to Warren Fine, my fiction writing professor in college. On the first day of class he wrote three telephone numbers on the blackboard. "The first is my home number, the second is my office number, and the third is the number at The Zoo Bar. If you can't reach me at any of these numbers, I don't want to talk to you." He taught me that there are no great writers, only authentic writers who become famous. Warren Fine described himself as the "foremost unpopular American novelist." I would gladly settle for honorable mention in that category.

To Harrison, because if I don't, he'll stop inviting me to his Memphis barbeques. To the McLean Mafia, because you rock, and nothing happens in this town without one of you knowing about it.

Finally, my undying gratitude to Becky, Nicholas and Alexandra. You encourage me to do what I couldn't imagine, yet keep my feet on the ground.

Also by Steve O'Brien

Bullet Work

PART ONE

Out of the Gate

ONE SECOND CHANGED EVERYTHING. One second altered fate for a lifetime. The winner zigged; the loser zagged.

One glance spotted true love, the next was blocked by a city bus. The victor reacted; the vanquished hesitated. Some called it luck. Some called it a gift. But it was just the second.

The second didn't care. The second was relentless. The second was waiting. It always waited, like a street mugger on a drizzly night. It waited in the shadows, emotionless.

The second was coming.

A series of seconds made a lifetime, two billion or more. Five, maybe six of those seconds altered one's life forevermore. Would they come in the beginning or at the end?

The second wasn't fair; it wasn't orderly. It would come on its own schedule, never revealed until it was too late.

Who would be wealthy, who would be poor? Who would have fame, who obscurity? Who would be loved, who scorned?

One moment a man cruised along a sun-drenched highway in a sporty convertible. The second appeared, and the car careened down the canyon wall, end over end, awaiting the explosion.

The second was unpredictable. The second was unforgiving. There was no bargaining with the second. It tested the strong and the weak alike.

Into each life the second would come, without warning, without hint. It could not be avoided. It could only be endured. Life became the response to the second.

In hindsight the second could be seen, dissected, and analyzed. Being in the second was like being in the eye of the hurricane: eerily quiet and completely beyond control. Only after the wind subsided could the story be told.

This is that story.

Chapter 1

THE BOY was a ghostlike creature—just a child. He and the mare circled the shedrow. Dan spotted him for an instant as he crossed the end of the barn and disappeared around the far side.

He'd be back around in about two minutes.

Dan swirled the stale coffee in his Styrofoam cup, then splashed it on the ground. He yawned and stretched his arms.

The boy wasn't that different from most backside help. All lacked a certain degree of cleanliness. But there was something memorable about the boy. His limp wasn't like others. He'd rotate on one side and swing his leg on the off stride. The right side was near normal; the left, a carnival ride. Nothing too striking, Dan thought—if you spent enough time around 1,200-pound thoroughbreds, one way or another, you wound up with a limp.

His was different, though. Something caught Dan's attention. The boy wore a tattered T-shirt with ripped jeans, just a shade lighter. The cardboard edge of his baseball cap was peeking its way out between the red fabric. Maybe it was his size, so small in comparison to the mare. Perhaps it was that someone so tiny in comparison to the horse could possibly be in control of the relationship.

Walking hots was the lowest level of the food chain on the racetrack backside. Hotwalkers were just that, walkers.

They stretched and paraded race horses either as the day's regimen of exercise or to cool out after returning from a workout or race.

A good hotwalker allowed the horse to take the walk, but he'd also pause when the horse wanted, let the horse graze when it wanted, and generally kept it from harm's way.

Hotwalking included talking, too. The best talked constantly. It calmed and reassured the horse. It also provided someone who would listen to the hotwalker.

Hotwalking was a safe harbor between dreams and reality. The steps didn't take either participant closer to anything; they were just steps.

The boy came around again. Fourteen, maybe fifteen, he was quickly obscured by the massive mare as he crossed the end of the shedrow again. Always walk on the inside. That way, the horse can see the hotwalker while being led into the turns.

Another odd thing—he held the shank in his left hand and had his right hand on the horse's neck, patting, stroking, sometimes just still. Certainly this wasn't the most comfortable way to walk a hot. A bond or closeness was apparent between the two, also not uncommon on the backside.

Dan watched as the boy went by again, then turned to walk toward the backside kitchen.

Jake Gilmore came out of his stable office and fell in step alongside Dan.

"Who's the kid?"

"Where?" Jake muttered while staring at something on his boots. He scrubbed the stubble on his neck and surveyed the area.

Gilmore stood just a shade over six feet. In the last decade of his fifty years, the once powerful upper body had melted around his waist, now supported by a sturdy leather belt and oversized rodeo buckle. Guy could give himself an appendectomy just sitting down wrong. Jake's eyes betrayed recent sleepless nights. For those like Jake who rose well before the sun each day, it wasn't out of the ordinary.

"The kid hotwalking the mare." Dan nodded toward the adjacent barn.

Jake looked over. "Don't know." Two or three steps later: "Just some kid." More silence. "Dick Latimer's barn."

"Recognize the mare?"

He looked over, turned back, and spat on the ground. "Nope. Latimer don't have nothing in his barn. Bunch a loose-legged claimers and two-year-olds he'll tear up 'fore the meet's over."

It didn't matter whether it was true or not. Trainers had to protect their relationships with owners and feed them information that prevented the owners from even thinking of moving their stock to a competitor's barn. It was all part of the game. Dan had learned the game.

Dan ran his fingers back through his short, dark hair and scratched the back of his neck. He was a good five inches shorter than Gilmore but significantly more athletic in tone. In contrast to the customary wardrobe on the backside, Dan's blue pinstriped suit pants and crisp, open-collared dress shirt said "owner." His well-groomed, youthful appearance said "new money." On the latter count conventional wisdom would be wrong.

A frenzy of activity dominated the backside from 5 A.M. to 11 A.M.; then, just as quickly, it became a sleepy little village. There was a system and rhythm to the chaos of the backside. Some horses going to the training track, jockeys and trainers discussed the latest workout. Jock agents hustled the latest Willie Shoemaker, just trying to get their boy a decent ride.

Vet vans parked in the roadway, with their doors

hanging open, displaying the meds and appliances necessary to keep the warriors in the game. Wraps hung on a makeshift clothesline. Stable hands mucked out stalls. The dull smell of manure and urine mixed with pungent hot salve.

The ever-present sound of water running provided the soundtrack. Stable hands washed down horses, filled tubs, or simply knocked down dust in the shedrow. The clip-clop of hooves on the narrow asphalt roads signaled horses crossing to and from the track. Pickups hummed as they crept along slowly enough to hear the gravel pop and churn as it was spit out by worn tires. The breeze carried a joke, laughter, and shouts of instruction. In many corners it was reunion time.

Today was Tuesday. But it was not just any Tuesday. It was Tuesday before opening day. The backside had been empty thirty days ago. Now a vibrant community had sprung up. Three hundred small businesses occupied the backside, complete with bosses, employees, payroll, and equipment. The most important assets of the businesses rolled in on fifth-wheeled trailers.

For the past three weeks the assets had been rolling in, some coming from campaigns at other racetracks, some from training farms, some returning from injury, and, this time of year, late summer, some were babies. These were the two-year-olds who would soon learn about their new environment and routine, far from the calm, consistent life of the training farm. For them, this was the equine version of culture shock.

Dan and Jake stepped onto the wooden landing. Jake pulled open the screen door to Crok's Kitchen. It resembled many other backside kitchens. The décor was totally utilitarian, filled with metal folding chairs and laminate-topped tables, none of which stood level to the ground. Each wobbled the direction of the newest elbow that rested on it. All random and disordered atop an uneven concrete floor.

Time stood still in backside kitchens. Revelations about cholesterol hadn't arrived yet. A remarkable place where the taste served as the only discriminator and fat grams were ubiquitous.

Crok was a seventy-something short order cook, by choice, and kitchen manager by default. She hovered like some relic left behind in an unexplained time warp. Barely five feet on her best day, Crok graced the kitchen like a blocking dummy on legs. Her gravelly voice bounced off the walls as she barked at customers. A black net pressed her gray locks down onto her head. Smiling wasn't her strength. All paid full fare, but she made sure those who were down on their luck had a meal. It might involve time served at a sink full of dishes, but no one was turned away if they were sincere.

The kid came in as Dan and Jake sipped coffee, surrounded by tables of similar groups, all talking about the meet, the stakes schedule, but mostly about how they were going to make money.

The boy limped through the line, filling his tray with biscuits, gravy, and grits. A large glass of milk finished the meal. Crok smiled and whispered something to him as he completed his journey through the stainless steel line. The kid didn't spill a drop of milk as he counteracted his limp across the room to one of the only empty tables near the door.

Jake continued his explanation about the outcome of throat surgery for Dan's three-year-old, Hero's Echo. A release of the trapped epiglottis required six weeks of rest. That meant six weeks of vet and boarding bills with no opportunity to recover costs. The surgery was needed and would hopefully move him to the next level. Jake was mapping out the recovery process as the noise level elevated in Crok's.

Three wiry grooms in muddy boots and weathered T-shirts had surrounded the kid as he sat alone at the table.

"Hey, retard," the tallest one spouted. "How's breakfast?"

The kid didn't look up. He just stared down at his plate.

Another of the three, the shortest of the group, scraggly blonde hair and overly tight blue jeans, reached forward and slapped the kid in the back of the head with an upward movement.

"Stupid, what's for breakfast?"

The shot wasn't meant to inflict pain, but merely to knock the kid's baseball cap into his plate of food. The three laughed heartily and high-fived one another. The kid still didn't look up.

He was used to this treatment, Dan thought. It was a battle he couldn't conceivably win, so he sat motionless, enduring the verbal and physical onslaught.

Crok flew from behind the serving counter, wielding a large metal spoon.

"You leave that boy alone." She took a swing at the nearest boy, but he leaned backward, like Cassius Clay taunting Sonny Liston. She missed. The boy stared at his plate. The trio scoffed at Crok but continued out the door.

"See ya, retard," the short one shouted.

"Have a nice day," said the tallest one.

Crok swept away the kid's plate, dusted off his ball cap, and in a matter of seconds returned with a clean, even larger plate of food. The kid said, "Thank you, ma'am"—still without looking up.

Dan watched the entire scene, glued to his chair. He just sat there. He didn't help. He didn't do anything. Finally, he looked down into his coffee cup.

"God, I hate myself."

About the Author

Steve O'Brien is the author of *Elijah's Coin* and *Bullet Work*. Both works have been the recipient of multiple literary awards. Since its release, *Elijah's Coin* has been added to the reading curriculum in multiple secondary schools throughout the US and has been incorporated in a university ethics course. Steve is a graduate of the University of Nebraska and George Washington University Law School. He lives in Washington, DC.

CPSIA information can be obtained at www.ICGtesting.com
Printed in the USA
BVOW040936300112

281665BV00002B/3/P

9 780982 073520